Praise for

CAROLYN DAVIDSON

"Carolyn Davidson creates such vivid images, you'd
think she was using paints instead of words."
—Bestselling author Pamela Morsi

"Davidson wonderfully captures gentleness in the
midst of heart-wrenching challenges."
—Publishers Weekly

"[An] unflinching inquiry into the serious issues
of the day."
—Booklist on Redemption

"Like Dorothy Garlock, Davidson does not stint
on the gritty side of romance, but keeps the
tender, heart-tugging aspects of her story in the
forefront. This novel is filled with compassion and
understanding for characters facing hardship and
hatred and still finding joy in love and life."
—Romantic Times BOOKreviews on Oklahoma Sweetheart

"This deftly written novel about loss and recovery is
a skillful handling of the traditional Western,
with the added elements of family conflict and a
moving love story."
—Romantic Times BOOKreviews on A Marriage by Chance

Available from HQN and

CAROLYN DAVIDSON

Redemption
Haven

Other works include:

Harlequin Historical

*Edgewood, Texas
**Montana Mavericks
†Colorado Confidential

CAROLYN DAVIDSON

Nightsong

HQN™

ISBN-13: 978-0-373-77285-8
ISBN-10:   0-373-77285-8

NIGHTSONG

Dear Reader,

As a writer I enjoy traveling in new directions, and writing this book was indeed a switch for me. I have the greatest respect for those who lived in this great land of ours before our forefathers ventured to these shores. I thought long and hard before deciding to attempt the telling of a story that would reveal some small part of the Native Americans and the impact they have had on individuals—those who knew them and those who joined with them in marriage, thus increasing the blend in the melting pot of our country.

Debra Nightsong was a very special heroine to me. She was strong, a woman of her people who chose to live her life with a man of another race, and did it well. The union she formed with Ethan changed her life, changed her as a woman and sent her on an adventure like no other. Unions such as Debra's with Ethan form the complex civilization we live in here in America, for such marriages seem to produce strong people, perhaps blending within them the finest of both races. And, like Debra, each of us has our own story to tell, an adventure that is ours alone, one I feel we are compelled to pass on to the generations who will follow. I hope my story will appeal to all of my readers, that your hearts will open to those who are a result of marriages such as that of Debra and Ethan. For beneath the skin we are all brothers.

Carolyn Davidson

I love brides…grooms, too, for that matter.
And none are so precious to me as brides and
grooms within our own family. My son Jon
has given three of his four daughters to the men
of their choice during the past year or so, and our
family has become all the richer for their presence as
couples in the far-reaching web of the Davidson clan.

So to the three beloved grandchildren who have
newly entered the realm of marriage, an institution
of which I am very fond, I'd like to dedicate this
book, with its own message of prevailing over the
hardships life has to offer to those embarking on this
course. To Rachel and David, Karen and Rob, and
finally to Jennifer and Tom, I offer my best wishes as
a grandmother and a veteran of marriage. May God
richly bless your unions, and may His presence be
alive in the years you spend together.

And, as always, I dedicate my work to my own love,
the man who has been a beloved companion and has
devoted himself to me for many years…
to Mr. Ed, who loves me.

Nightsong

CHAPTER ONE

Holly Hill, The Dakota Territory
June 1888

STEALING A HORSE was guaranteed to give a man sleepless nights. And Ethan Tyler was no exception. Only the fact that the poor nag should have long since been put out to pasture aided his insomnia, but the fact that he'd taken another man's animal weighed heavily on his mind. He was tired of running—it was time to call a halt and make decisions.

Even as he rode the trail from Holly Hill to the small farm he sought, he thought of the man who was even now missing his nag and his conscience bothered him with the theft he'd committed. Sending the horse back to town would be a problem, but one he'd figure out one way or another.

With that settled, Tyler looked ahead toward the farmhouse he'd been told was just three miles from town, at the end of a long lane, shaded by tall trees. A woman lived there, alone and unprotected. A woman whose parentage was in question, some saying she had a native mother, an unknown father and was probably no better than she should be. Others said she was to be respected, a woman alone, no matter her heritage.

Whichever she was, Tyler knew he could prevail upon her to hide him, for how long he didn't know, but at least he would convince her that he needed a hiding place for a while, and his skills at working around a farm would pay her well for her help.

He rode as quickly as the nag he'd borrowed would allow, hoping against hope that his arrival would preface hers by at least an hour. He needed time to put his horse behind the barn, should there be one, break in to her house and then lie in wait for her to arrive. His senses told him he was being followed and it was time to go to ground.

He would be gentle with her, for she was no doubt a crone, a woman of years who kept to herself and lived quietly. A grandmotherly sort, he imagined, a woman set in her ways, but perhaps thankful for a helping hand for a short while. Not a woman who would tempt him to abandon his celibate lifestyle for want of her charms.

He rode down the narrow lane toward her holdings, admiring the clean lines of her buildings, the neatly kept yard and the buildings surrounding it. There was a shed, less than a barn, but a sturdy structure, and a smoke house, side by side with another small structure, probably a milk house or corncrib.

The house was a typical farmhouse, with a wide porch and windows that looked out upon the backyard. Ridiculously simple to break in to, he thought, sliding a kitchen window upward without much nudging. He climbed within, relishing the scent of the bread she must have baked this morning. Before she went to town and left herself open to a scalawag such as he, a man who climbed through her window and into her house, awaiting her return.

The sun had set, painting the sky with soft colors, promising fair weather for tomorrow, and he waited, his patience long, his stomach well tended by the loaf of bread he found on the kitchen cabinet. Old or not, the woman could bake bread, he thought, and then tensed as he heard the sound of a horse, the soft whicker that sounded from the yard.

He rose and stood by the window.

The woman rode astride, defying the rules society back east had set down for a female on a horse. No saddle darkened the back of the golden mare she rode, only the flowing skirt that hung halfway down her legs, catching the breeze as she rode. Double saddlebags lay across the animal's rump, apparently balanced there, for they did not depend on a saddle to hold them in place.

As Tyler watched from the window in her house, she brought the horse to a halt there in the first light of the moon, never touching her reins. Only the pressure of her knees against the animal's sides caused the mare to slow her rapid pace and then stand, head lowered, next to the watering trough.

In a smooth motion, the rider slid to the ground, exposing a slender thigh as her dress pulled up, then she approached the horse's head, rubbing her knuckles against the mare's long nose, speaking to the animal as she removed the bit and bridle from the pale horse. The mare bent her long neck gracefully and drank from the trough, her rider waiting patiently. And then they were headed for the small stable that sat in utter darkness just beyond an enclosed chicken coop, the mare following her mistress as might a faithful pet. The woman's dress swayed against her body, exposing moccasins beneath its hem.

The barn door was opened and the woman and her mare went inside. In less than five minutes, the slender female emerged, tossed her dark hair back and lifted her face to the skies. The glow of moonlight illuminated her and Tyler inhaled sharply.

She was lovely, and definitely not what he'd expected when he'd heard of an Indian woman living alone beyond the edge of town. She couldn't be more than eighteen or twenty years. Her dress clung to her form, and the black hair she'd flung over her shoulders formed a dark cape that hung past her waist. She carried two sacks, one in either hand, hefting them easily. Tyler felt a heaviness in his groin as he watched her approach the house, and fought it with a sense of scorn. He wasn't here to take advantage of a woman, but to find a sanctuary of sorts. At least for a week or so.

Her footsteps were silent as she walked across the porch and the sound of the door opening seemed magnified in the stillness of the night. He moved swiftly to stand behind the door as it opened...and waited.

DEBRA SLIPPED HER FEET from the moccasins she wore, kicking them to one side of the open kitchen door, then stepped inside and pushed the heavy portal closed behind her.

Without warning, a rough hand covered her mouth, forcing her head against a solid wall of muscle, and the burlap sacks of foodstuffs she'd been carrying landed on the floor beside her. A powerful arm circled her waist, and held her firmly.

From behind the door, where he'd apparently been lying in wait, a tall figure shadowed her. He'd hidden there, and now he had the advantage over her. She was, of necessity, silent, his hand not allowing her mouth to open. But she could fight soundlessly, and her hands reached back over her head, fingers curved and aimed at his face.

She felt a fingernail dig deeply into flesh, and the indrawn breath of the man who held her. With a quick move he captured both her hands and drew them behind her back, turning her in his arms to face him.

"Hold still, ma'am. I'm not going to hurt you. You'll be all right."

His voice was graveled, rough and deep. She'd never felt less secure in her life, and he had the nerve to tell her that all was well. She stiffened in his grip, her breath rasping in her lungs, as she forced her bruised lips to open.

"I doubt anyone could hear you shout or cry out," he said mockingly, looking down at her from dark eyes that were barely visible in the light of the moon and stars from the windows. "You've chosen to live alone, a mile from the nearest neighbor, and let me tell you, that isn't a safe choice for a woman by herself."

"I have no intention of calling for help, you bastard!" she whispered. "What do you want with me? Or is that a stupid question?" A vision of violence filled her mind, with herself as the victim, and she shivered as if a wintry chill had passed down her spine.

"I've already told you that I won't hurt you, if that's what you're worried about," he said quietly. "You certainly weren't what I expected to find here. You're only a girl."

His voice rang with disgust, and he shook his head, as if denying his thoughts. "I just need a place to stay for a few days. You'll hardly know I'm here."

She laughed scornfully. "Somehow I find that hard to believe. You're too big to sweep under the rug, and I have nowhere to keep you. I only have one bed in the house. It belongs to me."

"Have you never heard of sharing?" A touch of

humor, bordering on teasing, colored his voice, and he allowed his index finger the privilege of tracing a line down her cheek. She pulled away from the touch, shivering as the rough pad of his finger took stock of her smooth flesh.

"I don't share my bed with anyone," she said adamantly. "If you insist on sleeping in the bed, I'll take the floor. I spent a lot of years without a mattress beneath me. Another night won't hurt me."

"Ah, you're wrong there," he insisted firmly. "You'll be where I can reach you. And I'll warn you right now, I'm a light sleeper. One move out of you and I'll be on you like a bear on a honey tree."

Somehow the picture that brought to mind lacked much, Debra decided. For a moment she wished fervently that she'd stayed in town with the storekeeper's daughter. The invitation had been given in an undertone, while Mr. Anderson was with a customer, and Debra had shaken her head, knowing that, if she were discovered in her friend's bedroom, there'd be hell to pay. And she'd be the one paying it.

A half-breed was tolerated in town, so long as she had enough money to pay for her purchases at the general store, but there could never be any friendships formed. Julia was the exception, having made it her business to drive her buggy out of town on the occasional Sunday afternoon, finding her way to Debra's small holding.

Now there was no choice, no friend to keep her

company through the night, only this stranger who appeared even more menacing as he warned her of the night to come.

"Do you have anything to tend to before you go to bed?" he asked.

"The cow will need milking, the horses will need feeding, and my food must be put up. I ate in town and the chickens were fed this afternoon."

He bent and picked up the bundles beside her, and she took them from him, feeling the warmth of his hands against hers. "Who are you?" she asked, wanting the truth from him, but not expecting to hear it.

"My name is Tyler."

"Tyler as your first name or your last?" she asked.

"Just Tyler," he said with finality. "Now put away your foodstuffs."

"I'll light the lamp," she said, walking toward the table, over which hung her kerosene lantern.

"No light," he said quickly. "I'll warrant you can find a place to stash your food in the dark."

"There's no one around to see the light," she told him, aggravated at being a prisoner of this man. Whatever he planned, it boded no good for her, she'd already decided.

He chose not to argue with her, apparently, for he simply waited as Debra opened the sacks on the kitchen table, feeling the familiar items within. Coffee, peaches, a tin of sugar, lard in a five-pound can, a bit of bacon and a sack of flour. With quick steps, only the faint light of moon and stars to guide her, she carried them into the small pantry, putting them in place on the almost empty shelves.

"Now we'll go out and tend your cow." His voice was low, his touch firm against her arm as he steered her toward the back door. She walked ahead of him, knowing her cow would be miserable if she were not relieved of her milk tonight.

Outdoors, the moon was high in the sky, illuminating the rough path to her barn—realistically more a shed, she thought, as the structure loomed before them. Her cow lowed impatiently from her stall, and Debra pushed the door aside, entering the dark, musty stable, able to find her way by touch, so familiar was she with the contents of the building. Her milking pail was covered by a towel, just inside the door, the three-legged stool she used beside it.

She bent to them, picking them up as she neared the stall where her Jersey cow waited. In moments she was seated near the animal's flank, holding the bucket between her knees as she began the process of emptying the bag of its burden. The small Jersey lowed once more, as if in greeting, and Debra murmured soft words to her, soothing her unease.

Fifteen minutes later, she'd given the animals their hay for the night, her horse in a standing stall nearby, three other mares tied in narrow seclusion farther down the aisle of the barn. Without words spoken, the man, Tyler, helped her fill the mangers, then followed her from the stable and into the yard.

She looked up at him, his face more distinct in the moonlight and her heart sank within her. Probably not more than thirty, but well-worn, she decided. He was hard, his features forming a harsh visage, a straight blade of a nose, dark hair badly in need of a barber's scissors and eyes that hid behind lowered lids and lashes.

Without speaking, he led her back to the house and as they entered Debra removed her shoes on the mat just inside the kitchen. Tyler followed suit and then stood silently behind her as she contemplated her next move.

"If that's all the chores you need done tonight, go in the bedroom and get out of your clothes," he said harshly, not offering any more excuses to put off the inevitable.

"I can sleep in my clothing," she said sharply. "I'm not getting undressed in front of you."

"I didn't expect you to. I'll wait out here 'til you tell me you're in bed."

She was abruptly released from his hold and with four steps she was in front of her closed bedroom door. She opened it, stepping inside and then turned to close it against him. It was not to be. His foot jammed it open and he laughed.

"I may not be allowed to watch, but I'm not taking a chance on you skinnin' out that window, sweetheart."

The moonlight was brighter in here, flooding her bedroom, and Debra sought out her nightgown from beneath her pillow. She went behind the screen in one corner, where her slop jar and basin were kept. In moments she had pulled her clothing off and the nightgown was in place. She hung her dress and chemise over the screen, then walked toward the bed.

"I'd be happy to sleep on the rug over here," she suggested and was not surprised to hear his gruff laughter again as he entered the room and closed the door.

"Not a chance, Nightsong."

"You know my name?"

"I heard it in town," he said. "I like it."

"It's only my surname. I'm Debra."

"Who named you Nightsong? A family name?"

"My mother gave me her name. She was The One Who Sings, and they called her Nightbird. When I was born she said I was the song she was meant to sing. She called me her Nightsong." She spoke the words softly, remembering the woman who had been her protector and champion during those early days of her life. They'd both been outcasts from the tribe, her mother because she'd borne a half-breed child, and Debra because she carried the blood of the white man in her veins.

"Get into bed." He gave the order with no inflection in his voice and she did as he said, knowing that she could not win a battle against him. At least not now. The sheets were cool against her, and she placed her pillow behind her, choosing to sleep without it, in order to keep a barrier between their bodies.

He only laughed beneath his breath as he slid into the other side of the bed, snatched the pillow up and put it atop his own. "That won't work, sweetheart," he told her. "You're going to be right next to me all night. We can make our living arrangements tomorrow, but for tonight, we'll just do our best to be friends."

"You're suffering a delusion," she said sharply. "We'll never be friends. I'm your prisoner for now, but…"

"It won't be easy to escape me, Debra Nightsong. In fact, I'd say don't even try. I don't want to hurt you, but I'll not let you get away from me."

She sat up abruptly and faced him. "You're in my house, holding me prisoner and threatening me. I don't owe you anything, mister. I don't know who you're hiding from, but I suspect it's the law, and I refuse to hide you here."

She saw the flash of his white teeth in the moonlight. "Right now, you don't have a choice, sweetheart. I'm the man with the gun, and about a hundred pounds on you. Not to mention that I'm a good foot taller than you are. That settles it, I'd say. You'll do as I tell you, at least for the next few days."

"Days? You plan on keeping me your prisoner for

a matter of days?" Her heartbeat increased as she considered his words.

His hand reached for her and his long fingers clamped around her wrist. "Don't worry about the days ahead, Nightsong. For now, we just need to get through the night. And you have only two choices. It's either me holding your arm or I'll tie you to my waist. What'll it be?"

She was silent. His fingers were hard against her skin, but not cruel, not enough to cause bruises, unless she fought his touch. The thought of being tied to him was unacceptable and she lay back down, accepting his imprisoning fingers binding her close.

He turned toward her, as if accepting her surrender, and laughed, a sound smacking of derision. "Close your eyes, Debra Nightsong. It's going to be a long night."

She did as he said, knowing that for now, she was under his control, and God forbid she make him angry with her.

But her mind was spinning like a child's top on Christmas morning. All she'd ever asked for was a peaceful life, alone here on the property her father had bequeathed to her. She'd done well, raising chickens, one of them a rooster who kept her hens in line, and awoke early every morning to hail the new day. Then there was the cow she cared for, and her golden mare. Now her herd had increased with the arrival of the three mares.

A garden thrived behind the house and her nearest neighbor cut the acres of hay she shared with him for his work. It was a good life, one she'd thought held a measure of safety and peace.

The dark-haired man beside her was a stranger, tall, well-built, and, as he'd said, probably a hundred pounds heavier than she. A big man, whose dark eyes had frightened her with their lack of emotion. As though he felt nothing, as if his feelings were locked up somewhere inside, he gave no hint of softness, no apology for his hands on her body, his presence in her bed.

She trembled, fearful of him, his presence in her home and the fate that might await her. Physically, she was no match for him, leaving her only her wits to depend upon.

The mystery was too much for her tonight, she decided. Just getting through the hours 'til morning was what concerned her right now. Her mind was whirling again, her wrist was held in an unshakable grip and she wanted to turn over. Away from his eyes that were even now focused on her. She could feel his gaze, knew he watched her.

"Let go of me," she said, as if she expected his co-operation. "I'd like to turn over."

"Go ahead." He dropped her hand and she turned away from him, only to feel his heavy arm slide over her waist, settling on her flat belly and then tugging her back against his warm body. "I'll just hang on to you this way," he murmured. "And don't give me a hard time, little bird. It won't do you any good."

"Don't call me that," she said sharply. And even as she spoke, she heard her mother's voice, soothing her, encouraging her and speaking the words in a gentle voice. *"My little bird. Don't worry. Your mother is here."* She inhaled sharply as a tear slid from her eye and dampened the sheet beneath her. His hand swept up over her waist and breast to spread across her cheek, and she shrank from the touch of those warm fingers on her face.

But to no avail, for the tears she'd thought to keep from him were swept away by his hand, holding the corner of the sheet, fingers that were gentle as he wiped her cheek.

"I upset you. What did I say to make you cry?" She thought his voice softened a bit, losing the harsh edge, the threat of violence she'd sensed earlier.

She resented his knowledge of her weakness and her voice was taut. "Take your hands off me. I don't cry. And, I'm not going anywhere."

He chuckled a bit, a low, husky sound and bent his head lower on the pillow, brushing his face over her hair. She felt his breath, warm against the side of her face, and caught the scent of him, that of saddle leather and fresh air.

"My arm and my hand will hold you against me. They will stay on you all night long. I offered you another solution, but you turned it down."

She shivered. "Tying me up wasn't much of an option."

His chuckle was low, offering her no hint of softening. "It's the only one you'll get, so make up your mind."

And with that, he pulled her even closer to himself, curling his big body against her back, his knees pushing her legs upward. "Close your eyes, little bird. I'll still be right here in the morning, and you can be angry at me then. It sure as hell won't do you any good to get all upset tonight."

She thought a trace of amusement coiled through his lazy whisper, and she felt her anger rise in spite of his warning. "I'm not used to sleeping with anyone," she said, wriggling in a vain effort to put him at a distance. To no avail, for he only pulled her closer and eased his hand across her belly to the hip she lay on, his fingers pressing into her flesh, almost guaranteeing bruises come morning.

"You're a little bit of a thing, aren't you?" he mused, measuring the width of her body with his arm. "Sassy and full of piss and vinegar, but not big enough to fight me."

"I'm big enough to take care of myself," she said stoutly, "except when a man uses his strength against me. And even then, I've been known to fight."

"Want to tell me about it?" he asked, his tone softly curious. "Who have you fought?"

She was stubbornly silent, and he chuckled again.

"I'll just bet you landed a few good punches before any man ever got the best of you. You're a brave one, I'll give you that." He paused and she sensed that he would speak a warning. "But don't try to fight me, Debra Nightsong. I don't play fair, and I always win."

"Especially against a woman," she murmured. "I was right about you. You're a bully."

"I can be kind," he told her.

He'd made his move, forced his way into her house, almost guaranteed a place to hang his hat for a few days at least. She'd just come from town, had brought supplies enough to last for some time in those burlap sacks. She wouldn't be expected by anyone to be seen in Holly Hill for a few days.

"I'll be up at dawn, when the rooster crows," she told him. "My cow likes to be milked early on and the chickens will need to be fed."

"Well, then rest easy. I'll be with you while you milk and tend your stock. Might even lend a hand," he whispered against her ear.

The scent of man, of his yearnings for a woman, enveloped her. For the first time in her life, she shared her bed, and resented it mightily. Enough that he held her fast, did she also need the constant reminder that this masculine being presented a danger to her?

He was clean, if she were any judge of it, smelling like the fresh hay in her field, a faint aroma of leather and horse surrounding him. An altogether appealing arrangement that tempted her senses.

He seemed not to be cruel, for if he'd so desired, he could have hurt her badly already, could have taken her body in an act of pure lust. He'd done neither, and for whatever rules of behavior governed him, she was thankful.

She must have dozed off, her body seeking the rest it required, for when she awoke, fully aware of the darkness and the man who lay beside her, she sat upright, his arm gripping her firmly.

"What is it?" he asked. "What's wrong?"

She sought her pillow, remembered that it was under his head, and settled for the sheet beneath her. "I need to use the…" She faltered, unable to speak aloud the need for privacy.

He released his grip on her and rolled from the bed. "Get up, Debra. I'll be right here. Don't think to escape or attack me with your hairbrush." A note of amusement touched his voice and she muttered a curse beneath her breath.

The screen shielding her personal space in the room concealed her from his eyes, and she hastily tended to her needs, then straightened her gown around her before returning to the bed. "Did you think I would be so stupid as to use a hairbrush as a weapon?" she asked, sitting once more on the edge of the mattress.

"You're not stupid, Debra. I was counting on your intelligence. I only warned you because I don't want a battle with you in the middle of the night." He gripped her shoulder and pushed her down against the mattress. Her pillow was soft beneath her head and she cut her gaze to him, his body barely visible in the moonlight.

"Thank you. I'll be more comfortable this way."

"I don't want you angry with me," he began, lying back beside her. "I know that sounds like a futile wish, but I mean it. I won't hurt you, Debra, and I knew you needed your pillow returned." He was silent for a moment and then his voice touched her again. "Decide which side you'll sleep on and get snuggled in, girl."

"So you can hang on to me?" She recognized the bitter tone of her own words as she turned to her side, facing the edge of the bed and the window that overlooked the yard.

"So I can make certain that you don't try to escape in the middle of the night."

"I'm not going to give you the chance to hold me down, mister. I'll lie where I am 'til morning."

"I wouldn't mind holding you down," he mused quietly. "As a matter of fact, I might like it more than I should. Let's not take a chance on it."

Awake now, Debra lay facing the lone window in her bedroom, watching as the depth of night, the darkness before dawn, began its morning journey into daylight. Her eyes refused to close in slumber and she resigned herself to several hours of waiting 'til the sun rose.

Yet, when she next stirred, it was to find broad

daylight in her room, the man behind her still holding her firmly against his body, and the unmistakable nudge of his manhood against her bottom. She'd not experienced such a thing before, but her feminine instincts told her exactly what it was, and she felt the danger as a viable threat, her rapid pulse sounding as a warning, vibrating through her body.

A man's urges are strongest in the early daylight. Her mother had said those words to her. Debra had filed the knowledge away in her mind, certain that such a worry would never be hers to own, that the challenge of a man's body in her bed would not be an issue in her life.

The rooster crowed and she became aware that it was not for the first time, for she'd no doubt slept through the sound. She'd spent the night with this man touching her, keeping her at his beck and call. She found herself, in the light of dawn, at Tyler's mercy, and realized the difficulty of ignoring the blatant presence of the man behind her.

CHAPTER TWO

THE MORNING SUN HOVERED just below the horizon in the east as Debra left the porch, the shed her destination. Behind her, the silent shadow she'd acquired last evening followed apace, and she shivered as she felt his mood, aware that he intended she be fearful of him.

The man apparently planned to move in to her home, and she seemed to have no choice in the matter. He'd already proven his superior strength, sleeping in her bed, giving her only as much freedom from his presence as he allowed, and she yearned for moments of privacy so that she might gain some sort of control over the situation. Living in his shadow was no option, and the thought of him in her home, watching her every move, caused a chill of fear to travel the length of her spine.

Now Debra bent to rinse her milk pail in the clear water that flowed from the pump, sloshing the water and dumping it away from the path before she sought out the relative privacy of the shed. Anticipating the soothing routine of milking her cow, the soft clucking of her hens, and the strutting rooster who claimed her attention, she pulled aside the shed door and entered the shadowed interior.

Then, milk pail between her knees, she squatted on the stool and rested her forehead against the Jersey's warm side. The milk sprayed the inside of the pail, the rhythm was one she'd learned early on, after much trial and error. The patient Jersey knew her well now, and they had established an unspoken communication. Not as satisfying as the presence of another woman might be, but better than nothing, Debra had long since decided.

The chickens were another matter. She tolerated their waspish behavior, aware that her own may not have been any better, should she have been forced to exchange places with them. They were at her mercy, being fed when she rattled the metal feed pan, having their eggs scooped up and stolen away for her benefit and only allowed the freedom to roam during the daylight hours.

And at that, they might be faring better than she, if the man behind her had his way. He'd apparently decided that Debra Nightsong would dance to his tune, that her day would be circumscribed by his choices.

"Debra." His voice spoke her name and she controlled the impulse to ignore him.

"Am I not milking this cow to your standards?" She knew her voice was cool, knew she invited his anger and cared little. It was daylight, her fear from the night just past had faded, and the thought of escape had invaded her mind.

Perhaps she could watch until he visited the outhouse, or even take a chance on leading her mare from the back of the shed later on. Once on the back of her golden horse, she would be gone, out of his control, and the thought made her smile.

He stood behind her, his shadow over her, and she refused to look up, concentrating instead on stripping the last of the milk from the cow's udder. "I wouldn't attempt to better your skills, Debra," he said smoothly. "Milking is not one of the finer arts, so far as I'm concerned. But I'm pretty adept at carrying pails. When you finish your chore, I'll tote the milk to the house."

"Why don't you gather up the eggs while you wait?" She shot a look beneath her lashes, noting his widespread stance beside her now. He was too close for her comfort, and she silently urged him to move away, only too aware of his presence.

"Chickens don't like me," he said flatly. "I don't choose to have bloody spots on my hands. I get along better with horses and dogs."

"Then by all means you need to become better acquainted with mine. The pitchfork is on the wall and the stalls are in need of cleaning."

He laughed, a short sound of amusement, and did as she suggested, lifting the tool from its place and bending to with a vengeance. He opened the back door of the shed and tossed the soiled straw toward a pile just outside.

"There's a wheelbarrow there if you'd like to use it," she told him. And then watched as he hauled in the conveyance and finished the task she'd assigned him. Loading the barrow from the straw stack behind the shed, he returned to where the horses waited and pitched clean bedding within their stalls.

The golden mare followed him tamely as he led her to the door. "I'll just stake her out back," he said. Not waiting for a reply, he walked into the brilliant light from the rising sun and snatched up her hammer as he passed the wall of tools near the door. The long stake she used for the mare lay against the shed and he picked it up as he went.

"Do you stake all of your horses?" he asked, motioning at the other three who stood placidly awaiting his touch.

"I just took delivery of those three days ago. I haven't decided yet what to do with them."

His words were decisive. "I'll figure it out. Maybe not right now, but by the time the day is over." He halted and looked back at her a moment. "I have a horse out back, tied to the wall of your shed. Not mine, exactly. One I borrowed from a farmer nearer to town. I'll feed him, too, and then decide how to return him to where I found him."

"Horse thieves hang in this part of the country," she said without pause, not deigning to look up at him.

"I know. Where I come from, too. But I didn't steal the poor creature, only borrowed him. I'll return him later today. Probably the poor soul who owns him won't even have noticed his absence. Probably had just put him out to pasture anyway. He's not exactly a fine example of horseflesh."

Taking an armful of hay with him, he went out the back door and she wondered briefly just whose horse he'd made away with. There were several behind fences between here and town, none of them much to look at, but probably all broken to saddle.

She heard the muted thumping of her hammer as he staked the mare, and in moments he reappeared, reaching for the milk pail as she rose and settled the stool against the wall.

"I'll gather the eggs, since you have a problem with my hens," she told him, holding her apron together to form a nest for the hen fruit. Nine eggs lay warm and waiting in the nests, an abundant harvest for one day, and she cradled them carefully against herself, taking care lest they bump and shatter the fragile shells.

Tyler watched her as she left the shed, followed close behind her as she walked the distance to the house, noting the easy stride she possessed, the natural grace of a woman, the fluid movement of her hips and the shimmer of the sunlight on black hair that hung like a curtain of midnight down her back.

She was a sight to behold, he decided. He'd come

here looking to find an older woman, a widow lady perhaps, living alone, in need of a helping hand. And found, instead, a beautiful woman who looked at him with eyes that weighed him and found him wanting. And he, who had so often been the object of a woman's admiring gaze, found only scorn in the dark eyes of Debra Nightsong.

He followed her into the kitchen, settled the milk pail next to the sink and then sat down to watch as she began preparations for breakfast. She washed quickly at the sink, dried her hands on her apron and lifted a skillet from atop the warming oven over her stove.

A small slab of bacon from the pantry made an appearance as she gathered up the food she would cook. Her knife was sharp, slicing with precision through the savory meat, and he watched the silver blade with a degree of appreciation for her use of it. She would be a formidable opponent should she decide to use her domestic tools as weapons.

The bacon was placed neatly in the skillet, and before many seconds had gone by, the meat began to sizzle and send forth an aroma that made his mouth water. It had been too long since his last meal, and breakfast had ever been his favorite meal of the day.

He went to the sink and washed up quickly. "Do you have any bread left?" he asked, his quick gaze searching out the kitchen dresser for a sign of her baking prowess.

"Wrapped up in that towel," she told him, nodding at a package on the surface before him. He picked it up and opened the clean towel, exposing almost a full loaf of unsliced bread, the end of the loaf ragged where he'd torn off a piece late in the evening while he awaited her return. Lifting her knife from the counter, he wiped it with a dish towel and turned his attention to slicing enough bread for toast.

"I should have used a knife last night. Looks like I made a mess of it."

"It doesn't matter. At least you left enough for breakfast. And if you hadn't, I have another loaf put up."

He sawed at the loaf before him, and then looked up. "Shall I put it in the oven?" He waited for her reply, three slices in his hand, and received a patient look from her direction. Her free hand waved at the oven door and he took the blatant hint, placing the bread on the rack within, backing quickly from the heat.

The eggs she'd brought from the shed rested now in a crock on the table and she lifted five of them, cracking them into a shallow dish, then waved a hand at the container. "Put this in the pantry, if you would. Right-hand side, second shelf."

He nodded, willing to be accommodating, since she held the spoon that would be stirring his eggs and he was of a mind to enjoy her cooking. The pantry was lined with shelves, Mason jars lined up precisely, many of them empty on the bottom shelves, awaiting the harvest to come from the kitchen garden.

Neatness seemed to be her motto, for even the canned goods she'd brought from town were stowed according to content, and beside them jars of coffee beans and sacks of sugar and flour vied for shelf space. She was an orderly sort, he decided quickly, her supplies sufficient to hold them for at least a week.

"Bring that churn out with you," she called from the vicinity of the stove, where he heard the splatter of bacon grease on the hot surface as she turned the thick slices in the skillet. "The bread should be toasted by now," she told him, and he opened the oven door, forking out the three slices of browned bread.

A generous slab of butter lay beneath a glass dome on the table, and he found a knife from the drawer, then set about slathering a thick layer of golden butter on his toast. He'd watched her put together a pot of coffee as soon as she made her way to the kitchen early on and now the aroma of the strong, fresh brew reached him.

His plate was readied, scrambled eggs with four slices of bacon edging the offering, a thick china mug filled to the brim with black coffee and toast he'd buttered on another plate. His mouth watered, and he did not hesitate, only taking time to find forks in the drawer before he sat down.

Debra sat across from him and her movements were

fluid, her hands graceful as she ladled jam from a pot onto her toast. For a moment, she paused, lifting her eyes to the window, her lips moving silently, and he thought she might be speaking a blessing on her food.

He picked up his fork and loaded it with eggs. The steam rose from the golden pile on his plate and he tucked in readily, the fresh eggs a delight to his taste-buds. The bacon was crisp, the coffee strong and black, just as he liked it, and he bent a look of appreciation on the woman seated across from him.

"You're a good cook, Debra."

She shrugged easily. "It doesn't take much talent to scramble eggs and fry bacon."

"Perhaps not, but someone baked the bread and churned the butter. I suspect you've learned well how to run a kitchen."

"My mother was a fine example to follow." She spoke softly, her eyes holding a faraway look. "She taught me all I know."

"Were you brought up in this house?" He found himself more than curious about her, his thoughts on the girl she'd been, the woman she'd become over the years. And yet, she was more girl than woman, he realized, surely not out of her teen years.

"How old are you?"

She looked up at him in surprise. "I was born and raised here. And now I'm old enough to live alone and take care of myself."

He grinned. "Maybe." The pause was long and

then he supplied her with his thoughts. "You weren't thinking last night when you walked into an empty house, Debra. You should have left a light on, or carried a gun."

"It would have been a waste of kerosene," she said sharply, "and my gun was already in the house." Her eyes met his with a dark look that offered scorn. "I've never had to fear having my home invaded before. This has always been a safe place to live. Until now."

"I mean you no harm, Debra Nightsong. I only need a place to stay for a while. I'll help you with chores, lend a hand wherever I can, in exchange for a bed and three meals a day. And when I leave, you'll be no worse for it."

"Entering my home uninvited makes you unwelcome. I didn't ask for your company, and I don't mind telling you that I don't appreciate your being here."

His grin was quick. "Sorry, ma'am. But, I'll be hanging around for a while. I'd thought to pay my way by working. I'd thought you might be some widow lady who needed a man to do some heavy work for her."

"Well, it must be obvious that I don't need a man for anything, Tyler, if that's really your name."

He thought her cheeks took on a rosy hue at that, and his chuckle appreciated her viewpoint. "It's my name, sure enough. And for your information, a good man can come in right handy, ma'am. For any number of things."

"I've gotten along without one for a long time. No

sense in changing my life now," she said pointedly. "I like things just the way they are."

"Living alone? Doing the work of a man? Trying to keep up a farm by yourself?" He knew his voice was impatient, and he modified it a bit. "I'd think having a man around for a few days might be a good thing for you. Give you a chance to order me around and have me handle some chores."

She looked at him from beneath dark lashes and he felt her mockery as she spoke. "How about weeding the garden then? Or perhaps putting up fence posts for a corral for my horse. I have any number of little jobs to be done."

She looked surprised at his smile. "I follow orders real good, ma'am. Where are the fence posts and a shovel?"

"I've had posts delivered from the sawmill. They're out behind the shed. The shovel is on the wall, next to the hoe. You'll need both if you plan on chopping weeds and digging holes."

"And what do I get in return?" He watched her as her mind worked, the smooth lines of her face giving him no clue as to her thoughts. And yet he thought she might be hiding a smile.

"You're not afraid of me, are you?" He'd startled her with that, he decided, for she blinked and looked unsettled for a moment.

"No. If you'd wanted to harm me, you would have already."

And if she only knew how tempted he'd been, last night when the moon had turned its face on her and illuminated the beauty of dark hair and smooth skin. Not to harm her, but to touch her woman's flesh, to bring her the warmth of his own. His control had been tried when he'd watched her as she slept. When his hands had craved the soft heat of her, his body had ached for the comfort of hers.

And yet, his intent would not have been to cause her pain, although that might have been an end result if he'd touched her slender form. She was no doubt a virgin, and would remain so while he lingered here, he vowed.

He'd never been prone to taking a woman who was not willing—indeed, not eager—to fill his bed. And there had been no lack of takers. Yet none of them had appealed to him in quite the same way as this female, this slim creature whose dark hair and eyes lured him with their mystery, whose slender fingers held the strength to milk a cow or wield a knife, whose home offered him a resting place where he might sort out his future.

And so he again spoke his intent, wanting to reassure her that his presence would bring her no harm. "I told you I wouldn't hurt you, Nightsong. I'll only be here as long as it takes to make my plans. As soon as I've decided my next move I'll be on my way and you'll be no worse off for having me here." And if he could tear himself away from the lure of her, from the soft scent of woman she exuded, the vision of beauty she offered to his hungry eye, he'd leave. And never forget the short time he'd spent in her presence.

"You'll leave me as you found me?" The question seemed to be as much a surprise to her as it was to him, and he refused to reply, only met her gaze in silence, not willing to offer an assurance he could not guarantee.

She rose and took her plate to the sink, then turned to retrieve his from the table. "Are you finished?"

He nodded, holding the last bit of toast in his hand. "Breakfast was good, Debra. Thank you." He watched as she poured hot water from the stove's reservoir into her dishpan, added soap from beneath the sink, and then sloshed her dishcloth to form suds.

"You didn't answer me." She turned to face him, holding the dishcloth in her hand as she approached the table. With smooth strokes, she wiped the surface clean, catching the crumbs in her hand and then looking up into his face, as if she would find some trace there of his intentions.

"Let's just take it one day at a time," he suggested. "For today, I'll dig post holes and lay out the corral for you. Do you have fencing or do you want a board fence?"

"I've had lumber delivered for the whole job. It's under a tarp behind the shed."

"Who were you planning to hire to do the work?" She sent him a look of scorn. "I have two good hands and I'm strong. It might have taken me longer than it will you, but I'd have done the job."

"I don't doubt that." He acknowledged her determination with a nod. "Let's leave the garden 'til tomorrow. Today, I'd like you with me out back."

"You don't trust me?"

"Should I?"

She laughed. "Probably not. But then, having my corral built without putting forth an effort on my part is tempting enough to keep me submissive for today."

"But not tomorrow?" His gaze held hers and he felt himself sinking into the depths of her soft brown eyes.

"I won't make any promises."

"I didn't think you would."

And so they left the house and within an hour, he'd dug several holes and the posts were leaning drunkenly into each of them, awaiting the dirt he would pack around each. Debra picked up a shovel and he shook his head. "I'll do that. Why don't you mark out the area you want to enclose? Use that stick over there and draw a line for me."

She nodded, shooting a wary glance his way, but did as he'd said, skirting a large tree and forming a rectangle that would give her horses ample room to exercise when she didn't want to stake them out in the meadow, yet still give them the shade of a tree during the heat of the day.

"You need a fence around the whole area, to pasture your cow," he told her.

"Right." The single word hummed with disdain. "Have you any idea how much it costs for wood from the lumberyard?" She looked beyond the limits she'd circumscribed for her corral and her gaze was wistful, as if she could see a fenced pasture, with her livestock feeding on the lush meadow grasses.

"Your problem is in finding cheap labor, I'd think," he said, following her gaze to where the trees offered shelter for animals from the sun's harsh rays.

"I can't afford to hire help, cheap or not. Things will get done when I'm able to do it myself. It may take a while, but I'll have a pasture full of animals one day."

"Animals? What do you have in mind?" He found he really wanted to know, had a desire to search out the crevices of her mind, seek out the dreams she sheltered there.

"Horses, maybe. I'd like to breed my mares. There's money to be made. It just takes time and a lot of effort."

"Do you have a stud available?"

She shook her head. "My nearest neighbor has a sorrel he might be persuaded to let me use for my riding mare. I need a bargaining tool, and I haven't figured it out yet."

Tyler nodded, thinking about the unknown neighbor and what he might ask for payment in exchange for the use of his stud, and found his thoughts straying into forbidden territory. The woman was too vulnerable, too open to hurt.

"How much hay do you have here?" He waved a hand at the far-off field, where the crop of hay was tall, ready to cut, awaiting the scythe of harvest.

"About twenty acres. I'm thinking about having him bring his crew over to cut it and keeping some for my own use. I had a man from closer to town come out last year and we worked out a share plan. I thought I might gain the use of the sorrel stallion for a few days in exchange for my hayfield."

"Keep what you need and offer him the rest," Tyler advised.

"Easy for you to say," she said with a harsh burst of laughter. "You're a man, and men make the rules in this world, I've found. I'll no doubt have to abide by whatever he's willing to offer me."

"So long as you have enough from the first cutting to fill your loft, you can stake your animals all summer and probably have another cutting of hay to bargain with in August." He looked around the space behind the shed. "Where did your straw stack come from?"

"The same farmer. He kept the wheat from my back acres and left me the straw for my animals."

"I think you came out on the short end of the stick." And he bristled as he thought about the neighbor who had taken advantage of a woman alone. "He kept all the wheat?"

"I have enough from my eggs and butter to cover what flour I need at the general store," she said readily. "I'm well aware that the man takes advantage of me, but as long as my needs are met, I can afford to be generous."

"Is your neighbor married?"

Her eyes widened again at his query and she nodded quickly. "Of course, with several children. He has a profitable operation."

"And is he a gentleman?" His gaze pinned her and he watched as his meaning struck home.

She shifted her gaze, her lip trembling as she sought a reply. "He hasn't had much choice. I won't put up with any shenanigans."

"You're a woman alone, Debra. You're in danger of his shenanigans, no matter that you have a gun and a lot of spunk."

She was silent for a moment and then her words told of the fear she lived with. "I'm careful. Usually," she inserted, as if she thought of her rash behavior last night, when she'd stumbled into danger in her own kitchen.

"If your neighbor knows you have a man here, he might not be so eager to take advantage of you."

"And he might spread the word around town that the Indian has taken a man into her bed." She spoke the words in a rush, as though she'd already considered the idea.

"And would that be difficult for you to live with?"

"Only if I plan on buying from the general store and being made welcome in town. A woman alone is always under scrutiny, with men waiting for her to make the wrong move. I can't afford to leave myself open to public scorn. I walk alone, and I have to watch every move I make."

"Well, your neighbor might be more amenable to a fair division of your hay if I'm out there in the field doing your share of the work. You can tell him you've hired a man to help out."

"And ruin my name in town? I don't think so."

"You'll let him take advantage of you instead?"

"It's the price I pay for being what I am." Her tone was one of a woman beaten down by circumstance, and Tyler could not countenance it.

"You're a woman alone, a woman who should be given the respect due her."

"I'm a half-breed." Her words were spoken firmly, as if they were familiar to her.

"And I'm a white man, which makes me neither better nor worse than you. You are a woman, first and foremost, Debra. Was your mother white? Or your father?"

"My father. He owned this place, and brought my mother here when they married. When he died, she took the deed with her. He'd made it out to me, and it was my legacy after my mother was gone."

"How long have you been here alone?" And how had she survived? How had a young woman alone been able to cope with the running of a farm?

"Three years, since I was sixteen. It hasn't been

simple, but I've managed to support myself. And now I have the beginnings of my herd of horses."

"Where did you get the mares?"

"Bought them from a man who sold his place and moved farther west. He had too many animals to take along, and gave me a good price on the three out back. One is already bred."

"I can see that." He looked out beyond the corral line she'd drawn in the dirt, out to where the meadow grasses grew and flourished. Where one of her mares stood apart, her sides bulging a bit with the foal she would drop months from now. She might one day have a herd of horses if luck was with her and the mares she cherished produced colts and fillies of merit.

"Have you thought of expanding? Buying more horses?"

She laughed, a short, sharp sound that scorned his idea. "And what would I use for money? Horses are expensive. I was fortunate to get the ones I already have."

"Where did you get your mare? The one you ride."

"I brought her with me from the tribe. She'd been running wild and I caught her and tamed her for myself. Then after my mother was gone, I left and came back home, brought the mare with me."

"You tamed her?"

Her chin tilted and a look of pride lit her eyes.

"Yes. The finest day of my life was when I got up on her back and rode away from the village of my mother's people."

"They weren't *your* people?"

She tossed him a look of scorn and disbelief. "I don't fit there, any more than I do in town. I'm an outcast, Tyler, as you well know. I don't have a place in this world, but the one I make for myself."

"Will you take my help, Debra Nightsong? Will you let me give you a hand, and work for my keep for a while?"

"Why?" It was a single word that asked for more than he was willing to give.

"Maybe because I'm an outcast, too."

She gave him a measuring look. "Are you? Or are you on the run?"

"You might say that. There are those who'd like to find me, and if I can find a safe place for a while, I'd be more than happy to earn a few weeks of peace."

"Should I ask who is looking for you? Or am I better off not knowing?"

"Just know that I mean you no harm, Debra." And with that she'd would have to be satisfied, he thought. For knowledge of his past would only frighten her, perhaps put her in danger.

"I'm foolish, I fear," she said slowly. "But I'm smart enough to know that your help would benefit me greatly." She inhaled deeply and let the breath escape slowly. "I'll take a chance on you. You can stay, I'll give you your safe place for a while, and you'll work for me."

His hand shot out, silently asking her to take it, to seal their bargain, and she responded as he'd thought she would. Her slender fingers formed to his palm, and he held them there, firmly, yet carefully, as he might shelter a small, helpless creature in his grasp.

But the woman who met his look with a level gaze of her own was not a creature who would ask for anything but what was due her. Respect, first and foremost. A measure of friendship, perhaps an honest day's work. He could do all of that. So long as she understood that the rules were his to make, hers to follow.

"I'll be staying in the house with you," he said firmly. "You'll not put up a fuss about me sharing your home. And I'll be sleeping in your bed."

She was silent, as though she accepted his terms, and then her head turned and he met the challenge in her gaze. "I'll not be tied to you at night, nor will I let you touch me during the day."

It was almost a dare on her part, for she lacked clout, and they both knew it. He was stronger by far, she perhaps more devious, but without the power to make him abide by her wishes.

"I won't tie you, Debra, and I'll keep my hands to myself. That far I'll go, not because I fear your knife or your skill with a gun, but because I respect you. Does that suit you?"

She nodded, slowly, but with a definite acceptance of his terms. "If you build my corral and set posts for a pasture fence for me, I'll give you a place to stay and cook for you."

His nod was a tacit approval of her terms, and he breathed more easily. Staying one step ahead of the man who followed him had been nerve-wracking. A respite would be welcome.

"Who are you hiding from?" Debra asked, as if the question had been fermenting in her mind and now begged to be spoken aloud.

If he expected her to give him refuge, he owed her an explanation, Tyler decided. "I killed a man." It was the truth so far as it went, and he watched as she digested his words, her eyes widening a bit, her mouth forming a soft "Oh" of surprise.

CHAPTER THREE

SHE LOOKED AT HIM with the level gaze of a woman set on having answers to her questions. And her query was what he might have expected. "Did you have a good reason?"

She indeed had the ability to cut through the deed to find the justification for his action. And he could do no less than answer her truthfully.

"I thought so. Still do, for that matter. He broke into my home while I was away, and killed my wife and son." The words were blunt, their message harsh, and he awaited her reaction.

Her hand reached for him, the sympathy in her action obvious and she spoke quickly. "No one could blame you for taking revenge on him, Tyler. Surely the law didn't accuse you of murder."

"The sheriff said I had no proof that he'd killed them. Said it could have been anyone, and I'd taken out my anger on the first available prospect."

"Had you no proof?" She awaited his words and he was willing to tell her what she wanted to know.

"His watch was attached to a braid of her hair.

And he didn't deny the killing to me, in fact he bragged about his taking of her body before he killed her. The fool waved his gun at me and told me how my son had run for his life, how he'd shot him down."

His voice broke on the words, and Debra's hand touched his, the warmth flowing from her bringing him back from the scene that haunted him still. He turned his hand to grasp her fingers and held them tightly within his own.

"He would have killed me," Tyler said, "but I was quicker than he'd expected. I shot the gun from his hand and then fired again. I didn't miss."

"How long ago?" she asked, and he looked beyond her, as if his eyes saw the past clearly.

"Almost two years ago. I was put in jail, and when there was a general jailbreak, I took advantage of the fact and escaped. The rest of the prisoners stayed together and were caught."

"You kept to yourself?" she asked, knowing already that he would not have relied on others to protect him.

"I ran as far and as fast as I could. Climbed into the first boxcar I saw at the train station and set off on my own. Been traveling alone ever since."

She felt herself leaning toward him, not physically, but somehow able to see within his actions to the man who still felt the pain of his loss, who didn't regret the life he'd taken in revenge.

He stood before her, tall, muscular, yet slim, as

though his meals had been sparse of late, and she could not fault the man. That he might be telling her a tall tale was a possibility, but Debra Nightsong was no fool, and she'd long been able to see the truth when it appeared before her.

Today was no exception. The man might be running from the law, but in his own mind, he'd done no wrong, only avenged two deaths. That his actions had brought the law down on him was perhaps not fair, but nevertheless a fact. Could she turn him away, believing his story as she did?

"You can stay here," she said. "I'll not turn you in, Tyler, even if I get the chance. Whether or not you killed in cold blood, I suspect you felt you had the right to avenge your wife and son's deaths. I'm not fit to judge you. I won't even try."

He loosed her fingers from his own and stood tall before her. His dark eyes met hers with a gaze that promised the truth, and she was prone to believe him.

"I'll not play false with you," he said. "I'll stay here and help you." His eyes measured her and he smiled. "I don't know how far I can trust you to keep silent about me should the occasion arise, but for now I'll have to give you the benefit of the doubt."

Her hand was warmed by his, her flesh still aware of his touch, and she thrust it into her apron pocket, where her fingers curled in upon themselves. He was strong, a man taller than most, his shoulders wider than the men of her mother's tribe, his ability to force her to his will not an issue, for she was wise enough to gauge the muscle beneath his skin, smart enough to recognize a man with the ability to hold his own.

The sun shone down brightly on the meadow behind her shed, the horses and her cow grazed peacefully at the end of their tethers and the man beside her had made his position clear. Debra looked beyond the animals and the lush pasture where they grazed, to where the hayfield lay, awaiting the scythe and the men who would reap its worth.

"Will you help me put up enough hay before I allow the neighbor to take his share?" It was not what she had planned on saying to the man beside her, but the knowledge that he was strong and capable of helping her hold her own, of lending his strength to hers for a time, made her seek out his promise.

"Where is your scythe?" he asked. So simply he agreed to her plan, so readily he acceded to her need.

"Hanging on the wall. I keep all my tools inside the shed," she said. "If you'll use the scythe, I'll rake the hay. A day or so in the sun will dry it enough so I can bring it to the barn for storage."

"We have a deal, Debra Nightsong." His hand reached for hers again, and she slid it from her pocket, allowing him to grasp it in his own, warming it with the heat of his flesh. His eyes narrowed as he looked past the pasture before them, his sights on the same hayfield she'd measured with her own gaze. The hay was ready to be mowed, the sun promised to shine, probably for several days, for no rain clouds threatened in the west.

Debra felt a surge of satisfaction at the deal they'd formed. For a week she would have the help she needed. Her loft would be full, her animals would have their needs supplied for the winter to come. Perhaps the garden might thrive under a man's touch, for she was not able to plow up the soil as she should. Her strength was not enough to turn over the earth for the space she required.

As if he knew her thoughts, Tyler leaned against the wall of the shed and mulled over the needs of her farm. She turned her gaze to him as he spoke, pleased that he seemed to so readily fall into the role she had set for him.

"I'll use one of your horses to plow more space for a garden, Debra. Have any of them been broken to harness? Have you used them for plowing?"

"I've only used a shovel," she said. "I don't have the strength to hold a plow steady. It takes a man's muscles to force the blade into the ground. And using the shovel takes me forever to prepare the ground for my garden."

"I can handle that for you," he said. "I'll add to the space you've already set aside if you like."

"I'll plant corn if you prepare the ground for me," she said quickly. "I only have room now for beans and tomatoes and such. I've got peas and carrots coming up, almost ready to pick."

He looked back through the shed to where the chickens had strayed into the yard, pecking at the bits and pieces of food they found there. "Corn makes good feed for chickens through the winter. Can you have it ground at the gristmill in town?"

She nodded, feeling her spirits lift as she thought of the crop she might plant and then sow in late summer. If she could trust this man... And why shouldn't she be able to? He was as good a prospect as the neighbor who had taken her wheat and left her the straw. As willing to help as the man who had mowed her hayfield and taken his greater share for granted.

"Can we work together for a while, Debra?" He asked the question softly, his voice falling on her hearing as a temptation, perhaps luring her into believing that he could be trusted, that his help would be hers for a time.

"Yes." She accepted him so readily it shocked her. So easily did she acquiesce to his offer. "Yes," she repeated. He was behind her now, looking over her shoulder at the animals in her pasture, his chore of putting up a corral for her well under way and she was comforted by the knowledge that for now, for these few days, she was not alone.

THE FENCE POSTS stood straight, the boards joining them nailed in place, each level with the next. Debra crossed her arms on the top rail, looking beyond the boundaries of her newly built corral to where her animals grazed in the sun. Another horse had joined her stable, a bay mare already with foal, purchased from a neighbor who needed ready cash. Already broken to the saddle, the mare would provide cash income if Debra chose to sell her after the birth of her foal. For unless she had a stud available on a regular basis, she would not be able to breed her mares at the right times.

Her resources sorely strained by the additional purchase, Debra consoled herself with the idea of a second colt or filly in the spring when the mare would deliver the first addition to her newly formed stable of animals. Her bank account was down to rock bottom, but the purchase was sound, Tyler had said, and she felt able to trust his judgment.

One dark night, astride one of her mares, he'd returned the gelding he'd confiscated as his own to its owner's field, not divulging its origins to her, only saying that it had probably not been missed by its owner. Showing no guilt for his misdeed, he'd made her smile with his simplistic notion that his theft had only amounted to a loan from the farmer.

She admitted to herself that she would have hated the thought of his death at the end of a rope, should his crime have come to light, but not for the world would she let him know that she had ignored his theft and the subsequent return of the evidence.

His help had been invaluable over the past weeks, and she was reaping the results of his work. Her garden flourished, with corn hilled in neat rows, tomatoes forming small fruit on their vines and beans cooking in the big kettle in the house even now. A pan of peas had been shelled and cooked before she canned them in pint jars just yesterday. Carrots showed their orange shoulders just above the ground, awaiting her hand, and she planned the stew she would make from the last of the potatoes in her fruit cellar, plus a piece of beef she'd bartered from her neighbor.

A peck of peas and enough beans for a meal had earned her a chunk of stewing meat from his butchering. Summer was not the usual time for a steer to be sacrificed for the family's needs, but the herd of cattle in the fields to the west of her property was prosperous, and her neighbor had killed one and cut it up for his wife's use.

A quarter of the beef hung even now in the woodshed, and Debra planned for its use. She would cut it up, cook it in large chunks in her stewing kettle and then can it for her use over the next few months.

Tyler had said he was familiar with butchering and had given her neighbor a hand with his chore, earning her the beef as a part of his salary. The neighbor had quizzed him at length regarding his presence at Debra's holding, and Tyler dutifully gave her chapter and verse of their conversation.

"I made it clear to him that I was merely a hired hand here, a man in need of money, and willing to work for it. I let him know that I admired you and respected you, Debra."

"And did he believe you? Or did he seem to think the half-breed had taken a white man to her bed?"

Her blunt manner surprised him, although he wasn't certain why it should have caused him any surprise. She was a bold woman, not afraid to speak her mind. He spoke again, wanting to ease her mind.

"He didn't make any backhanded remarks, if that's what you mean. Just seemed to accept my word for it. I think he admires you, Debra. He spoke highly of you and your ambition, your work here on the farm."

She nodded, accepting his words of praise, almost as if they were due her. He could only hope that the townspeople were as well informed as to Debra's conduct in the community. Putting the stain of a woman without honor on her was far from his intent. But people talked, gossiped when things didn't seem to their individual standards, and putting Debra's name on the line was not to be considered.

Their association had proved thus far to be profitable to them both, Debra considering herself the winner with a new corral and a pasture already partly fenced in.

Tyler said the neighbor had seemingly been satisfied regarding his presence at Debra's farm, nod-

ding agreeably when he was told that Tyler was helping with the crops and caring for the livestock.
Agreeing that Debra needed help and hiring a hand
to work for her seemed logical.

But, as Tyler said, the man had smiled broadly as
he spoke of Debra's hard work and her need for a
husband. As if he considered Tyler an applicant for
the position. Perhaps that would settle any gossip to
be found in town, Tyler thought, and tucked the notion into the back of his mind to consider further.

He'd managed to work enough hours for the
neighbor to earn himself a horse, not a prize package
to be sure, but a ten-year-old gelding who promised
to provide his owner with years of use. Debra didn't
own a saddle and had convinced Tyler that he could
ride without the aid of leather between himself and
his horse. His determination to purchase a saddle at
the earliest opportunity was pure stubbornness on
his part, she was sure, but it was an argument she
knew she would not win. The man was determined
to fit his animal out with all the requisite tools—
bridle and bit and a saddle that would make his riding a comfort.

She scorned his need for such trappings, happy
with the golden mare she rode, who obeyed the touch
of her knees against her sides, the rope she tied about
the animal's neck enough of a guide for what she
required of the mare she rode with pride. Tyler
watched her, his eyes admiring her skill when she

rode, and she delighted in the knowledge that he did not deny her ability to control her horse so easily.

Indeed, she could have ridden without even the rope in her hands, for the animal had been trained to obey her voice, and there existed between them a rapport that made their relationship a joy to watch. Yet she did not deny Tyler the right to his need for a harness for the plowhorse and the saddle he planned to purchase for his gelding.

The amount of hay she had decided to keep for her own use was cut in three days' time, Tyler wielding the scythe, she spreading the harvest to dry in the sun. Raking it into rows the second day, she examined it and found it dry. By the time he'd cut enough hay to fill her loft, she'd spread it out, then raked it into piles, ready for loading onto a flat wagon from the shed.

Tyler hitched her pack horse to the wagon and together they scooped great armfuls of hay to the flat bed. Her rake gathered up the scattered bits and pieces and she added them to the pile that grew quickly. Hauling the hay back to the shed was but a small task, with Tyler doing the hardest part of the job, loading the hay into the loft for her use later on in the year.

Together they carried the fragrant piles up the ladder, tying it up in a quilt and hauling it through the hole in the floor of the loft, only to dump it and then rake it up into great piles in the drafty loft.

Debra looked about her with a sense of pride, that she had managed to harvest so much of her crop with Tyler's help. She felt rich with the knowledge that her animals would have feed for the long months of winter, thankful for the man who had lent his greater strength to her aid, and thus helped her make gains against the cold weather that was sure to come.

She stood looking at the bountiful piles of winter hay and caught the grin Tyler sent in her direction. He bowed with great ceremony, and approached her diffidently. "Does my work merit a reward?" he asked.

"What did you have in mind?" Her heart beat more rapidly as he surveyed her slowly, his dark eyes lingering on her lips, then traveling down the length of her body.

His words were bold. "Maybe a kiss. Even a hug, if you're so inclined."

She thought him a scamp, but reserved her opinion, judging that he'd earned at least a kiss, since it seemed so important to him, and she had more than enough to suit him. Approaching him, she tilted her head a bit, the better to reach his lips and brushed her own against the firm line that awaited her. His mouth softened beneath her touch and he reached for her, not allowing her to escape his embrace.

"How about the hug?" he asked, already taking possession of her with both arms wrapped about her.

"Was I to give the hug, or receive it?" At odds with

her own response, she felt a blush climb her cheeks as his muscular frame pressed against her softer body, knew for a moment the heat of his embrace, and then as he bent his head lower, felt his lips snatch another kiss from her willing mouth. It wasn't a peck, as she'd thought it might be, but a full-blown kiss, involving the damp touch of his tongue against her, edging between her lips, into the warmth of her mouth. He sought the length of her tongue with his, tangling them together, taking her breath with his venture into an intimacy she was not confident with.

She trembled in his grasp, feeling exposed as these waters were too deep for her to gain any sense of balance. "Tyler? Tyler, what are you doing?" She tried to catch her breath as she pulled from his grasp, only to catch a quick glimpse of his lips, curved into a superior sort of smile he'd slanted in her direction.

"What do you think, sweetheart? Just claiming my kiss, and about half a hug."

"Half a hug? How do you figure that?" She brushed at her dress, unable to meet his gaze, and he laughed.

"I hugged you, but you didn't hug me back. That's half a hug in my book, lady. Can you do better?"

She shook her head. "Would you settle for a cup of coffee and fresh coffee cake? I've got a pot brewing on the stove and the cinnamon cakes are still warm."

He grimaced. "Better than nothing, I suspect. But

I'm not letting you off the hook, sweetie. I'll get you another time."

And that was exactly what she feared, she decided, climbing hastily down from the loft and heading for the house, as far and fast as she could march from his arrogant grin.

And yet, all of his teasing aside, it was a good feeling, she thought, pouring his coffee and cutting the cake, knowing that she was at least halfway prepared for the winter months, knowing that her stock would be fed. And wondering who would be pitching the hay from the loft?

THE FARMER WHO HAD CUT her crop last year was notified to come and take his share, and Tyler spoke with him about the price he should pay for the crop. Apparently surprised that Debra had a champion in residence, Samuel Shane agreed on a price for the hay, and bartered part of his butchering in the fall, plus apples from his orchard for his share of the harvest. If Mr. Shane was curious about Tyler's place here on her farm, he did not speak of it, only nodded as he agreed with the conditions set out by Debra's hired man.

Debra was pleased, cautious about expressing her thanks to Tyler, but aware that having a man standing in her stead was indeed a thing to be pleased with. In fact, she found herself thinking about his presence in her home and wishing fervently and silently that his time with her would not soon come to an end.

It was almost as if they shared the farm, she thought, pulling carrots from the garden, plucking beans from their stems. He, with the hammer and his greater strength forming the fences she needed, she with her skills in the kitchen, and throughout the house, making a comfortable place for them to live.

He appealed to her senses, his clean scent, his habits of cleanliness matching so closely her own. He swam nightly in the pool in the pasture, sharing the water with the animals that drank there after dark. His clothing was washed and hung on the clothesline, his trousers and shirts side by side with her own dresses and undergarments. She wondered sometimes what the neighbors thought of the man who lived on her farm with her, but had not sought out their opinion.

That there was talk in town was a given, but she could not bring herself to worry overmuch about gossip. What she did was her own concern, and not fit for speculation by anyone else.

With whom she chose to make her life was private business, and she chose for now to allow Tyler access to her farm and to the house she lived in. They seldom spoke of his past, only living with the knowledge that he might one day take flight from her life.

She had not offered him any glimpse into her own past, living in the present and walking a fine line in his presence. He slept on the floor in her bedroom, changing his mind apparently after the third night of sleeping beside her.

He'd spread his quilt on the rug beside the bed, and without a word had gone to sleep there. Unwilling to question his decision, lest he repent his change of mind, Debra had crawled into her bed each night and slept peacefully, knowing he was nearby, yet not fearful of his presence.

He rose early, stoked the wood-burning cookstove and went out to do chores while she cooked breakfast. Her privacy was not invaded by his presence, for he used the parlor in which to dress, storing his clothing in a drawer in her dresser, but keeping himself apart from her.

It was a strange arrangement, she knew, but it suited them both, and she found comfort in the companionship he offered. They spoke but little, only words that related to the work they did, he with his building, she with the gardening, and only when she sat on the porch in the evening and watched the sun dip beneath the horizon did she feel the need for more from him.

That he might fill a permanent place in her life was not considered, for she knew he would not linger longer than it would take for him to plot out his future. He had a horse now, and a bit of money set aside, due to his work on the neighboring farm. Soon he would surely be on his way, leaving her alone again.

But better off than before, for he had laid out the fencing for the pasture and by the time the second cutting of hay approached, he had completed the job. Her horses and the milk cow roamed at will beneath the trees, spending their days with heads lowered to the ground, where the meadow grass grew in abundance. The sides of her bay mare rounded more each week it seemed, and it seemed that by the end of winter she would see her own golden mare producing an offspring of her own.

Whether the mare had been covered by a wild mustang or perhaps the neighbor's stud, a stallion who had frequently escaped confinement and roamed the far pastures and meadows, was a moot question. That her golden mare had had an encounter with the stud was a probability, she knew, and she spoke of it to Tyler.

"If she drops another golden foal, it will have been from the sorrel stud," she said, watching the horses one day. He stood beside her, and his nod agreed with her prediction.

"I've heard that a mare such as yours only breeds true if a sorrel is the sire."

"It's what my mother's people said. And they were experts at the art of raising horses."

He turned to her, a question alive on his lips. "Did you have any problems in town yesterday?" She'd gone in to the general store with her supply of eggs and butter, and made the trip alone, Tyler remaining at the farm.

"The storekeeper asked if I had a man living with me." Her voice was quiet, but he sensed the pain behind her reply. "He wanted to know if you had serious intentions where I was concerned. I suppose it was a backhanded way of asking if you were going to marry me."

"Did he give you a bad time? Or didn't you tell him the truth?"

"It was none of his business, but he knew already. My neighbor no doubt told about your working for him. And I made it clear that you were a hired hand, and not a permanent fixture here.

"At any rate, he was reluctant to sell supplies to me, but he needed my butter and eggs, so he had no choice. The townsfolk who don't have animals of their own depend on farmers to supply their needs, and my butter is always rich from the Jersey's cream." Her smile smacked of the victory she'd known, there in town, where she had attained a degree of respect.

"So they talk about me being here. Has anyone asked you who I am?"

She shook her head. "I wouldn't have offered anything anyway. I'm not known for being talkative. One of the ladies was curious about you, wondered if I'd known you sometime in the past, and was curious about your living here. She suggested that it didn't look good for me to have you living here, what with me being a woman alone, but I made it clear that it wasn't her concern. She only smiled at that and I suspect that there's talk that we're..." Her pause was long and he felt a pang of regret that she should be considered the less for his presence in her life.

"Have you ever thought of marriage? Has anyone ever approached you and asked to court you?"

She offered him a look of such surprise he almost laughed aloud. "What's so strange about such a thing, Debra? You're a beautiful woman, with a thriving farm, and surely there are men about who would want to possess both you and your property."

"I'm still a half-breed. No matter how much land I own, or how well my land produces, I'm not a woman to appeal to white men. Perhaps for other reasons, but not for marriage."

"Have you had problems with the men hereabouts? Have they bothered you?"

She shook her head, then seemed to hesitate. "A bit, but my shotgun has been sufficient to keep them at bay." She clutched the top rail of the fence tightly. "I fear that I may be taken by surprise someday, that someone may come upon me when I'm in the garden or the shed and my gun is not with me."

"You don't carry it, Debra? Would it be wise to keep it by your side?"

She turned to him and her gaze was level. "Not with you here. No one will approach me as long as you stay." Her smile teased him. "I consider you a form of insurance against predators."

"And when I'm gone?"

Her head drooped and he thought her shoulders

sagged a bit, as if she were troubled by that thought. And then she straightened and her chin lifted, perhaps with pride.

"I'll be as I was before you got here. Alone, but able to care for myself and what is mine."

He reached out to her, his fingers brushing the fine skin of her cheek and she inhaled sharply, her eyes widening as if she would withdraw from his touch. He would not allow it, but stepped closer, curving his palm against her face and turning her to better see the expression she wore.

"What if I stayed, Debra? What if I made this my home, and you…" He took a breath, knowing she might flee from his words. "What if we were to marry? Could you spend your life with me, knowing of my past? Knowing I've taken a life?"

The words fell between them and she twisted from his touch, her eyes wide with panic, as if she feared him. He would not have it. She had not feared him, had not flinched from his presence in weeks, and now she acted as if he had grown horns.

"Don't pull away from me," he said harshly. "I'm still the same man I was ten minutes ago, Debra. I'm not going to pounce on you or hurt you in any way. I thought you knew me well enough by now not to fear me."

She shook her head. "I don't fear you. My hesitation is not because you've taken a life, for I know you were justified in what you did. I just can't accept the idea of marriage to a white man. Nor to a man of my mother's people, for that matter. I will live my life alone."

"Why?" His question was bold, he knew, but his need to know her thoughts was heavy on him. "Why can't you be my wife? I wouldn't expect more of you than what you give me gladly. I'm not a harsh man, nor will I change overnight if you bear my name. I'm free of hindrance, with no family to tie me. And I'm a hard worker, surely you've seen that. I wouldn't be a bad husband."

Her eyes were dark, black with what appeared to be fear, and he failed to understand what she dreaded. "Do I frighten you, Debra?" And if she nodded, he would mount his horse and leave, for the thought of her fear made him feel less than a man.

She placed the flat of her hand on his chest, and he felt the warmth of it radiate throughout his body. Unmoving, she measured him with her gaze, her eyes taking stock of his face, his arms, the length of his legs and the width of his chest where her palm had laid claim to the body beneath it.

"Your heartbeat is strong," she said quietly. "It is the beat of an honest heart, Tyler, and you are an honest man. I can not deny that. You have been good to me, you've worked for me and taken hold as if this were your own place." Her tongue touched her upper lip as if she hesitated to speak further and he held his breath, for surely her words would frame his future.

His hand lifted to cover hers and he felt the warmth of long fingers and the fragile bones of a woman beneath his touch. "I would take you as my wife, Debra, if you agree. I'll work for you and provide for you as a husband, and if I'm hunted down, I'll leave you as I found you. You won't bear shame because of my past."

"You will expect to share my bed." It was a statement of fact, not a query, and he considered it as such. Her mouth trembled as he watched, the first sign of feminine weakness she'd shown in his presence. His index finger rose to touch the line of her upper lip and he caressed it carefully.

"Yes." It was a single word, but it spoke volumes, and he recognized her hesitation for what it was. She had not known a man's body, and feared being used as a wife.

He watched his hand, saw the trembling of his fingers as they spread once more against her cheek. "I need you as a man needs a woman, but I won't take what you hold dear. Unless you offer your body to me, I'll do without the comfort of your woman's flesh."

"Men aren't usually so willing to—" Her voice broke off as if she could not bring herself to speak the words that filled her throat.

"I'm not most men." He bent to her, lifting her chin with his palm and touched her lips with his own, brushing lightly against the softness he found there.

"I would treasure the kiss you give me," he said softly.

Her lips were a temptation he found it almost impossible to turn from and he coaxed her gently, his own opening but slightly, not wanting to frighten her with the desire that filled him. She was soft, gently formed, and he had been long without a woman in his arms. Not since his wife's death had he yearned so for the pleasure to be found in the depths of a female's body.

And now his yearning was great, his arousal prominent and obvious as he pressed her against himself. His arms around her were firm and she accepted his touch, leaning against him as if his heat drew her. His hand slipped down her back, pressing her closer, and he felt her warmth enclose his need.

It was all he could do not to hold himself against her more firmly, but he knew she would be frightened if he kept her captive, and so he relaxed his arms a bit, offering her the space to move from him.

Debra felt her body still, knew a moment of fear as she sensed his man's arousal against her belly. She'd not known the feel of a man's flesh, but knew the look of a man before he takes a woman to his bed. The braves of her mother's tribe had made no secret of their prowess with the women of the tribe, and more than one had come to her mother and offered himself to her.

It had frightened the girl who watched, and she'd

buried her head in her bedding as the sounds of a man using her mother had hammered into her memory. Now she knew the body of an aroused man for herself, knew the feel of his need for her and felt a returning desire for his touch.

"You're a virgin, Debra, and I would not hurt you or take you to bed unless you become my wife first." His words penetrated her sense of fear and she relaxed against him. "Does my need for you frighten you, little bird?"

She nodded, once, and then stood with her face buried against his chest. Her words were soft, poignant, and her voice faltered as she spoke. "I saw the men of my mother's tribe. One of them came to her while I lay nearby." She could not continue, and her voice broke.

"It was not for a child to see or hear such a thing," he said roughly. "You didn't understand what was happening, and you were but a child, too young to be exposed to your mother's—"

"She wasn't willing, but he took her anyway," Debra said. "I heard her cry when he used her body, and he laughed at her, told her she was but a woman and good for nothing else."

"And did you believe what he said?" Tyler held her close, wanting only to cherish the young child she had been and the woman she was now.

"I suppose I did then," she admitted. "For I knew no better. But now I know that he only tried to shame her in order to make himself look more a man."

"He was less than a man, to take a woman without her yielding to him gladly," Tyler said softly. "He had no right. Men have no rights but those a woman gives them."

"You come from a different world than I. Women are not cherished by men in my remembrance, all but my father, and the way he was with my mother when I was a child."

"Then try to remember that and forget the rest," Tyler told her. "Recall only the good things that happened in your life, the family you lived with here on your father's farm, the good times you shared with him and your mother. He must have loved you to leave you his land. He must have known you would care for it and keep it as it was."

"My mother said he loved me." It seemed but little for a woman to cherish, the secondhand knowledge of her father's love, but it was obviously a comfort to the woman he held, and Tyler added what warmth he could to the knowledge she held so dear.

His arms were strong, his body warm, and she nestled against him as if she'd come home. Her breath was shattered as she inhaled deeply, the sound faltering, as if she suppressed tears, and he would not shame her by acknowledging her sadness.

"Marry me, Debra. Be my wife, little nightbird. You may not feel any desire for me now, but it will come, I promise you. One day you'll want me as I want you."

She tipped her head back and met his gaze, her eyes dark with a look he dared hope might be desire for him. His mouth touched hers again and his kiss was welcomed, her own lips warm against his, her breath sweet. He did not press for more, only the touch of her flesh comforting his own.

Her arms slipped around his neck and she pressed her body closer to his, fitting herself to the length of him, her breasts against his chest, allowing his hips to nestle in the cradle of her own. And if his arousal frightened her, she did not draw back from him, only shifted a bit as though she wondered at the pressure of his manhood against her.

His mouth lifted from hers, his lips closed, for he would not frighten her with his passion, knowing she would fear the touch of his tongue should he use it to force his way into the warmth of her mouth. She clung to him, her hands strong as she held the nape of his neck, her body conforming to the shape of his own.

"You give yourself sweetly," he said, his voice a low hum in her ear. "I can barely keep from lying you on the ground and taking you for my own."

She shook her head, rubbing it on his chest, denying his need. "I don't think I can do as you want, Tyler. My mother told me once that there is pain when a man takes a woman for the first time, that his path is not smooth, that he must forge a way into her body that gives her only pain."

"There is pain in that," he admitted. "But it is overcome by the pleasure to follow, if a man is careful, if he is gentle and cares for the woman he beds." His hands touched her sides, measuring her waist and the width of her hips, then met at her back, soothing the line of her spine with tender strokes.

"I would be gentle with you, little bird. I would not cause you pain if it can be helped."

She trembled against him, and he knew her fear was real, that she held memories of a time long past, when she had been exposed to the dark side of a man's needs.

CHAPTER FOUR

THEY SPOKE NO MORE of the offering he'd made to her, Debra only thinking of it, considering the idea of being the mate of a man such as Tyler. And at that, she hesitated, recognizing that she only knew him by that name, and not even certain if it were his first or last.

Tyler. She spoke it beneath her breath, and yet he heard her, for his head came up and he made her aware of his presence. He was near her on the porch, his arm resting on his knee as he sat leaning against the post near the steps. His gaze was dark, and she wondered what it held, for he gave little away, only looked on her as a man might look at a woman he considered to be available.

His eyes touched her but lightly, as if he would not show his desire for her, and yet it lingered there, a potent presence between them. For he'd spoken it aloud, only a day ago, when he'd asked her to consider marriage to him.

Her answer hovered on the tip of her tongue, and she held it quiet, for trust did not come easily to her.

He'd done as he said, had given her no reason to doubt his word, had not made any approach to her person but for those few minutes behind the barn, when he'd held her close.

Still, she hesitated, for to accept the man as her mate would allow him access to her bed, and she didn't know if she could accept that. If she could give him her body as he would expect her to. For men were not prone to patience, she knew. The men of her mother's tribe had proved that with their pursuit of the women they wanted. She'd been apart from all of that, protected by the mixed blood that flowed in her veins.

But no such protection existed now. For this man knew what she was, knew the shame she bore from her mixed heritage and cared little for that stain on her worth. He seemed to look at her as a female who appealed to him, who caused his passions to rise in his body. A woman he would wed and call by his name.

Then she would be…Debra Tyler? Somehow she didn't think that was his name. That knowledge spurred her to the query that sprang from her lips.

"What is your name? Truly your name," she asked, looking at the man who sat with such a relaxed demeanor on her porch. His arm did not shift, his leg did not straighten at her words, and he sat as he was, only moving his head to better see her expression.

"You don't like calling me Tyler?" His mouth twisted in a grin that made her smile in return.

"It's a fine name. I just don't think that's all there is to it," she answered, knowing that she was right in her assumption. Knowing that he teased her by his words.

"You may be right," he said quietly. "On the day you marry me, I'll tell you the rest of it. Will that be enough to merit an answer from you?"

"You're a determined man, aren't you?"

"And you are as equally determined, Nightsong. Shall I know your name also?"

"My father's name was David. I didn't know his last name until he died. My mother only called him David and I was too young to care about any other name but my own. I've been Debra Nightsong my whole life. I never took his name."

"And what was it?"

"David Thornley. I found it on the deed to this place when my mother gave it to me. I suppose I could have taken his name then, but I didn't. I've always been more Indian than white anyway, and there seemed no reason to change what I'm known by."

"I like your name. It sings to me."

She was silent, amazed at his words. That this strong man should be willing to speak his thoughts to her so plainly was more revealing than he could know. *It sings to me.* The beauty of the phrase determined her in that moment and she stood from her chair to face him boldly.

"I will marry you, Tyler. No matter your name, no matter your past, I will marry you and be your wife.

I can't make any promises to you, other than this. I'll do my best to be a good wife to you. I'll work hard to make this a thriving farm for both of us, and I'll be faithful to you."

He seemed stunned, his eyes wide, his look one of surprise, and then he smiled, and it was as if the sunlight had come to dwell in that expression of his joy.

"I'll accept your word, Nightsong. I expect no more from you than what you are willing to give me. If you say you'll be my wife, that you will work with me to make this place a success, I'll believe you, and honor your faith in me."

He raised his body from the step he'd claimed as his seat and rose to face her. His hand reached for hers and he held it firmly, lifting it to his lips. His mouth touched the backs of her fingers, then turned it within his grasp and kissed the palm—a soft, sweet caress that spoke silently of his need for her.

She allowed his touch, indeed welcomed it, for she'd thought of little else since the day he'd first kissed her. Now she wondered if he knew that his kiss was the first she'd shared with a man. And if he did, had he thought her worthy of his attention? Had she responded as he'd wanted?

The questions flew through her mind, and his words put them all to rest as he drew her close to himself, his arms encircling her waist, his hands lying flat against her back. "You are untouched, little bird, a woman without the knowledge of a man, and

I'll treat you as such. I promise you that I'll be a good husband to you, that you'll not regret accepting me into your life…and, in time, into your bed."

"In time?" She couldn't believe that was her voice, speaking those simple words, repeating his vow to her. The sound seemed too soft, too gentle for the voice of Debra Nightsong, for she'd always been strong and her voice that of a woman of courage. Now she sounded as if she were an unknowing child, asking for explanation of his simple words.

He seemed to understand her need, for he smiled down at her, his hands making soothing movements against her back. "Perhaps not as much time as you want, Debra, but as much as I'm able to give you. I'll be patient with you for I'm smart enough to recognize that you're a stranger to the meaning of the marriage bed."

"I know nothing but what my mother told me of men," she said simply. "She might have given me instructions of my duty to a husband if she hadn't died so young, but as it was I came here to the farm as a girl, not yet a woman, and probably not ready to hear such things."

"Don't girls of your tribe marry young?" he asked, wondering that no young man had craved her attention during her growing-up years.

"Many of them long before my age," she said, nodding as if she remembered such things happening. "But my mother kept me away from the men who would have asked for me. She said I was too young to have a husband."

"And she was right." Tyler's voice was strong, his words definite, as if he were thankful for the intelligence of her mother.

"I'm glad she protected me," Debra said softly, remembering the woman who had cared for her during those years with her tribe. "She taught me to cook, and sew my clothing. My father had shown me how to skin and gut a rabbit. I suppose I could do the same with a deer, but I've never shot one. I didn't know what I'd do with all that meat, and so I just use whatever I can barter with my neighbors for. And I sacrifice a chicken once in a while."

"On the altar of your hunger?" he asked, his face sober, while his eyes laughed with pleasure at her words.

She smiled, pleased at his humor. "I guess you could say that. Although I'm not often hungry."

His look was critical. "I've noticed. You're entirely too slim. Almost thin, in fact."

"Thank you," she said, and frowned as she recognized that her tone was as chilled as a December morning. "I'll try to add some weight to make you happy."

Allowing a grin to curl his lips, he shook his head at her. "You don't need to do anything but breathe to make me happy, sweetheart. I'll take you just the way you are, and as often as possible."

What he'd meant by that remark was a puzzle, she thought, allowing her mind to repeat his words silently.

"You look like I've said something to upset you, and I didn't mean to. I was only being—"

She cut him off with a wave of her hand. "I'm not upset, though I'll admit I don't understand some of the things you say. I'm afraid I'm a simple soul, Tyler. You'll have to speak plainly to get through to me." Her hands pushed at his chest and she stepped away from him, from the hold he'd managed to maintain on her waist.

But even that small move didn't keep him from her, for his face darkened, as if with anger, and yet he was not harsh as he reached for her again. Perhaps it was fear that spoke aloud, maybe only the innocence she hated, even as she acknowledged its presence.

"Don't manhandle me, Tyler. I've never allowed any man to put his hands on me. And you'll not be given that privilege, either. Until I marry you, you'll let me be."

"Wrong, Nightsong." His eyes narrowed as he scanned her form, his gaze seeming to dwell on each small part of her, and she felt her breasts beneath her clothing, knew they swelled to fill the fabric of her chemise. His hands were warm against her waist, his long fingers resting just beneath the heaviness of her breasts. He had no right, no reason to treat her so. And she turned on him in anger.

"I'm not sure I'm ready to speak of marriage any longer. Allowing you into my bed doesn't seem like such a good idea, and unless I miss my guess, you think I'm going to submit to whatever you have in mind for me."

"All this because I like to touch you?" he asked, his smile lacking humor.

"Is that what you call it? I had to put up with your shenanigans the first few days you were here, Tyler. I've managed to get you out of my bed and onto the floor, and unless I change my mind in the near future, that's where you'll stay."

"I don't think so."

As a statement of intent it could not be bettered, she decided and she turned from him, the need to hide her tears of major importance right now. And why the man had the ability to make her shed those hated salty drops was beyond her. She only knew that she somehow allowed him to make her feel helpless, like a woman without strength to make her own choices. Debra Nightsong was not a woman to be subdued so easily.

"Have I frightened you again?" His words angered her and she felt her face burn with humiliation.

"You don't frighten me. You never have. I fear no man, Tyler whoever you are."

He grinned, the challenge of his frown, the dark anger he'd directed at her a thing of the past. "I think we're having an argument, Nightsong. Our first, if

I'm not mistaken. And I'd just as soon not be exchanging harsh words with you."

"Then just be quiet and leave me alone." She turned away, her hands peeling his from her body, and went into the house. The kitchen was dark but she knew her way well and walked across to the hallway and from there to her bedroom. In a house this small there was no trick to gaining the one room she could claim as her own and hope for privacy to be granted her.

The door closed with a solid sound behind her and she leaned against it, her mind spinning. She was so angry at him, and for the life of her she wasn't sure why. He'd handled her as if it were his right, and that alone was enough to fire her temper. But his intentions were honorable, she'd stake her life on that fact. Yet, she could somehow not give her total acceptance to his proposal, for he asked more than she was willing or perhaps able to give him.

Behind her the door moved, and she recognized that he had lifted the latch, that he was putting his weight against it, moving her from her position. In mere seconds he would be trespassing in her domain—*a domain he shared,* she reminded herself. Yet, it was the only place she felt safe, and once he intruded, she would no longer have the privacy her heart craved.

"Step away from the door, Debra. I don't want to hurt you when I push it open."

She trembled at his words, knowing that he would not back down, that his determination exceeded her own in this matter. Her head bowed, she walked into the center of the bedroom, and behind her, heard the door swing open, knew the moment he entered the quiet of her bedroom.

"Why are you running from me?"

She turned to face him, knowing she was but a dim shadow in the darkness of her room. He was limned in the doorway, the kitchen lamp glowing behind him, and she was struck with the size of him, the width of his shoulders, the way his head brushed close to the lintel. "I haven't run. Only tried to find a place by myself, where I can think my own thoughts without you…"

He walked closer to her, almost touching her clothing with his own, so near did he stand. The warmth exuding from his body touched her with fingers of fire and she withdrew, almost trying to shrink within the contours of her dress. "I've never tried to infringe on your privacy, Debra, only tried to speak with you, to make you understand my thoughts and ideas. I don't know how to convince you that I'd be a good husband to you, that marriage for us would be a good choice."

"You're infringing on me now," she said harshly, her voice lifting with the anger behind it. "Go away, Tyler, and leave me be. I don't want you near me."

He smiled, and she was almost convinced by the gentleness that expression conveyed. "I think your problem may be that you *do* want me near you, Nightsong. And you're not sure what to do about it. I don't think my touch is repulsive to you, for you tremble beneath my hands, and your mouth softens when I touch it with mine."

He would touch her now. She knew it, in the depths of her body, where the gentle fires of her newborn passion burned. And when his hands were on her, when she yearned to crush herself against his greater strength, those fires might burn out of control, and she would no longer be able to refuse him.

As if her thoughts reached his mind, as if he knew exactly what she feared, his hands gripped her waist, drawing her closer to his form, and then slid behind her, capturing her in the warmth of those muscular limbs that held her with the tenderness of a mother with a child.

She wanted to melt against him, her body cried out for the heat that radiated from him, and her legs trembled with weakness that was not usual for Debra Nightsong. She'd always been strong, capable and certain of her needs. Now this man held her body next to his, and suddenly her needs were those he'd brought to life within her.

She craved his fingers beneath her breasts as they had been only long minutes ago on the porch, and at the same time, she hated the yearning she felt. For it could only make her weak to so cling to a man. She must be strong, as her mother had bid her. She must stand on her own two feet and make a life that would be safe and under her control.

Yet, the strength of the man before her drew her inexorably into his shadow, and she felt almost a part of him, her breasts crushed against his wide chest, her legs parting for the intrusion of his muscular thighs between them. He smoothed the fabric of her dress down the full length of her back and his hands cradled the firm rounding of her bottom, lifting her against himself, holding her high so that her face was on a level with his.

His words were soft, but firm, and she watched his lips, barely moving as he issued his will aloud. "Kiss me, Debra. Touch my lips with yours and taste the desire I hold in my heart for you."

She could barely breathe, her heart pounding in her chest like the drums in her mother's village. His lips lured her, softening before her eyes, parting as if he strove to catch a breath, glistening from his tongue's movement across them, and she was drawn into his spell.

Her mouth opened a bit, and she offered him the caress he had demanded, for she would not allow him to think she only did as he asked out of fear. Her lips were soft against his, her mouth a vessel to be filled by the length of his tongue, and though the caressing movement against her teeth and her own tongue was still new and strange to her, she felt warmed by his taking of her in this way.

He tilted his head a bit, the better to gain his goal, his mouth opening over hers, his tongue suckling hers in a gentle motion that sent shards of sensation to the depths of her belly. He tasted of the coffee he'd drunk for supper, of the peppermint candy he kept in his pocket. A mixture of sweetness, of masculine strength, of all the things she loved about him.

And that, she realized as his tongue traced the ridges of her mouth, was the sole reason she would accede to his demands. For she loved not only his taste, his touch and the look of him, but the man himself, the man who had entered her life so harshly, with no warning, and taken over the running of her farm as if it were his due. And perhaps it was, for she knew she had given him reason to take his place here as a helpmate, as a husband.

In all but name and physical possession, she was his already, his wife, his woman.

He left her mouth then, touching her cheek and the fragile skin of her throat with the warmth of his lips, whispering against her ear with words that wrote upon her heart, words that claimed her as his own, that promised her his troth, his love and support in all she did, all that she hoped for.

"I'll take care of you, Nightsong. You'll never want for anything—food, clothing or love. If you'll share your home with me, I'll protect you and keep it safe for you and our children. And before many days have passed, I'll find a way to clear my name of the charges against me."

"Our children?" Her mind had been focused on those words and she pushed against his chest. He allowed it, allowed the tilting of her head as she looked up at him and, in the dim light of her room, saw his smile, knew the strength of the man who held her. Whose arms kept her above the floor, tight to his body, yet did not threaten her with the arousal she felt through the layers of clothing that separated them.

His words were firm. "The children we will form between us." He wanted her body, as a man wants a woman, but he would not force her to his will, would not demand she perform as his wife. Not now, not until she spoke the words that would determine her future with him. A future it seemed he had already considered and planned in detail.

"Marry me, Nightsong." It was a demand, the strength of his voice resounding in her ears as she heard his insistence vibrate in each syllable. "I need you, Debra. I need your nearness to me, your woman's warmth in the night, and your strength in the day. I need to know that you will be mine for all the days of our lives, that we will share the joys of marriage, and perhaps the sorrows that will come to us. I can't promise you that it will be a smooth road that we take, but I can promise that I'll be with you every step of the way. I'll never betray you or make you sorry that you've become mine."

Her arms lifted to encircle his neck and she leaned forward to rest her head against his shoulder, needing the knowledge that he held her firmly, that he would not loose her from his touch, that his promises were true and she would be safe with him.

"I'll marry you, Tyler. It will turn you into an outcast, as I am, but if that is your desire, then I'll not tell you no."

"I need no one but you, Debra. I need no one's acceptance but yours."

"Then we'll go into town and find out the way it should be done," she said quietly, her words muffled against his shirt.

"Will you marry me in front of a man of the cloth? Or will that not be according to your beliefs?"

"I'm half-white, Tyler. My mother and father were married that way, but they had to go miles to find a preacher man who would do it for them. The church in town was not willing to accept them."

"And are the same people there now?" he asked. "Is the preacher there the same man now, as then?"

"I don't think so. He's a young man, with a young family. The other preacher was gone when I came back to the farm. My mother had not had good things to say about him, but I think she would have liked this man. He's young, kind and has warm eyes."

"Then we'll ask him to perform the ceremony for us. And if he refuses, we'll find someone else. Even the judge for this district will do, but I'd feel better if we were married in a church."

"We'll do whatever is right in your eyes," she said, willing to allow him his way in this.

His arms tightened around her, holding her against him more firmly and she felt her woman's flesh soften and gather heat from his body. Inhaling sharply, she moved against him, needing to be free of him, of the temptation of his body against hers. He loosed his grip on her bottom and she slid down the length of his torso, until her feet touched the bedroom floor.

He turned her in his arms, 'til she was facing the open doorway, and she felt his hands against her belly, then at her waistline, long fingers forming to her contours until they rested just beneath her breasts.

"I want to touch you." His murmur was against her ear, for he'd leaned his head to rest on her shoulder, the heat of his breath penetrating the fabric of her dress. She shivered at his words, for it was not a request, but a statement of intent.

"Are you afraid of me?" His head had turned a bit, and his words brushed her ear, his whisper hesitant, as if he feared her response.

Her head moved, just a bit, an imperceptible turning from one side to the other and her words emphasized the movement. "No, I don't fear you, Tyler. I know you won't hurt me, and I know you won't take advantage of your greater strength." She felt his hands move against her, knew the warmth of his palms beneath her breasts, then the measuring caress of his fingers as he cupped her in those broad palms and allowed his thumbs to move over the crests that budded in his path.

His hands trembled on her, and she smiled, aware that he was willing that she should set the pace in this. Willing for her to deny him what he asked for so silently, if she so chose. Her head bent and she looked down at his big hands, watched as his fingers flexed, felt the rush of sensation those long digits brought to life in her breasts.

"Debra?" He waited for her answer and she tipped her head back, leaning it against his shoulder. He accepted the offer and inclined a bit to touch his lips against her cheek. His breath was warm against her skin, his lungs seeming to work at a frantic pace, as though they would not expand as he willed them.

"Will you wait until we're married?" she asked, her bold question spoken before she could consider it.

And as if he had expected her reticence, he nodded his head against her, his beard a bit rough on her cheek. "I'll wait. I've been biding my time for weeks. I don't suppose another few days will matter. It will only make it harder on you, though."

She turned in his grasp to face him and her brow furrowed at his words. "How so? What will be more difficult for me?"

"It's been a long time since I've been with a

woman, Debra. I fear hurting you as it is, and the longer I wait and yearn for you, the more of a problem you may have with accepting me as your mate."

He paused and she thought he looked a bit embarrassed, chagrined, perhaps. And then he grinned and shrugged as if he would dismiss the problems he'd referred to so obliquely. "I'm a large man, Debra, and you are a small woman. The longer I have to wait for you…"

She reached up her hand and pressed her fingers against his lips. "It's all right, Tyler. When the time comes, we'll work it out."

He tilted his head a bit lower and his forehead touched hers, the movement a caress in itself. "Will we go into town right away?" he asked. "I don't mean to rush you, but if we're going to do this thing, I'd as soon do it now. That floor is getting harder by the night."

And so am I. He grinned at the thought that spun through his mind.

She bit at her lower lip. "Are you laughing at me? What did I say to amuse you?"

"Nothing, sweetheart. Nothing at all. I was just making plans, and enjoying it."

THE NEXT MORNING seemed to be planned ahead of time, Debra thought as she filled coffee cups and dished up eggs onto their plates. Tyler had come in from doing the chores with his schedule already set in place.

"We'll leave for town as soon as I get washed up," he told her. "I'll need to change and put on clean clothes. These smell like the barn."

She laughed, eyeing him as he settled at the table. "I can't imagine why. After all, you've already spent your morning with five horses and a cow. Not to mention a flock of ornery chickens."

"The eggs are still in the shed," he said gloomily. "I started gathering them, but that white hen got her feathers ruffled and wouldn't let me touch her nest, so I decided to let you cope with her later on."

"I didn't think a big strong man like you would flinch from a chicken," she said, imagining his aggravation with the recalcitrant hen.

"I told you the first day I was here. Chickens don't like me. And I'd rather see a chicken cooked up into soup than sitting on a roost."

"Get your breakfast done and get cleaned up and I'll tend to the eggs." She sat down across from him and they ate quietly, Tyler seeming lost in his thoughts.

The ride to town was long for Debra, her mind busy with the reaction they would receive from the preacher and the townsfolk once their marriage was a fact. That they would be ostracized was a given, for a marriage of mixed blood was not condoned. In fact, there was a good chance that the new minister might not conduct the ceremony for them, and she sorted through the options they might have to consider.

Their first stop was at the general store and Julia Anderson stood behind the counter, adding up the purchases for Mrs. Henry, the wife of a local farmer. The list was long and she cast a look of impatience at Debra as the figures refused to cooperate with her.

"This will just take another minute, Mrs. Henry," she said hurriedly, and then turned her attention to Debra. "I'll be right with you, Debra."

A simple nod acknowledged her recognition of the couple's presence in the store and Debra turned away to look at a display of shoes on a nearby counter. She lifted a sturdy half boot in her hand and considered it. Too heavy and not as comfortable as her leather moccasins, she thought quickly, moving on to a lighter pair of ladies' shoes that might be fit for Sunday church or a party at the Grange Hall.

"Do you need new shoes?" Tyler stood beside her, speaking in a low tone.

"No. I have my riding boots and my house shoes. That's all I need." She shot a grin at him. "I'm a woman and I always like to shop, even when I don't plan on buying anything."

"I didn't think to ask if you wanted a new dress to be married in," he said, regret alive in his words. "We can find one right now and you could change into it in the back room."

She shook her head. "No. I'm happy with what I'm wearing. I'm really only here to ask if Julia might be able to stand up with me when we get married."

"I didn't think of that. I suppose I'd better think of someone to hold me up, too, hadn't I?"

She allowed her eyes to travel his length. "I don't know. You look pretty sturdy to me. And probably the preacher can suggest someone. You don't know any of the men in town anyway, only my neighbor."

"Or the fella out front who told me about a woman living alone outside of town who might need some hired help. The best advice I ever got," he said, as if he were recalling that day many weeks ago.

"You asked about me?"

"Not you, Debra. Just asked in a general way if anyone in these parts was hiring extra hands." He turned to look out the window. "See that old fella on the end of the bench out there? He was the one sitting there that day, and he said that running a farm was no job for a woman alone and there was a lady down the road a couple of miles who might be able to use a hand."

"And you thought I was an old lady?" She recalled his words early on when he'd admitted to his error.

"I got quite a jolt when you rode in the yard on that pale horse of yours, and then when you came in the house and I got my hands on you, I was more than surprised." He grinned at her and winked. "You weren't at all what I expected, but I sure wasn't disappointed in you."

Mrs. Henry gathered up her purchases and cast a long, reproving look at Debra and her male companion before she left the store. As the bell over the door rang, announcing her departure, Debra stepped up to the counter. She was greeted with a wide smile and the man behind her received a curious look.

"Julia, this is Tyler. You know about him, I'm sure. He's been working at my place and…" Her voice trailed off and she found herself the recipient of a glowing look from her friend behind the counter.

"I'd heard there was a man out there at your farm, Debra. My father was kinda concerned that someone might be taking advantage of you, but your neighbor, Sam Shane, said that the man you'd hired was a good worker. And some of the ladies in town had a bit to say about the arrangements at your place, wondering if the man you'd hired was taking advantage of you."

"There was no need of that. He's a gentleman and a fine man." Debra leaned closer to her friend and spoke softly, her smile a measure of her happiness today. "And a fast worker, too." She lowered her voice. "He's asked me to marry him, and I was wondering if you could leave the store for a bit and go to the preacher's house when we've got a time set up for a wedding."

"He wants to marry you?" Julia's mouth formed a small circle and she whispered an exclamation then that made Debra smile. "Oh, my. Oh, my." As if her mind had stalled midstream, she only nodded quickly and reached for Debra's hand. "I can't tell you how happy that makes me. You've been all alone out there on that farm for three years, and now this. I'm happy for you, Debra." And then she assumed a sober look. "At least I will be if you're excited about it, too."

"Oh, yes," Debra said, shooting a look at Tyler. "I'm couldn't be more pleased. Tyler's been wonderful, helping me on the farm, getting in the hay and building my corral and fencing the pasture."

"Whoa!" Julia said, cutting off her friend's spiel. "I guess you'd better marry him and keep him around. Sounds like he's gonna come in right handy."

"Well, there is that," Debra said, blushing as Tyler laughed aloud at what bits of the conversation he'd caught. "Anyway, I'll come back and let you know when we can have the ceremony. Will you be able to stand up with me?"

"You'd better believe it," Julia said quickly.

CHAPTER FIVE

TYLER ESCORTED DEBRA from the store with Julia's good wishes still ringing in their ears, and they climbed onto the wagon seat and headed for the small church at the far end of town. Beside it stood the white house where the minister lived with his family. Two children played in the front yard and when the wagon pulled up at the gate, one of the little boys ran into the house, calling for his mother.

The young preacher's wife came to the door, wiping her hands on her apron and smiled welcome. "Come on in, folks. Edgar has gone to the hardware store, but he'll be home right shortly." She held the screen door wide and they entered the parlor at her invitation. "I'll fix us some lemonade while we wait," she said. "And I'm Laura Temple, by the way."

"My name is Tyler, ma'am, and of course you know Debra Nightsong." Tyler nodded his head at the young woman and escorted Debra to the parlor sofa. "We'd be happy with a glass of lemonade," he said nicely, and grinned at Debra as he took his place beside her.

Within ten minutes, the three of them were talking a mile a minute, Laura obviously in need of a listening ear, and Debra more than willing to hear the ups and downs of a parsonage. "And so, what with the ladies' circle and the men's study group, Edgar and I are busy with running hither and yon, and then there's my two boys, always needing something and the garden to tend and the chickens to care for. Land sakes," she said, her chatter running down as she took a deep breath, "I don't know where the time goes, but it sure is busy living with a preacher."

Her eyes lit as they heard the screen door slam and she rose quickly. "And here he is now," she said as the tall, young man walked in the door. "Edgar, these two want to get married, and they want you to do the honors."

"Well, let me sit down here and we'll have a little talk," Edgar said, his gaze taking in the two who awaited his presence. "I know you're the Nightsong woman, aren't you?" he asked Debra, and then he smiled at Tyler and offered his hand. Tyler took it and again introduced himself.

Studying them with kindly eyes, he seemed to relax and come to a decision. "You're wanting to get married, is that right? And is today the day?"

"Yes," Tyler said quietly. "We thought if you had the time, you could do the ceremony for us this afternoon. Julia down at the general store said she'd stand up with Debra and I thought perhaps you knew of someone to perform as a witness for me."

"My wife is real good at signing her name on wedding certificates," Edgar told him. "She's made a dandy best man more than once." He shot a quick smile at his slender, young wife, and she nodded her agreement.

"That'll be just fine," Debra said, looking to Tyler for his approval. He gave it with a smile of agreement and the deal was arranged. Tyler would go back to the store to pick up Julia and they would be married within the hour.

LAURA LED DEBRA into the kitchen while her husband prepared a marriage certificate for the couple, talking at a rapid pace. "My, my. I've not had this much excitement in a month of Sundays. Usually we go about this with a few weeks warning," she said. Once in the kitchen, she poured warm water from the stove into a pan and offered Debra a towel.

"I thought you might want to wash up a bit, after being on the road, and besides I wanted a chance to talk to you without my husband hanging on our every word."

Debra accepted the towel and used the warm water to advantage, washing quickly at the sink as Laura talked about the ceremony to come.

"I just picked some flowers from the yard this morning," she said, drawing a small posy from the water glass it had been sitting in. "Just daisies and violets, but it will look just right with your orchid-colored dress, Debra." She spun in a half circle, the flowers clutched in her hand. "I'm just so excited for you."

Debra laughed at the woman's exuberance. "I'm pleased, too. I'd never thought to be married, but Tyler has been such a help to me on the farm, and he's a good man."

"Well," Laura said in a quiet voice, as though she didn't want to be overheard. "I've heard bits and pieces at the general store about you having a man at your place, and a couple of the ladies were offering some opinions, but Julia Anderson set them straight, told them that you were a lady and they had no right to suggest that there was anything improper going on out there."

"I figured that there'd be talk about us," Debra said. "Folks always need to be discussing someone or something or they're not happy. This ought to put a stop to it though."

"I suspect it will," Laura said with a laugh. "My, just think. A wedding today, and I'd thought nothing exciting would be happening 'til the Fourth of July picnic."

A quick knock on the front door resounded through the house and they heard Edgar welcome Julia and Tyler back from the store. "Come on in, folks," he said. And then called out for the ladies in the kitchen to make an appearance.

With much laughter and excitement they gathered

together before the big front window of the parsonage and Edgar drew a slim volume from his pocket. The silence that accompanied his gesture was sudden, and the air seemed to take on a different quality, almost as if they had managed to turn this humble parlor into a chapel in which they might find the presence of the Almighty himself.

The words spoken were familiar to Tyler, and he wondered if Debra had ever heard a wedding service read before. With soft inquiries, Edgar asked them their names in full, and then proceeded with the ceremony.

In a solemn voice he asked for their responses and Debra listened raptly as Tyler spoke his vows. "I, Ethan Tyler, take thee, Debra Nightsong…" She heard the words as if in a dream, loving the cadence of the men's voices, dwelling on the words of promise given to her by the man she'd promised to wed.

Ethan. His name was Ethan. She listened to him repeat the words, following Edgar's directions, and thrilled to the message. He would love her, honor her and cherish her. And somehow, she knew that he would do all of that. Oh, maybe not all at one fell swoop, but eventually, he would learn to, would give her more than the words spoken in the heat of his passion, but the declaration at a time when his desire for her was not a part of the conversation. Not that his words would change anything, for she was willing to wait for such a thing to happen. After all, she hadn't come to that point herself, had not given him claim to her heart. The honoring part, those words he'd spoken so glibly, was truly easy for her to live with, for he'd already proved himself to be an honorable man. As to what the cherishing meant, she wasn't quite sure, but whatever it was, Tyler would do it well.

But, his name wasn't Tyler, was it? He was Ethan, and she dwelt on that name as the minister turned to her. It was a part of the vows she pledged in those minutes, repeating the words from the prayer book Edgar held in his hands.

For richer, for poorer, for better and for worse… They were beautiful sounds, promises for the future and she held them close to her heart to think about and reflect on later. And then Edgar said in a voice that rippled with joy. "You may kiss your bride."

Ethan Tyler bent to her and his eyes shone with a light she'd not seen before, his lips curved in a smile that spoke of his happiness as he took her shoulders in his big hands and bent to place a warm kiss on her mouth. She felt a blush cover her cheeks, to think that they would perform such an intimate act before others, but Edgar and Laura seemed to think that it was but an ordinary thing to do, and so she quickly smiled at them as the ceremony ended.

Julia hugged her quickly, then shook Tyler's hand. "I'm so pleased for both of you," she said. "You're a lucky man, you know."

And Tyler nodded quickly in agreement, his arm sliding around Debra's waist, his eyes warm on her as he accepted the congratulations of the witnesses and the man who had pronounced them husband and wife.

IT WAS HEADING TOWARD late afternoon by the time they gathered together the purchases Debra had on her list from the general store and climbed again into the wagon. She felt different, conspicuous somehow, as the vehicle rolled out of town and they were given the once-over by folks walking past the stores and shops. Two ladies stood in front of the hotel and Debra watched as they stared after the wagon, then bent their heads together to whisper.

"We're going to be the topic of conversation tonight, I'll be willing to wager," she said, sitting up straight and trying her best to look dignified. She still held the small bouquet Laura had given her, and the violets were wilting, victims of the late afternoon heat.

"I'm getting hungry," Tyler said. "Did we get anything good for supper in those boxes of supplies?"

"I thought maybe we'd celebrate and cut off a piece from the beef that's hanging in the smokehouse. I can make a pot of stew or roast it in the oven. I'm a good hand with dumplings if we have stew."

"I'll eat whatever you fix," he said, and he reached his hand to cover hers, squeezing gently. "Your skin is cold," he said. "And I don't know how it can be. Lord knows it's plenty warm out."

Debra shrugged and looked down to where her palm was cradled in his. "Just excitement, I suppose," she said.

"You're not worried, are you?"

"No, not really. Well, maybe just a little."

He laughed aloud. "That's what I like. A woman with a definite opinion." He turned his head to look into her eyes. "Another thing, Debra. If you want to, you can call me Ethan, sweetheart. I told you I'd give you the rest of my name when we got married, remember? My stepfather's name was Mason, but I no longer use it, only my mother's maiden name, Tyler." His grin turned into a tentative smile that begged her understanding. "So now you know all my secrets." His look was pensive as he hesitated and then he stilled as if at a wonderful memory. "I guess names aren't really that important, but my mother always used Ethan when she spoke to me."

Her concern was evident as she asked "Why don't you use your father's name? Was your mother married to him?"

His mouth thinned and he shook his head. "No, legally I don't have a father. Only my mother. I've never heard the whole story, but I know he refused responsibility for me. We·didn't talk about it, and I knew it was a sore point with her, so I pushed it into the background."

"Well, I kind of like *Ethan*. I don't care about names, but if I have a choice with yours, I'll choose

Ethan. After all, with me using my mother's name instead of my father's, I can understand. I think we're two of a kind, Ethan," she told him, and then whispered it beneath her breath as they traveled toward home. It was a soft name, she decided, a name to be whispered in the dark, perhaps. And at that idea, she blushed again, her mind racing ahead to the night that was to come.

Supper was a quiet affair, with Debra cooking a meal she was certain he would enjoy. She cubed into chunks the beef he brought her from the smoke-house, simmering them while she cut up vegetables and prepared the dumplings to place on top of the savory stew. He watched over her shoulder every chance he got, in between doing the chores and putting away the supplies they'd brought from town.

And then they sat together at the table and he surprised her with his words, reaching across to take her hand in his as she was about to lift her fork from the table.

"Debra, would you mind if I said grace before we eat? My mother thought it was important that we be thankful for our food when I was a child, no matter how poor we were or how much or little we managed to put on the table. I'd kinda like to follow her example if it's all right with you. Maybe start a new custom between us on our wedding day."

"Of course, Ethan." There, she'd said it aloud, and enjoyed the smile he sent in her direction.

"I like that," he told her. "It sounds almost like…"

"Like an endearment?' she asked.

"Yeah. I guess that's what I mean. It makes me think about my mother and the home she made for me. She was the most important person in my life. Until I met you."

"That's the nicest thing you could have said to me," Debra told him. "I want to be important to you, Ethan." She waited as he spoke soft words of thanksgiving and ate then, watching his obvious enjoyment as he devoured the meal she'd prepared for him. Too soon, it was over and the day was coming to an end. Her wedding day.

As if he knew her thoughts, he rose and took the dishes to the sink. "I'll help you with these before we go to bed, Debra. I don't want you worrying about anything tonight. There'll only be you and me in that bed, no thoughts about dishes or chores or what will happen tomorrow, just the two of us, loving each other."

Loving each other. His words resounded in her mind, and she examined her feelings for him. There was respect, admiration and a bone-deep liking for the man. She loved the way he treated her, cared about her and tried to make her life easier by the things he did to please her. If that added up to loving, then she would put words to her thoughts. Later on, when it was dark in her bedroom and they were alone and together in her bed.

It would not be as other times, at the beginning, when he'd forced his way to lie by her side. For now it would be his place, his right, to sleep with her as a husband. The thought was exciting, but still she felt a trace of apprehension, knowing that her body was his to possess.

He was a man, first and foremost. A man probably in need of a woman, and she had made herself available to him, a woman he could claim in any way he chose.

Even as she considered the hours ahead, he led her to her bedroom door, escorted her over the threshold and turned her to face him. His hands were gentle on her, cupping her shoulders in his palms, then moving to touch the line of buttons down the front of her dress.

"Can I help you take this off?" She thought his fingers trembled against her buttons, and only nodded her agreement to his query.

"I didn't realize there were so many layers to your clothing," he said with a grin, as he unveiled the fabric of her petticoat, then the soft cotton of her chemise beneath it. "Well, I guess I knew you were well covered, but this feels like I'm unwrapping my favorite Christmas present."

His fingers moved quickly over the ties and buttons he discovered and his movements were deft as he undressed her, lowering her finally to the edge of the bed, clad only in her stockings. He knelt before her and slid the practical cotton hosiery from her legs, allowing his fingers to linger but for a moment on each increment of flesh he touched.

"Do you want your gown on?" he asked, and she shook her head.

"You'll probably just take it off anyway."

The light was dim, only the glow of stars and moon through the window providing them with but the view of shadowy images. It was enough, she thought, watching as he stood and began to undress. He made short work of it, as if impatient to join her on the bed, and she watched as each item of clothing was tossed to the floor.

He stood before her, naked and beautiful, his body tall and strong, his shoulders wide, his waist and hips narrow. His legs were long, his thighs solid and muscled, and she thought his body was the most beautiful thing she'd ever laid eyes on.

"I've never seen a naked man before," she told him, reaching to touch the firm flesh of his thigh, flesh that seemed made of ivory in the moonlight. He jerked and she withdrew her fingers, flashing a stunned look in his direction.

"No, don't pull away. I didn't mean to startle you," he told her. "I want your hands on me, sweetheart. I want mine on you." His eyes were dark with a look she might have feared, did she not know him so well, but her faith in the man she'd married gave her courage, and she lifted her hand again to brush her fingers across his skin, even as her gaze touched the male parts of him that seemed so strange to her, so foreign to her own female form.

As if her scrutiny affected him, he groaned softly, and as she watched, the part that proved him to be a man seemed to grow and thicken before her eyes. She looked up at him, at the stern, almost cruel look that masked his face, and her heart trembled within her. What damage would he do to her with that powerful weapon? She'd only heard scant snatches of gossip from the women of her mother's tribe, bits and pieces whispered while the women cooked or stitched their clothing.

They'd talked between themselves of men, of the size of their masculine parts, and she'd been left in the dark to wonder of what they spoke. And now, before her eyes, she saw proof of those whispered words.

She'd heard of young girls and their fate when taken by men of another tribe, knew that such a fate was considered worse than death at a man's hand, yet her mother had been married, had loved her father. Certainly she would not have cared for him as she had if he had caused her pain during their times of mating.

"Debra." His voice came to her, even as his hands reached to rest upon her shoulders. "Don't be frightened of me. What you see is only evidence of my need for you, for my longing to love you and make your body mine. I can't bear it if I've made you fear the pain you will feel at our first mating."

"Will it only be the one time?" she asked, unsure of her ground.

"Unless there are problems, and I'll have to be honest, I've never heard of a woman having pain every time she makes love. I'd think it would discourage the bravest souls if that were true."

"I've never been a coward, Ethan. I don't think I'll start now."

"Then will you let me lie down with you? Give me space in your bed?"

She only nodded and then rose, turning to pull back the quilt, then the sheet, opening her bed to him, offering herself as she stood, facing him.

He accepted her invitation, drew her to rest against his body, his long fingers tracing the line of her spine, his head lowering as he sought the warmth of her mouth. She felt his male part pressing against her belly, and knew, contrary to her brave words, that she doubted she would be able to contain that masculine organ in her depths.

On the other hand, he seemed to have no such doubts, for his movements were certain and sure, his arms lifting her high before he bent to place her on the bed. He lay beside her then, lifting himself on his elbow, the better to examine her, from the smile that trembled on her lips to the tips of her toes, curling upon themselves, displaying her state of confusion, the sense of embarrassment she could not help but feel at his scrutiny.

"You're beautiful, Debra." His hand touched her breast, curling beneath its weight, lifting it a bit as he bent his head to touch the furled crest with the tip of his tongue. She shivered as a shard of fire seemed to fly from that bit of shriveled flesh to the very depths of her belly. And he smiled, a masculine, triumphant grin that told her he was pleased with her reaction. He rubbed his cheek against her breast, gently, as though he feared the faint stubble on his face might scratch her tender flesh. But not so, for she lifted against his gentle movement, and he laughed, a soft, teasing sound.

"You're more than I expected, sweetheart. I'd thought to coax you, try to talk you out of your clothing, maybe even put off our coming together until another time if you were hesitant." He lifted up and met her gaze. "You surprise me."

"I want to mate with you, Ethan." She couldn't put it any more bluntly, couldn't have opened her heart to him more readily had she thought long and hard about what she might say to him. "You're my husband, and I want to belong to you."

"You will, love. Now—tonight—you'll be mine."

She touched his face, her palms curving to cup his cheeks. He was warm, his skin a little rough from the stubble of his beard, and his mouth opened a bit, as if he must catch a breath. Lifting her head from the pillow, she touched his lips with hers and he accepted her encouragement with the pressure of his mouth against hers. His teeth touched her lower lip, nuzzled it and suckled the tender flesh and then skated across her cheek to the side of her throat, where her heart beat at a frantic pace. His mouth opened a bit and he sucked there, a tender caress, as if he would take her life's blood into himself.

"You're sweet, your skin is like honey." The words were low, almost a growl and his breath was hot on the flesh he bathed with his tongue. She heard a moan, a faint trembling sound that arose from her throat, shivering as his touch sent fingers of heat down the length of her, to where her woman's parts ached for his presence.

That she would want, would crave, a man's hands on the places she'd almost ignored for all the years of her life seemed impossible to believe, yet the fingers that coaxed her legs to part were welcome, and she did as he directed, silently, but surely.

"I don't know what to do," she whispered, wishing she'd listened closer to the women who had gossiped and spoken of such times with their menfolk.

"That's all right," he said, smiling as he lifted his head to meet her gaze. "I know enough for both of us."

"I thought you would."

He frowned. "Don't think I've been in bed with any great number of women, sweetheart. I won't make a list for you, but believe me when I say that I've been kinda picky about the women in my life. None of them, except for my wife, meant anything to me, but a way to relieve my body when I'd gone for too long a time without…" As if he feared saying words that would offend her, he shrugged and burrowed his head against her shoulder.

"A man is different from a woman in his needs. I know that." She wanted to say more, but could not find the words to express her thoughts. He was dark, leaning over her, his skin deeply tanned where the sun had warmed it, yet, his body was pale against her own. They were people of two races, from different backgrounds, different parentage and not much in common to warrant hope for their marriage. Yet, she knew that together they would forge a future together.

This night would be the beginning, the start of their family, for surely there would be children born of their union. And with that thought, she managed to relax in his arms, found herself molding her body to his in a way she hadn't known was possible.

Ethan felt the tense muscles beneath his touch relax, knew the instant that Debra lost her last trace of fear for what was to come, and he touched her lips with his own in a kiss that praised her courage, even as he rejoiced in the bravery of the woman he had wed.

His mouth had become acquainted with her body

over the past minutes, his tongue tasting the skin that drew him with a flavor and scent he craved to the depths of his being. She was clean, pure and lovely, a woman built to fit well into a man's embrace. Her sleek form was fitted against his, even now, as though they were two parts of a puzzle, being brought together by some magic of the night.

Her breasts fit in his palms, firm and yet soft and tender, and how that should be so was a mystery to him. Women had long since seemed to him to be made of finer flesh than that of a man, their female parts more delicate, more gently put together, and he found himself seeking out now the most intricate bits and pieces of the woman he'd married. Her fingers were strong, straight and narrow against his chest and shoulders; her neck a slender column, the flesh tender and finely pored. He'd spent hours watching her over the past weeks, noting the elegant formation of her body, her throat and ears, the long, slim legs that he'd been reduced to merely dream of, for they had not been exposed to his view before tonight.

Now he ran his hands down the length of her thighs, cupped the rounding of smooth calves in his hand and circled slim ankles with his fingers. Her feet were narrow, high arched and small, and he touched the toes with his long fingers, his rough, callused hands holding them in his palm. His mouth touched her knees, heard her gasp of breath as he moved up the curve of her thighs, tasting of one, then the other, his lips ever nearing that place where he would soon seek his pleasure.

And in seeking his own release, would endeavor to give her the joy her woman's flesh was capable of.

His lips touched the patch of dark hair that hid her woman's parts from him, indeed the darkness had already done that, but she flinched as he brushed the curls with his chin. He soothed her, rising over her with soft words of assurance, and she reached to hold him against herself.

His hand settled there, where he'd longed to taste of her sweetness, and his fingers sought out the hidden treasures of her flesh that would soon bring to her a knowledge of her own need. She was untried, not used to the touch of a man, and he was careful, gentle in his handling of those tender places he visited. She would know no pain from his explorations, only the giving way of her maidenhead when he took it as his own. And for that he repented ahead of time. But his need was greater than his mercy to her, and he could not find it in his heart to regret the act he was about to embark upon.

She had lifted to his touch, her body twisting beneath him as she met his hand, as if she ached for the pleasure he was bringing to her. Small sounds from her throat reached his ears and he reveled in the knowledge that he was pleasing her with such simple actions. That her knowledge of him in a more intimate way would bring pain was inevitable, but delaying any longer would not make it easier for her to bear.

He levered himself between her thighs and found the entrance to her body readily, stretching her once more with his fingers, recognizing the small withdrawal she instigated as he widened his pathway as much as he could. And then he returned his agile fingers to the place that gave her the most pleasure and she whispered words in his ear that he did not recognize, only knew that the tone of her voice urged him on to the next step in this process of loving his wife for the first time.

The heat of her body called to him and he entered her carefully, pushing forward a bit at a time, even though his body urged him to completion. He would not ravage her soft flesh, would not bring his full strength into being, but instead eased his way carefully, gently, until he felt the unmistakable barrier her body offered.

"Sweetheart, hold tight to me." His voice was raw, rasping in his throat, but she obeyed his edict and her hands clung to his back, her head buried in his shoulder as he thrust his way, in one strong movement, through the flesh that proclaimed her a maiden, a virgin, a woman who had not known a man.

She was hot, tight, her body the stuff of a man's most carnal dreams, and he closed his eyes, unwilling to take his own pleasure before she came to a knowledge of the joy awaiting her. He was patient, touching her firmly, lifting from her to suckle her breast as he moved within her, his hand still against her warmth.

She moved beneath him, her movements untutored, unskilled, those of a girl who had not trod this path before, and he strove for the patience to bring her with him to the fulfillment of this night. She cried out, her body jerking against him, her head twisting on the pillow and her legs capturing him, wrapping him in the embrace he'd craved.

And even as she sobbed her release, he found the depths of her womanhood, plunged carefully, ever aware of untouched flesh that opened to him, his body shuddering in the throes of a climax unlike any he'd ever known in the years of his past.

As if he'd traveled to some other plane, some unknown place, where he'd been given the privilege of discovering a rare beauty, he rose beyond the commonplace into a realm of perfection, where ecstasy enveloped him like a warm blanket and soothed his tortured soul.

The pain of loss, the aching need for tenderness in his life, the yearning he'd lived with for the past years, was as a thing of the past. He'd found a place of safety, a haven that welcomed him, took him in and held him close. There in the arms of a woman he'd come upon by chance, a golden creature with the form of a female and the heart of a warrior, he'd sought and found the home he'd needed for so long.

"I love you, Debra. You're my own, my Nightsong." The words were slurred, his speech still trembling from the powerful spasms that shook his body. He kissed her, his lips traveling from her throat to her forehead, her eyelids, her cheeks and ears, her neck, the rounding of her shoulders and the soft slopes of her breasts. The warmth of his breath, the rough touch of his tongue and the edges of his teeth explored and charted each inch of her he could reach.

And she allowed it. She reveled in it, her sighs and moans of pleasure giving him assurance that her body belonged to him, that she accepted him as her mate, that she had given him the warmth of her body and the spirit within her was his. She was his. His wife, his mate…his heart rejoiced in the knowledge that he had taken her as his own.

CHAPTER SIX

ETHAN WAS PROVING to be a good hand with the horses, Debra decided. He'd spent hours gauging their knowledge of the trappings he was familiar with, the bridles, saddles and the weight he placed on their saddles, evaluating which ones were used to being ridden, which ones had not been used for such a thing as yet.

"Your mare won't take a saddle, will she?" he asked, leaning on the corral fence beside Debra as they watched the horses in the pasture.

"She's never had one strapped to her back. I don't need one to ride, and she is docile enough that I don't worry about her dumping me off. I know how to hold on without the use of a piece of leather beneath me."

"I saw that the first time I caught sight of you," Ethan said. "You rode into your yard like you were a part of the mare, and she followed you to the barn like a pet dog waiting for a handout."

"She cares for me, as I care for her." As though it were an everyday occurrence, Debra described her relationship with her mare. "I treat her as I would have her behave toward me, and we seem to see eye to eye on the subject."

Ethan laughed softly. "You've just given proof to the white man's code of Christianity," he said. "The idea of doing unto others as you would have them do unto you is from the book of faith they honor."

"And are you one of them, one of those who honor this book?"

"I was born into a family in which we attended church on Sundays, asked a blessing on our food three times a day and were read to from the written words that we believe are holy. I suppose that makes me a man who honors the Bible."

"I'm pleased," she told him, smiling into his eyes. "A man is stronger if he has a true faith. My mother knew of your white man's faith, and she believed that much of it was not unlike that of her own people."

"Do you think we might go to the church in town some Sunday morning?" he asked knowing he risked the possibility of recognition, and he awaited her reply.

"You are my husband, Ethan," she said slowly. "I will do as you ask, so long as it does not clash with what I believe in."

"Was that a yes or a no?" She thought his eyes lit with amusement at her answer.

"A 'yes,' I think. I want to please you. It is the role of a wife to make her husband happy, to ease his way, to fill his needs as best she can."

He gathered her close, and she thought his hands trembled against her back. Resting her head against his chest, she knew a surge of joy, that this man should so cherish her, that he delighted in her presence and enjoyed the warmth of her body against his own.

"You've given me much. You're a passionate woman and I think you'll make a wonderful wife for me, Debra. I'm pleased that our wedding night went so well and that the week since has been so filled with joy. You accepted me and made me welcome in the depths of your body and made me feel I'd found a resting place, a haven for my heart and soul."

She turned her head and buried her face against his shirtfront. "You make me blush," she told him. "I didn't think we would talk of such things. Only do them in the dark and then not think of them until the next time of mating occurred."

He laughed and she felt the rumble of his happiness beneath her ear. "You please me, little Nightsong. You are so innocent, so fresh and lovely. I've never known a woman to be so able to express herself."

She looked up at him in surprise. "Not even your wife?"

He shook his head, his eyes bleak as his thoughts left her and seemed to retreat to another place, another time. "She was a woman raised by older people. Her mother and father were almost beyond the age of having children when she was born, and she grew up with old people. She never had the chance to express herself to them, for they were of another generation, and thought children should be silent unless spoken to."

"And was she still that way when you married her?" She was hesitant to ask her questions, not knowing if it gave him pain to speak of the woman he had loved first.

"She was a good woman, but she didn't offer me her thoughts," he said, speaking slowly as if he chose his words with care. "She was grateful that I treated her well and she loved our child." His eyes seemed shadowed and she thought he looked far into the past.

"My son." His words were quiet, yet bore a trace of harshness, as if he freshly mourned the loss of his child. There was much about this man she had yet to learn, she thought, wisely deciding not to pursue the matter while his grief was so exposed to her.

"Did she love you? Your wife? Was she beautiful?' A plaintive note seemed to enter her voice and she rued the persistence of her questioning. She should not nudge him further with her curiosity.

He lifted her chin with his index finger and looked at her with a depth of intensity that surprised her. For long moments he scanned her face, as if memorizing each feature, each expression she offered him.

"Not as lovely as you, little Nightsong. She was pretty enough, a woman sought after by other men, and I felt lucky to have won her. But she didn't have your…" His eyes narrowed as he looked into hers, as he put her away from his body and his gaze traveled the length of her.

As if he chose the word he'd sought and was ready to speak it aloud, he continued his train of thought. "She didn't have your grace, your elegant lines, the ability to walk as a queen. And you possess all of those things, Nightsong. You hold your head high, and you know your worth. That makes you of greater value than as if you questioned your own importance to me."

"My mother told me that unless we valued ourselves, no one else would see us as we really are." She'd all but forgotten those words spoken to her as a child, yet now, she knew them for the truth they were. "My mother was a wise woman," she said firmly.

"And she raised a daughter to be proud of."

She felt a burst of pride within her at the words he spoke. Ethan was not a man to speak without forethought, and to know he regarded her so highly was a thing not to be taken lightly.

"I am only what I am," she said, as if she would soften his praise, for she would not have him think her proud.

"What you are is what makes you the woman I love."

She was stunned by his admiration, thrilled by

the words he offered her, and she bowed her head before him.

Drawing her back into his embrace, he held her firmly, as if he would thus claim her anew, and she allowed her weight to rest against him, in silent pledge of herself to his will. A man must always be the stronger of the two, her mother had said; must always be acknowledged as the sole leader in a home; and given the place freely and gladly by his woman.

"Debra, is there more about me you would know?" He offered her an open book, full knowledge of his life before this time, and she thought for a moment of what she might ask, and then her better sense prevailed.

"I need know nothing else for now," she said, looking up into his stern face. "If you will leave this book open and this page of your life exposed to me, so that at some later time I may know more of you…" She saw the tightening of his mouth, the narrowing of his eyes as she spoke, and for a moment regretted her words. Perhaps he had regretted his offer, decided she needed to know nothing more of him. Maybe, upon second thought, he had told her all he could and still keep his privacy.

"And will you share with me whatever I ask of you?" he wanted to know, his voice strong as he demanded her compliance.

"If I can. If I'm able to remember whatever it is you want to know about my past."

"Tell me one thing, sweetheart. Had you ever thought of marrying a man not from your mother's people?"

She'd not even considered such a thing, she realized, and her mind filled with the memory of the young men she'd known in her youth. "I suppose I thought to have a marriage with someone of her people, but when I left there and came to live alone on my father's land, I decided to forego marriage. I'd thought not to ever have a man or children from him." She knew her face showed the surprise she felt.

"I wasn't prepared for you, Ethan. When you entered my life, it was like a thunderstorm within me. You took hold of my thoughts and made a place for yourself in my home. I had no way of holding myself back from you, for you seemed to fill a need in me that I hadn't even known existed."

"All of that?" His grin spoke of satisfaction as she told him her thoughts.

"And more." Her admission was given with reluctance, but she knew the value of honesty, and had determined that she would ever give him that part of herself that she might have hidden. The part that craved his mind and spirit, the aching need within her that only he could fill.

"I didn't know I could love another woman, Nightsong. I thought my love was locked away and would be frozen forever. When my wife and son were killed, I buried the soft part of me that lent itself to loving, and when I committed murder, a wall was built around the tender parts of my heart. I knew I'd never be the same."

"And have you become a new man? Are you not the person you were as a youth? As a young man finding your way?"

"I've changed, perhaps for the better. I no longer accept things at face value, but find I seek a deeper knowledge, a deeper meaning in life. I knew you would be important to me when I first touched you, Debra. You filled me with desire for you that night, the touch of your hand, the flesh of your arm beneath my grip, the fire in your eyes as you defied me—they all seemed to fuse together in my mind and became a woman I knew I would someday have as my own. I wanted you then, and now even more."

"Should I have feared you that first night, when you threatened to tie me?"

He shook his head. "I wouldn't have caused you pain or hurt you in any way. I only wanted to be here with you, to find a place in your life, and foolish as it may sound, I determined that night to make you mine."

"I didn't know," she said quietly. "I might have run from you if I'd known you were so set on this thing between us."

"And now? How do you feel now, Debra Nightsong? Will you accept my love and live with me for all of your life?"

She felt a melting deep within her at his words, and her acknowledgment of his challenge was automatic. "I'm already Debra Tyler, and that says it all, Ethan. I've vowed to be yours. Don't ever doubt it." She reveled in the knowledge that never had she been given so great a gift as what this man offered her. "I will be your wife for as long as I live," she promised quietly, and felt as if she took her marriage vows anew, so firmly did she believe in the words she spoke to him.

"And will you bear my children?"

"If I am granted that joy, I'll hold it dear. I can think of no other pleasure so great as that of giving you a son."

"And a daughter? A girl with dark hair and shining eyes. A girl who can ride a horse without a saddle and gather eggs without fear?"

She thought he teased her with his query and her lips curved in response. "My daughter will never know fear of anything, least of all an insignificant chicken. I will tell her, as my mother told me, you are no better than any other living thing, but you're just as good, just as capable and just as strong as you want to be."

"Your mother was wise." He spoke the words softly and Debra took them as a gift, knowing that he did not grant them to her lightly, but spoke the truth as he saw it.

THEY SPENT HOURS in the garden later that day, with ripened tomatoes and the second planting of green beans ready to pick. Her basket was filled with the fruit of the vines she'd cultivated so carefully, and she told Ethan of the jars beneath the house, shelved in the fruit cellar, jars she would fill with the tomatoes that she used in her cooking.

"My mother had never eaten tomatoes until she married my father. They are a part of the nightshade family, and eating them was not done," she told him as they carried the jars up from the cellar into the kitchen. She poured hot water into her biggest pan and lowered the jars to soak, the rubber rings and lids with them. "He told her how to use them in soup and with meat, and she canned bushels of them the next summer. I remember slipping the skins from them at the table, helping her to cut them up and prepare them for the canning jars."

"You have good memories of her, don't you?" He smiled at the warmth of her smile, the light in her eyes as she spoke of her parents.

"They gave me what I needed to be prepared for my life here. While I was yet very young, my father taught me to shoot with his shotgun and rifle, how to clean the game I shot and how to bury the parts we did not use."

"Did he wish for a son?" Ethan thought the man could have had no greater gift than the daughter he'd helped to create, but knew that some men yearned for a copy of themselves to live on into the future.

"I don't think so. I remember that time in my life

so well, even though I was young, almost too young to learn all the things he thought I should know. Perhaps he recognized somehow that he had only a short while to teach me what he must, that our time together would be limited by the years of his life.

"He said I was all he wanted, that any child to come after me would be but an image in the window glass, a shadow of the woman I would become." She laughed, the sound almost a sob caught in her breast, as she spoke of the man who had given her life. "He thought I was perfect, and it took many scoldings from my mother to disabuse me of that idea."

He'd released her from his embrace long moments ago, but now Ethan felt the need to touch her again. His hand lifted hers to his mouth and he kissed the smooth skin that stretched from her fingers to her wrist, turned it in his hand to bless her palm with his lips.

"You're perfect for me," he said, hoping she would believe his words, wanting to impress upon her his admiration for her, his love for the woman she had become.

"I think you may be just a bit prejudiced," she told him, laughing a bit as if she found his words more than she could accept.

"Perhaps I am, but then what would you expect? I'm married to you, Debra. I know you as a wife and I admire you as a woman. The thought of nightfall and the joy it will bring is a big part of my life right now. Perhaps because we are newly married, and yet, I think I'll still yearn for you in the long years to come, that I'll crave the possessing of you as long as I live."

Her hand touched the nape of his neck and she coaxed his head lower, lifting her face to his. She kissed him, and he wondered if she was aware that it was not her custom to initiate affection between them. That she gave of herself sweetly, but usually only at his persuasion.

It was too good to pass up, he thought, lifting her into his arms and striding toward the house.

"What are you doing? Where are you taking me?" She asked questions, but the look in her eyes told him she was well aware of his reply even before he spoke it aloud.

"It's time for you to rest awhile," he said, his mouth pursing as if he spoke some great truth. "I think I need to lie beside you to make sure you do as I ask."

"In bed?" Her brow lifted teasingly and she smiled.

"Can you think of a better place for us to spend the afternoon?" He stepped onto the porch and opened the screen door easily, turning to carry her over the threshold so that she did not collide with the doorjamb. He closed the entry door with a foot and took her to the room they shared in the night hours.

"We've never done this in the middle of the day," she whispered as he placed her on the bed.

"I've always been willing to try something new once in a while," he answered, his fingers busy with the buttons that held her dress together. He opened the bodice and worked at the smaller buttons on her vest. "Will you let me do this?"

He was surprised at the soft laughter she could not seem to contain. "Do I really have a choice? I think you've made a decision here, Ethan and I'm just a part of it."

"Not true," he said lightly. "I'll never do anything to you that isn't agreeable. I'll only love you when you think it is right and proper. And I'll tell you now, little bird, I think this is about the most proper thing we can do this afternoon."

"Who am I to argue with a man who's already made up his mind?" She worked at the buttons of his shirt as she spoke and, in moments, she had stripped it from him and tossed it to the floor.

A flurry of clothing followed that garment and the afternoon sun, shining through the window, lent its warmth to the man and woman who lay beneath its rays and sought an ecstasy they had every right to own. Their bodies meshed and parted, and then, with kisses that stirred her to passion once more, Ethan formed his wife into a shivering, shimmering creature who clung to him with a desperation he gloried in. His hands were careful, his touch gentle as he brought her to a knowledge of pleasure she seemed not to have known before. Her body writhed, her hips lifting to his touch, her words a tangled hum of delight as he sought out the secret places that wept for the blessing of his fingers and palms, and the touch of his lips upon them.

And then he rose over her once more, lifting to match his masculine form to hers, his hard length finding a haven in the softness of her feminine warmth. He slid within her, his groan of pleasure almost smothered against her throat as he pressed her into the mattress. Her hips rose, meeting his in the rhythm he had begun, and she caught his tempo readily, each sigh, each whisper seeming to goad him on in his quest for the joy he knew he would find in her slender body.

He felt the spasms rend him then, his body trembling, his harsh cry sounding her name, his jaw clenching tight as the frantic throes of his release shattered his control and he was but a weight upon her. His body jerked once, then again in a reflex action that brought a matching movement from the woman beneath him.

She whimpered, a soft cry, accompanied by an upward thrust of her hips and he felt his manhood stirring once again, responding to the movement of the woman who tightened strong muscles to capture it in her depths.

"Ethan…don't leave me." Her plea gladdened his heart and he bent to her, his arousal swelling even more as he felt her need surround him.

"I'm here, love. I'm here." Carefully, gently, he renewed the rhythm of loving he had abandoned for long moments, and felt the shiver that flowed the full length of her body. Triumph filled him, the knowledge that she could not bear to end their time of loving adding strength that promised a fulfillment of her need.

With a thrust into her depths, a soft cry of consummation burst from his lips and she held him close, her body writhing beneath his. She twined her arms tightly around his neck, her face turning to his throat and her soft murmurs of pleasure met his ear.

"Thank you, my Ethan. You fill me with joy, my love."

Her whisper against his ear pleased him to no end as he strove to catch his breath. His bride had come close to exhausting him, her demands matching and even surpassing his own, and he delighted in her willingness to match him in this endeavor.

"I love you, my sweet," he whispered. "I want you to know happiness in my arms."

She nodded, as though words escaped her, and her body relaxed in his arms. In moments, the deep, even tones of her breathing gave him the knowledge that she slept, that her body needed refreshing from the hours they had spent together. He pulled the sheet over her and nestled her against himself, his thoughts soaring to the heavens as he sought the favor of his mother's God, and lifted his thanks for the gift of the woman he held.

THEY AROSE FROM THEIR bed just as the sun began its descent to the western horizon. The water had cooled in the kettle holding her canning jars and Debra bade Ethan to put it on the stove to heat while she began supper preparations. They ate later than was their usual schedule, and Debra washed her canning jars and covered them with a clean dish towel, claiming that the afternoon spent in their bed had ruined her scheduled chores.

Ethan helped her with the dishes, over her protests, for she felt it was her place to do the work in the kitchen. He did not agree and, without much fuss, won the argument. They did the tasks together, as usual finding a peaceful pleasure in the joint operations of her farm. Debra washed the eggs and stored them in the crock while Ethan set the milk aside for churning in the morning, when she would skim the heavy cream, adding it to that of the previous days'. Then according to plan, she would churn it into the golden butter that brought a high price at the general store.

The day had been like a dream come true, Ethan thought as he readied himself and his wife for bed. With hands that cherished each small particle of skin he touched, he took her clothing from her, tucking her into the bed where they had only recently found their pleasure together.

He pulled the sheet over them as he settled beside her, turning her then to face him, his arms surrounding her lush form, so slender, yet so rounded and feminine. He thought her perfect, as he'd told her earlier, and his touch gave witness to his thoughts. She arched beneath his hands, moaned her needs into his hearing, accepted the caresses he bestowed upon her as an offering at the altar of love.

A great outpouring of emotion swept over her, and Debra rose over the man she'd married, wanting, yearning to give him the completeness of her love, not knowing what form such a thing could take. Her mouth blessed his body, his throat, his chest, the flat line of his belly and the strong, muscular length of his legs. She tasted of the salty, clean scent of him, her mouth opening as she heard his words of praise, touching him with her tongue, wrapping his most private places in the expression of her love, until he rose up, catching her by the waist to draw her over him, coaxing her into the position he desired, seeking and finding the warmth of her that might form to contain his arousal.

She acceded to his wishes, melding her body against his, teasing and tempting his masculine parts to fit where they yearned to be contained. Rising over him, she cried out her rapture as the moonlight cast its magical glow over her taut features, her lithe body, the length of black hair that teased his flesh with its sweeping beauty.

And when she awoke, it was to find herself still atop his form, her soft parts cushioned by the muscular planes of chest and belly, her legs caught between his, her head resting on the curve of his shoulder. And she thought it might be the place where she would be content to spend all of her life.

CHAPTER SEVEN

IN THE WEEK THAT FOLLOWED, the horses in her pasture had increased in number yet again, Ethan having found another young mare available in town. He'd taken money from his cache for the purchase and now Debra looked at the small herd from her post at the corral fence. Leaning on the top rail, she watched as Ethan worked with one, then another of the mares who fed on the grasses in the pasture. They nuzzled him, coaxing the bits and pieces of carrots he had hidden in his pockets for them, and the grooming he performed on their lush coats caused them to preen before him.

As though they would do him honor, they presented themselves to him for their share of his soft words, the gentle rubbing of their ears and the sweep of his hands over their flanks. He was surrounded by them, this man who had a gift with her animals that might be envied by the people of her mother's tribe.

The man who employed those same tactics with his woman. And at that thought, Debra laughed, recognizing her own susceptibility to Ethan Tyler's charm. He clipped a lead line onto one halter, urging the young mare to follow behind him, then causing her to trot in a circle around him, tempering her with the length of line he held, speaking to her firmly as he directed her where he would have her go.

That the mare performed as he wanted came as no surprise to Debra, for she had seen him working with the mares for the past weeks, with an ever-growing sense of admiration for his skills. She knew she had a good hand with the horses, had trained her own golden mare without aid of any man, and yet there was a skill in Ethan's hands she did not possess.

She hoped he would be as adept at helping with the delivery of the foals when that time came. And at that thought, she shivered. The idea of having a pasture full of frolicking colts and fillies in the years to come was thrilling, and the chances of that very thing coming to pass were growing stronger by the day.

For even now she beheld five mares who carried young in their bellies, none of them over four years old themselves. The beginning of a herd to be proud of, with perhaps one of the number, yet unborn, a stud to breed with other mares yet to come. She thought of the neighbor, Samuel Shane, who had offered to buy a foal in the spring, when they had all made their appearances in her barn, when she might be persuaded to sell one or two of them.

If they could trade one of the newborns for the presence of his sorrel stud in her pasture for a month or so, it would be well worth the price of one of her prized foals. With the strong blood of that red stallion running through the veins of her mares' offspring, she would have the beginnings of a stable of truly superior horses.

The prices they could demand for them from willing buyers would aid her in the building of her farm, would put money into the building of a true barn, a structure that would hold stalls for twenty or more horses. They would be able to build a shed to house her chickens, taking them from the shed they shared now with a cow and an assortment of horses.

She thought of the larger smokehouse they would build, with Ethan working at her side, where they might hang the meat they butchered, steers from their own pasture. And to that end, she determined to have Ethan ask their neighbor about buying a young steer from him when the young bullocks had been denuded of their masculine parts and were more fit to have in her pasture.

Perhaps even this fall they would be able to butcher a steer of their own, instead of bartering with the neighbor for a side from one of his herd, butchered for his own family's use. She floated easily on dreams of her own making as she watched Ethan working in the pasture, elation at the joys inherent in her marriage washing over her, as a spring rain might fall upon her hayfield.

And the results were the same, for the hay would

grow and green and ripen into hay for the taking, and so would her eager spirit grow and ripen into the soul of a woman, a woman who would be a fitting mate to the man she watched.

Thankfulness for the care her mother had taken with her, the protection she had provided during her years with the tribe, was alive in her thoughts. She might have been taken by one of the braves, relegated to a position as second or even third wife, made to be a slave to another woman and a sometimes companion to the man who ruled over his own small kingdom.

She had seen it, had known of the fate of those younger women who lived at the bottom of the family ladder, whose youth was robbed by those who would make such females into mere shadows of their former selves. She had been spared such a fate, for her mother had kept her apart, filling her with the knowledge that she was not made for such a life, that she would one day have a man of her own, a man she would not share with another woman, but would keep unto herself.

And it had come about as her mother had wanted, for Ethan Tyler had come to her, not as a suitor, but as a conqueror, as a man setting out on a mission. That his mission was to stay from the public for a time, that he needed a safe place, a haven from the law, was not important. He was a man such as her mother would have wanted for her.

And that was the crux of the matter, Debra decided, thinking of the woman who had taken a husband from another world herself, who had married into the white man's world, and found happiness.

From the pasture, Ethan looked her way, his hands busy with a mare, holding the lead line, coaxing the pretty little bay to his will. He smiled, a grin that made her think of the night just past, when he'd loved her so well, and she lifted a hand to acknowledge his smile, to let him know she watched him with approval.

He took the line from the mare's halter and strode across the pasture toward her, his long legs making short work of the path he took. He stood on the other side of the fence and bent to her, his mouth finding hers with unerring precision. His lips were warm, damp from the touch of his tongue on them as he'd labored in the sunlight, and she inhaled the aroma of him, the sweat of his brow, the aroma of hay and horse he carried with him.

It was a good scent, she decided, a manly odor of horse and man, of daylight and sunshine, of strength and arrogance, of the man he was and the father he would be to the child she knew she carried beneath her breast.

She had thought it strange that her monthly flow had not come as expected, and had not spoken of it, certain it would only be late. And then, when four weeks passed without a sign of the bleeding she had come to accept as a part of her life as a woman, she knew. Knew with a certainty bred within her, a part of her blood, a sureness she could only accept and not explain.

As a woman of her mother's people, she knew things that were not as yet visible. Not as a shaman might know them, not with visions in the night, but as particles of truth that sprang full-blown into her mind, knowledge she could not comprehend or explain, but only accept as a part of her heritage. Her mother had known of things before they happened sometimes, indeed had warned Debra that she would be alone while still a young woman, a girl of sixteen, not a full grown woman in the white man's world, although her life in the tribe could have been set by that time in her life.

She had known she would leave her mother's people even before the time came, and when she felt the day was upon her, she'd leapt unto the back of her golden horse and set out, only a bedroll and a change of clothing with her, the deed to her father's farm tucked into her undergarments.

Those first months and years had been harsh, a time of testing for the young girl who lived by herself and existed from one day to the next. Only the gift of a cow and three chickens from her neighbor had enabled her to begin her life as she now knew it. She would never forget his kindness, that of his wife as she taught her to milk the cow, showed her how to skim the cream and churn the butter she was able to sell for the supplies she needed at the general store in town.

The equipment for survival was there, at her father's farm, the stove, the butter churn, the fruit cellar with cans of produce from her mother's garden, left for her use by the woman who had known her daughter would one day return here. She used the same kitchen cabinets her mother had stored her belongings in—indeed, those same kettles and spoons were used now for Debra's cooking.

She watched now as Ethan's smile recognized her musing, as he was silent, awaiting her words that would tell him of her thoughts. He knew her well. He knew the times when she was silent, when the memories of her yesterdays filled her, and when the time of overflowing came, she told him that which he yearned to know.

Thus she had given him her days, telling him of the struggle she went through that first winter, when the snows fell and she fought her way to the shed, how she slept out there with her animals when the storm caught her unawares and she could not find her way back to the house.

It was warm there, with the breath of the cow making clouds upon the air, the horse welcoming her into her stall, where the warmth of the big, golden animal was shared in the hours of the night. Ethan had frowned at her memories, holding her tightly against himself as she spoke of hardships that he felt were too harsh for a woman so young to face alone.

He would be with her from now on, he'd said, more than once giving her the assurance of his love, his presence in her life.

They went to the house together, Debra still silent, Ethan patient with her withdrawal, knowing it was not a part of him, that she held some small piece of herself separate from him, a part he would patiently draw from her through the years to come. His patience was a revelation to Debra, for she had not known that a man could be so tender, so ready to wait upon another, giving time as a gift, without intruding where he was not yet welcomed as a part of her past.

They spent the hours of the day as was their wont, working in the kitchen to prepare meals, eating together and then returning to the shed to settle the animals for the night. The mares were brought inside for shelter, for the sky was leaden with clouds that promised rain before dawn, and Ethan would not leave the vulnerable mares to the elements.

He tied them in stalls, crowding three of them into the box stall Debra used for birthing, feeding them well and leaving them with water and hay for the morning. They would be released in the light of day into the pasture once more, once the storm had passed and the blessed rain had greened the grass for their enjoyment.

Now, he took Debra to the house, speaking of the trip to town they would make in the morning. "I think we need to see how far we can stretch the money you have on the book at the general store, Debra," he said. "We need a good storehouse of supplies for the winter months, and it isn't too early to begin stocking up the pantry. We'll have the fruit cellar to depend on, but there are things we'll need to have in case we have heavy snow in a few months.

"There's something else I need to talk to you about, sweetheart. I have money put aside from my earnings at the Shanes' farm, plus a bit left over from my travels before I got here. I don't know if we should put it in the bank or just go ahead and spend it on fixing up things before winter."

"You have that much money?" She was surprised at the news, sure he had traded off work for his horse, and then the beef hanging in the smokehouse. He carried funds in his pocket when they left the farm, but that he had any amount of cash put aside was a surprise. Welcome, but a surprise nevertheless.

"I wasn't trying to hide it from you, Debra. I hope you know that. It just hasn't come up, but most of my cash is in your dresser. You'd have found it in short order had anything happened to me, or if you'd looked a little deeper than my drawers in there."

She laughed. "I look into your underwear frequently, Ethan. Every time I wash the clothes, in fact. I guess I didn't look deeply enough."

"Well, you know where it is if anything comes up, if you should ever need it and I'm not here."

A chilly finger of fright traced the line of her spine at his words and she turned to him, her arms looping around his neck. "Don't even talk that way. Where else would you be, but here with me?"

He shook his head, his look solemn. "That's something we don't know, love. Things happen, sometimes without warning, and I want you to be prepared."

"You're frightening me, Ethan, and I'm not easily put off by scary things."

"I know that. You're the bravest, most courageous woman I've ever known. But emergencies arise at the most unexpected times, and I wanted you to know about the money, in case you needed it."

"I have you, and you'll take care of me. I don't need anything else," she said stubbornly.

He laughed. "You're hopeless, do you know that? You have the idea that I'm invincible, Debra. Trust me, I'm not. You may have to face things on your own one day. I want you to be prepared."

MORNING DAWNED with bands of pink in the eastern sky, the promise of early sunshine welcome on his head as Ethan headed for the shed, milk pail in one hand. He'd left Debra busy with breakfast preparations and he looked forward to a speedy session of milking, more than ready for the pancakes she'd promised him.

The cow was most obliging, giving her milk without a stray kick or baleful glance in his direction. The chickens forsook their nests when he opened the door, and scattered feed across the yard, leaving their nests available for him to forage for their daily offering of eggs. He filled a blue-speckled pan he found in the shed, counting the number to himself.

"You got eight eggs today, Debra," he announced, entering the kitchen, the milk pail swinging from his right hand, the pan of eggs clutched against his shirt.

"Where'd you find that pan?' she asked. "I'd forgotten it was in the shed, and I worried that you wouldn't have anything to put the eggs in. That is, if you were brave enough to shoo the hens from their nests." Her smile mocked him and he bent to kiss the tip of her nose on his way to the pantry.

The milk pail was covered with a clean dish towel, the eggs placed on the pantry shelf, and he readied himself for breakfast. Washing quickly at the sink, he told her of the chickens scavenging the yard for their morning snacks, of the grasshoppers he'd seen them snatching up, the bits and pieces of previous feedings they'd managed to scratch up from the dirt.

"I'll shake a panful of feed in the shed before we leave. I don't think I want to let them run while we're gone to town," she said, dishing up his pancakes and then retrieving the syrup from the pantry. She tipped the bottle to one side, measuring the scant amount remaining.

"We should buy some more, I suspect. Although I may see if Mr. Anderson has any maple flavoring. I can make syrup myself that way."

"Don't you have any peddlers in this part of the country? We had a fella who stopped by every month or so back home. He had a great big black bag he'd open on the kitchen table and my mother would pick and choose things for the kitchen and herself. We even managed to get a few candy sticks out of him when Mama bought a goodly amount."

"Julia told me once at the store that a man was going to set up a route in this part of the territory, but I don't know what happened to him. I haven't heard any more about it."

"It's kinda handy, knowing that someone will be stopping by every once in a while to sell stuff you might not find at the general store." As if his memories of such a man were happy ones, Ethan spread his arms wide and laughed.

"I'll bet his suitcase stretched out at least this far by the time he unfolded all the pockets in it. Had everything from soup to nuts. Mama used to buy needles and thread or a new thimble. Sometimes she got salve for our scrapes, or spices for the kitchen. Seems like he was with a big company from east of here."

"I'll ask Julia if she's heard any more about such a thing going on around here when we go to the general store."

The ride to town was but a short jaunt, the gelding

stepping out smartly as if he were headed for a barn full of hay. "We need to think about getting a buggy for trips to town instead of using the wagon. I'll bet Jack up there would be happy to haul something that weighs less than half as much as this farm wagon. And I'll bet you'd like the trip better without the sun full on your face. There's a lot to be said for a new buggy."

Debra shot him a look guaranteed to make him hesitate before he put in his order for a new conveyance. "And who can afford such a thing?"

"We can. I'm going to sell the hay this time instead of bartering for it. We'll be ready to cut it in a week or so, and if your neighbor wants it badly enough, he can pay for it. The money would pay for a buggy for you, and trust me, you'll find it much easier to drive than this wagon."

"Well, with you around I needn't drive the wagon anyway," she said smartly. "Why do you think I feed you and keep you happy?"

"Tell me, why don't you?" he challenged, his grin wide, his eyes sparkling.

"Because I love you." The words were spoken before she had a chance to think about it. They were the secret she'd kept guarded in her heart, not willing to make such a declaration up until now. And why today seemed to be the day for such an event, she could not have said, only that the time for a final commitment had come, that she was willing to offer him everything she held dear.

"You haven't told me that before, Debra." His look was sober, his eyes warm with pleasure at her words. "Why now? Why today?"

"Because I haven't spoken the words aloud before now doesn't make them any less important now. I've felt true liking and respect for you almost since the beginning, but there is an element of trust that I hesitate to give any man. Any woman, for that matter. I'm not a warm, trusting person, Ethan."

"Now, there you're wrong," he said, his voice firm. "You've been as warm as a man could ask for. I think...no, I believe you trust me more than you even admit to yourself. You've married me, put yourself under my control, and I think you trust me not to take advantage of you, Debra. I could claim all you own as mine. According to the law, you turned over everything that is yours to my name when we married. Does that worry you?"

She shook her head. "You'd never do anything to hurt me, Ethan. I know that."

"Is that what you'd call trust?" He waited for her to think about it, watching the road ahead, as if he had dismissed the matter from his mind.

"I hadn't thought about it before," she said. Her brow furrowed as she considered the idea. "I suppose I trust you more than anyone else in my life. My mother represented security to me for a lot of years, especially after my father died and we were left alone. I was but twelve years old when she took me back to her people. She kept me safe, and I trusted her to do that, never for a second of time did I fear that she would let anything happen to me that was not right and proper."

"And do you think I'll give you the same support as did your mother? Do you believe I'll look out for you and keep you safe?" He turned toward her and caught her gaze, his eyes dark with promise.

"You know I do, Ethan." She smiled, her heart free from doubt. "The respect you earned during those first few weeks here turned into love without my recognizing it. I still hold you in high regard. The respect I feel for you has not changed, only risen to a higher lever." The words rolled from her as if she had scripted them, and she felt a blush cover her cheeks as she spoke.

"You're the most important thing in my life, Ethan Tyler. I've given you everything I have, my heart, my body and the whole of my existence. You have my farm, the one thing I brought into this marriage, and all that it contains."

"I don't want to own your farm," he said harshly. "I hope you don't think that was a factor in my proposal to you. I only want to claim you as my wife, live my life with you and have a family of my own."

She smiled at him, a great truth dawning upon her as his words soothed her soul. "I want you to own my property, Ethan. I'm dependent upon you, and I like it that way. I can claim your protection for me and the children we will share. I was alone for too long, and I've found a joy in our life together that I didn't know existed until now. I'm not sure why you feel the way you do about me, but I accept that it is so."

"Your mother felt this way about your father, didn't she? Is it so difficult for you to understand that I want to keep you safe as your father did your mother."

"I've been on my own for a long time, Ethan. I'm trying hard to bow to your place in my home." Considering all that she knew about the woman who had borne her, she attempted to answer his question. "Yes, I think she did, I think she truly loved him.

"She'd had an unhappy time as a girl, married to a man who was cruel to her, a man who gave her a son and then took ownership of that child as though my mother was of no account. When he died, his family took the boy and she was not allowed to see him again. Especially after she left to be with my father. They said the boy had been told that his mother was dead to him, and that he didn't know she existed."

"You have a brother, then? With the tribe?"

She smiled a bit at that. "It seems strange that it should be so, but I do have family, now that you put it that way. I wouldn't know him if I walked past him on the sidewalk in town, but somewhere out there, living with my mother's people, he exists."

"Would it be out of the question for you to find him, to let him know you belong to him, as a sister?"

"I'm not welcome in the village any longer. When I left, I was told I would be shunned by the tribe, even my mother's family."

"Who is left of her family?"

"A sister, her children and my old grandmother. I don't even remember speaking to any of them. My mother was an outcast when we returned after my father died, and she was not given the respect due her."

"Does it bother you? Not to know them?"

She considered the idea, and as though a light had been lit within her, the answer came to her. "No, Ethan. I have you, now. I need no one else, and I'll not seek them out."

The outskirts of town surrounded them, small houses on either side of the road, children running and playing, dogs barking, some women sweeping porches and others sitting to watch their young ones play together.

A brown pup scampered beside the gelding, barking and playful. "I hope he doesn't get run over by the wagon," Debra said, frowning as she watched the playful antics.

"He won't," Ethan assured her. "He probably chases every wagon and buggy that passes by. He's pretty agile," he noted as the pup scampered to one side and sat on the verge, his tongue hanging out after his exertions.

"Ethan?" She was hesitant, unwilling to allow him the thought that she wanted for anything, and yet this was a dream of her childhood and she felt safe in confiding it to him. "Do you think we might have a dog at the farm? It would be good to have a watchdog, I think, and when we have children, they would have a natural protector."

"I'll ask around for a puppy if you want one," he said, immediately and with no doubt attached to his words. "I've thought a cat would be a good idea, out in the barn. It would keep down the mice that keep getting into the oat barrel."

She bounced in the seat at the idea of animals, remembering the yearning she'd had as a child for a pet of her own. "Who do you suppose might have pups?"

"We'll check into it today," he said, the words a promise, and she was satisfied.

"I DIDN'T KNOW IT would be so simple," Ethan said, smiling at the vision beside him. The wagon was headed for the farm, the supplies stored in the back in three boxes, one of which he'd said would be just the right size for a bed for the puppy Debra held.

"Maybe it was just luck that the doctor's dog had a litter and he was set on giving them away," she said, deeply involved in petting the small animal in her lap. A tiny pink tongue had claimed her fingers, and the spotted pup seemed to have claimed Debra as his own.

"I don't believe in that sort of thing," Ethan said firmly. "I think everything happens for a purpose, and we were meant to have a pup at the farm. The time was right, and things worked out for the best. Now all we have to do is locate a cat."

"I think a full-grown animal would be better than a kitten," Debra told him. "I'd rather have a kitten to raise, but an adult cat would fit in better in the barn. I wouldn't worry about her being alone out there."

She lifted the pup in her arms and buried her nose in the soft fur atop his head. "He smells so good, Ethan. He's so soft and warm."

He thought he'd never known a woman so easy to please. She had taken to the pup like a cat takes to cream, holding it close, thanking the doctor's house- keeper three times before Ethan could load her up on the wagon. Her eyes shone, her mouth could not seem to stop smiling, and she had patted his hand and thanked him numerous times since they'd left town.

"We'll keep him in the house till he's old enough to sleep in a doghouse outdoors," he decided aloud. "I think he'll do well behind the stove where it's warm. I'll put his box there and we'll find a piece of blanket or something to keep him warm."

She stilled suddenly and he glanced at her with a question in his eyes. Her even white teeth bit at her bottom lip and she spoke her thoughts aloud.

"I wondered if we could keep him in the bedroom at night. Then if he gets restless and needs to go out to relieve himself, I'd hear him and know. It might save puddles on the kitchen floor."

He grinned at her. "You just want him nearby so you don't worry about him, Debra. You can't fool me."

"I wasn't trying," she said, her voice a bit snippy, he thought. It pleased him, that she had no fear of retaliation should she dispute his advice, or not agree with him on any small thing. She bent her head low to press her lips against the downy head that had sagged against her hand, the pup relaxing into sleep. He was limp in her hands, and she folded her arms across her chest, cuddling him close.

"I think you'll spoil him rotten," Ethan said. "He has to know his place in the house, Debra. He can be a pet for you, but he has to know that he's still a dog, not people."

She looked indignant. "I know that. He'll have his own place, but I can't help but love him. I feel like he needs me and I want to keep him safe and protect him."

"I can see that, love." He put his arm around her shoulders, drawing her closer. "Do you see that some things are alike? That the way you feel about the puppy is similar to what I feel for you? I want to keep you safe and protect you, too. The difference is that I love you as a wife, a woman to be cherished, and that little mutt is just a dog. A cute pup, to be sure, but not due the care I give you."

The long lane leading to the house was upon them now and Ethan turned the gelding down the narrow lane, passing lush fields on either side, where daisies and wild mustard grew in profusion. The house ahead seemed to welcome them, a homelike feel about it, and he gathered Debra closer.

"Do you think we might consider painting the house this fall?" he asked. "I'd like to put a coat of white on it, and I thought about making some shutters, painting them black. That ought to dress it up, don't you think?"

She looked pleased at the idea. "I'll help you. Mama and I painted the kitchen walls years ago, and I was pretty good at it."

"Maybe we should give those walls another coat of paint, too. What color would you like?"

"Color? I hadn't thought about changing it. We just got white paint from the hardware store in town." She hesitated, her mouth working as she thought. "How about yellow? I could make some pretty curtains for the windows, and maybe a tablecloth to match."

"Whatever you want, sweetheart," he told her, pleased that she had taken to the idea so quickly. He pulled the wagon up to the back porch and jumped down, reaching up for her, gripping her waist and lifting her to stand before him. His arms encircled her and he held her close.

"I love you, Debra Tyler." He bent and claimed her lips with a kiss that seared his very being. She was warm, responsive and obviously willing to accommodate his desire, should he ask it. A thought that appealed to him mightily.

"Let's get these supplies in the house," he said, his voice husky with a passion he could not hide.

She looked up at him in surprise. "You sound almost angry," she said, frowning.

"No." Without explanation, he released her, turned her toward the porch and sent her on her way. "Go in and pull the coffee to the front of the stove to heat, will you? I'll be right there with a box of foodstuffs to put away."

She did as he asked, looking back at him over her shoulder as she opened the door and stepped across the threshold. Her eyes seemed puzzled and he grinned, pleased that he had perplexed her. Hurriedly, he picked up a box of the supplies and followed her into the house, depositing his burden on the pantry shelf before he returned to the wagon for another load.

The woman had a surprise coming, he decided. Unwilling to wait any longer than it would take to unload the wagon and take care of the horse, he'd give her fifteen minutes to consider the idea, and then he was going to haul her off to the bedroom for a little talk.

And if he had his way about it, the conversation would be short and sweet. Merely an affirmation of his intentions, hopefully plans that she would fall in with, without hesitation.

CHAPTER EIGHT

SHE'D NOT SLEPT WELL, at least not since the black of night had given way to the gray sky that comes just before dawn. Something had been poking at her, some stray thought that would not be banished, no matter that she dressed quietly so as not to wake Ethan. There was no reason for him to be up before time for the chores, and the sun had a good hour before it would crest the horizon.

A pot of coffee was put on to boil, a handful of fresh grounds and a pinch of salt added to a half pot of water. She'd done it almost automatically, having become accustomed to the early morning ritual since Ethan's arrival. She had settled for leftovers or a cup of tea before he'd entered her life, with his insistence on early morning coffee.

So easily she had come to do his will. At least in this one small thing, she thought, even as she recognized that her whole way of life had changed over the past months. The kitchen was warmed almost beyond comfort with the heat from the wood-burning stove reaching each nook and cranny. Opening the back door and allowing the fresh, early morning breeze to enter might work, she decided, turning the lock and twisting the knob.

As if hit by a lightning bolt, she felt it again, that same strong knowledge that something awaited, just over the horizon. Behind her, the pup sniffed at her skirts and whined, an obvious plea to be let out of the house for his early morning rituals.

She unlatched the screen door, opening it far enough for the spotted pup to escape the confines of the house, and watched as he scampered to the nearest tree to sniff its trunk, perhaps in search of some stray predator. Lifting his hind leg, he put an end to whatever scent he'd found there and continued on, his nose close to the ground as he quartered the yard, investigating his territory, so new to him, yet, after his late night jaunt last evening, familiar.

She moved onto the porch to watch him, amused at his antics, for he seemed bound to imitate whoever had been his idol at the doctor's place in town. Perhaps his mother, maybe even his father had been close by. Used to the outdoors, the pup trotted past the barn, rousing one of the mares into a sharp whinny. Casting a superior look at the shed that contained that pent-up creature, he went on, crouching on all fours to squeeze beneath the pasture fence.

His head lifted, his nose apparently scenting some new flavor that intrigued him, for he ran full tilt toward the far side of the pasture, and then under that fence to the wooded area that bound the east side of her farm. Something had caught his attention, she thought, and he wouldn't be returning in any great hurry.

The chores in the kitchen faced her and she pulled open the screen door to reenter the kitchen. As she did, the same pull on her senses urged her to halt. Door half-shut, she closed her eyes and concentrated, luring whatever strayed on the outskirts of her consciousness a bit closer.

It was not to be, for the sound of Ethan in the bedroom broke her mood and in a few minutes he'd joined her in the kitchen. "Why didn't you wake me?" he asked, rubbing at his hair, the dark strands falling over his forehead in disarray.

"I woke early and thought to start breakfast, but the pup wanted to go out and I watched him for a while."

He looked toward the porch. "Where is he?"

"Beyond the pasture a ways. He won't go too far, will he? Do you think he might get lost in the woods?"

Ethan crossed to the door and stepped out on the porch. A shrill whistle from his lips surprised her and she followed him outdoors. "It always used to work when I was a kid and I wanted my dog to come running," he said with a grin.

"Hasn't done much for this one," she said, pursing her lips. "I don't even see him now. And I don't like it."

Ethan put his arm around her shoulder and squeezed a bit. "Don't be a fussbudget. He'll be fine. When he gets hungry, he'll be back."

From the barn, one of the mares sounded an early morning whinny, and Ethan frowned. "Wonder what got her started?"

"I heard her when the dog was out by the shed," Debra said. "She must have scented him and realized it was a strange smell."

Ethan shook his head. "There's more to it than that. She's heard something else." With long steps he left the porch and set off for the shed. "I'll do the chores and be ready for breakfast," he called back to her.

Again, she felt the rush of heat in her blood, a sense of something out of the ordinary, and she hugged herself, a chill taking possession of her. Across the meadow and beyond she saw the pup's tail, held high as he raced back and forth, and her anxiety seemed to calm. She didn't relish the thought of something happening to the dog when they'd just gotten him, and begun to make plans for his future.

Back in the house, she put the skillet on to heat and found the slab of bacon hanging in the pantry. Her sharp knife made short work of it, and eight slices soon lay in the skillet, sizzling gently as the pan heated.

"Eggs," she murmured to herself, heading back to the shelf where the egg crock sat. It was empty, the trip to town having included selling eggs along with her butter. She'd have to wait 'til Ethan brought in this morning's eggs before she could stir up anything.

Again the dog yelped, a high shrill bark that drew her back to the door. He stood just beyond the pasture fence, his tail high, wagging ferociously, as he sounded another alarm. Something was wrong, she was certain of it, and with a quick trip back to the stove, she pushed the skillet to the far corner, where the fire was not yet felt to any great extent, and hastened outdoors.

Her heart was pumping as she ran past the shed, climbed the fence quickly and made her way across the pasture to the far side. The dog saw her coming and scooted under the fence, meeting her before she reached the boundary between pasture and open meadow. Nipping at her skirt, and growling softly in his throat, he was agitated and she shared his mood.

A man. She felt the presence of a man, and halted her steps at the boundary fence. The pup slid beneath the bottom board and turned to look at her, his ears peaked, his head high. "What have you found?" she asked him quietly, even as she climbed the boards and slid down the other side.

He raced ahead of her and she followed apace, making her way through the tall grass carefully, lest she trip and fall on a gopher hole or some other obstacle to be found there. Fifty feet or so beyond her, the pup skidded to a halt and turned to watch her progress, impatient with her slower speed.

She slowed even more, apprehension swelling in her throat. Beyond the dog, some unknown object drew her, and yet she was hesitant to go farther. The sure and certain knowledge that whatever lay beyond her vision was a threat enveloped her. Yet, nothing could be seen from here, and she would feel foolish, should she call Ethan from the shed for no visible excuse.

As her feet began to move again, the dog turned and raced farther afield, coming to a halt a hundred yards away from where she paused. He nosed at something on the ground, only his head and tail visible as he turned to look for her again.

"I wanted a dog, and now look at me. Chasing him halfway to town and back." That her words were an exaggeration was beside the point, she decided. Something else was drawing her, something besides the dog, who ran back to tug at her skirt with sharp teeth.

For a moment, she wished futilely that she had her shotgun clutched in her hand, and then banished the idea with a shake of her head. There was nothing to fear in her meadow, probably a small animal, either dead or dying. The meadow grass reached above her knees at this point and she looked ahead to where the ground rose a bit, there where the pup had once more taken a stance, perhaps that of a conquering hero, she thought with a grin. A riderless horse stood at the edge of the field.

As she neared the base of the small hill, she raised her skirts, holding them high so as not to trip over the fabric of her dress, and climbed easily the small rise before her. Something blue lay ahead, just beyond the dog, perhaps a piece of fabric, she thought.

And then, as her heart seemed to collide with her ribs, she recognized a black boot, and then another. She halted, her hand at her throat, the knowledge of danger alive in her chest. Whoever it was, man or boy, he was unmoving, and she thought quickly of her neighbor. Might he have walked through the woods and come upon trouble of some sort?

The wish that she had called out earlier, for Ethan, was futile and she recognized it as such. Running now, she saw the form of a man, a man full grown, his blue shirt and trousers dark against the grass. His eyes were shut and she looked closer, trying to gauge whether or not his chest rose and fell in the rhythm she would have expected.

A groan left his lips and she saw his eyes flutter, perhaps he'd heard her. No, more likely, he'd been roused by the puppy's barking. In any event, he opened blue eyes, squinting at the sunlight that had just begun to shine from over the trees behind him. A spasm of pain contorted his features and he tried to speak, lifting one hand in her direction as if he would call out to her.

She moved closer, fearful of being the victim of a hoax, for if he were a troublemaker, he might reach out for her foot, grasp her ankle and bring her to the ground. Another look at his waxen features changed her mind and she spoke to him.

"Are you hurt? What can I do to help?"

His eyes opened wider and he spoke but a single word, one she dreaded to hear, given its deadly portent.

"Snake." As though it had taken all of his strength to utter that lone syllable, he inhaled deeply and closed his eyes, obviously losing consciousness.

"Snake. You've been bitten," she murmured, even as she recognized that he could not hear her. She looked back toward the shed, wishing for a moment that she had the ability to whistle as Ethan had done just fifteen minutes ago. Torn between trying to lift the injured man and running back for help, she hesitated.

It was then she saw the back door of the shed open, saw three mares come through the opening, then another, followed by Ethan, leading the fifth horse behind him, one hand on her halter. He stopped in the sunlight, the horses running past him, traveling the limits of the corral to wait for him on the opposite side where the gate led into the pasture.

She spoke his name. "Ethan." And then realized he stood no chance of hearing her unless she sounded an alarm he could not miss.

Her shout for help was not any sound he had ever

heard before, for it was as best as he could tell, a war cry from some native who had strayed onto the land beyond the pasture. Ethan lifted his head to scan the horizon, catching sight of a woman—Debra, waving at him with wild movements, even as the puppy barked in a shrill warning of a sort.

Releasing the halter he held, he ran for the gate, opening it and racing toward the back of the pasture. With one hand on the top board, he sailed over the fence and ran full tilt, barely breathing as he raced the distance to where she waited.

His heart pounded with abandon as he took in her stance and, coming toward him, the puppy that seemed to be pleased with his prowess, still barking, his tail waving like a banner in a parade.

"Ethan, I'm all right," she said, her voice carrying to him, his fear for her somewhat abating by the words she called out in his direction. She turned from him then, and he saw her kneel in the grass, only her head and shoulders visible to him now. In moments, he'd scaled the slight rise atop which she awaited him, and skidded to a halt in the grass.

Before her was the body of a man, perhaps not a body as such, for unless he was mistaken, the chest moved a bit, signifying life, the presence of lungs expanding and filling with air. He dropped to his knees beside her.

"Who is he? Do you know him?" The face was not familiar to Ethan, yet he'd seen men of this ilk before, and his skin shriveled with a chill that would not be banished.

"I feel that his name is Jay," Debra said quietly, "and I think he's here because of you. I don't feel any danger directed at me, but I sense that he's looking for you, Ethan." Her voice broke and she looked at him with eyes that were wide and shiny with tears that glistened on their surface.

"How do you know that?" he asked sharply, aware that her words might be all too true. He'd known that his name was on the lips of lawmen from here to New York, but this wasn't a sheriff, or a deputy. He knew what to look for and a small town lawman would be wearing a badge, most likely, and carrying a gun.

This man wore clothing designed to blur his purpose here, a common blue chambray shirt and dark trousers such as any farmer might possess. His hat lay a few feet from him, a broad-brimmed sort, much like his own.

"He's been bitten by a snake," Debra said, her voice trembling. "I don't know if he's going to be all right or not. But we should get him to the house so I can take care of him."

"How do you know? Where's he bitten?" Ethan's questions were sharp and rapid, and he pulled her back from the stranger.

With a jerk, she turned to face him, almost falling as she lost her balance, hovering there on her knees. "He said one word before he lost conscious-ness. He said 'snake' and then closed his eyes again. I don't know where he's bitten, but we need to find out. In a hurry."

Reaching into his pocket, Ethan pulled out his knife, opened it quickly and searched out a starting place. "Undo his shirtsleeves and check out his arms while I cut his trouser legs." Without hesitation, he slit the man's pant legs from ankle to knee, his sharp blade finding no resistance in the harsh denim material.

"No need to undo his shirt," Debra said, pointing at the stranger's left calf, just inches below his knee, on the side of his leg where the flesh was fuller. A double puncture in his skin looked reddened already and Ethan did not hesitate, but bent closer to make a slit between the two holes and watched for a moment as the blood flowed to soak into the ground beneath the man's leg.

With a sharp exclamation, he bent low, put his mouth against the wound he'd created and sucked strongly at the blood and fluid issuing forth. With a shake of his head, he turned to the side and spat the mouthful on the grass, then repeated the act. Twice more, he sucked fluid from the man's leg before he rubbed his mouth on his sleeve and spat again.

"I don't know if I got it in time or not. Or even if it was a rattler bite, but I suspect it was," he said. Debra nodded her agreement.

"I've seen several rattlers out here. They come out of the woods in the morning and sun themselves on the grass."

Ethan rose and looked at her, noting the pale tone of her skin, the trembling of her hands. "Are you all right, sweetheart?" he asked, aware that she had been badly frightened by the events of the morning. "How did you happen to come out here, anyway?"

"The dog." Simply, without wasting words, she waved a hand at the animal who sat behind Ethan, quiet now that he'd sounded the alarm and warned of the problem. "I heard him out here and I knew there was something wrong. I'd felt it for a half hour or so, since before I got up."

Ethan looked at her questioningly. "You *felt* it?"

She nodded and shrugged. "I knew there was something going on. Something wrong, but I didn't suspect what it was. Then when I saw the dog raising a fuss, I realized it was a man out here somewhere. It didn't see him until I was almost on top of him."

"You realized there was a man out here, and you didn't call me first?" He knew his voice had risen and its tone was rough and harsh, but the anger that flowed from him would be expressed. "You could have been hurt or even killed if he hadn't been hurt, if he'd been lying in wait for you."

She shook her head. "But he wasn't, Ethan. He needed help. And if we don't get him to the house, we may lose him yet."

So sanely she spoke, so quietly she argued her point, and he could only tremble as he thought of what might have happened, how easily he could have lost her, when he'd only begun to recognize her worth to him.

"And what if you'd been alone here. If I weren't here with you?" he asked, knowing that his words were foolishness, that he was grasping at reasons to hold onto his anger, that his fear for her had overcome his good sense.

She stood beside him now and bent to press a kiss on his lips. "I'm not hurt, Ethan. I wouldn't have taken any chances with my life. I *knew*."

He rose slowly, grasping her arm, drawing her close to himself. "I'm not angry with you, sweetheart. Only worried and frightened for your well-being. I could not live without you in my life. I haven't found you only to lose you."

"I'll ask forgiveness for causing you worry, Ethan, but not for trying to help a man in need." She leaned back in his embrace to meet his gaze. "We must help him, Ethan. Now."

She looked up, seeking the horse she'd seen earlier, but it had strayed off somewhere out of sight. Ethan nodded shortly and released her from his grasp, then bent low to lift the stranger from his bed in the long grass. "I'll carry him. Why don't you run ahead and bring a horse. Maybe we can put him on top one of the mares and get him to the house faster."

She didn't deign to answer, only turned and sped away, her feet sure against the uneven ground as she headed for the corral fence and from there to where the mares grazed in the grass beneath the trees. With a sound he barely heard, she called her golden mare to her side and with a lithe movement he could only admire, she jumped to the back of the sleek creature and the mare headed in his direction.

With a smooth, strong leap, she sailed over the corral fence and, without hesitation, ran across the pasture to where he waited. Debra rode her as if she were one with the animal, her knees firmly gripping the mare's barrel, her hands buried in the pale mane.

Halting beside him, she slid from the mare's back and the horse stood quietly, her dark eyes focused on the woman who held one arm around the animal's neck.

"You didn't waste any time, did you?" Ethan asked with an admiring grin. He faced the mare's left side and shifted the man he carried over his shoulder, turning him so that his body rested on the back of the mare.

"Will she protest his weight?" he asked, and Debra shook her head.

"I'll lead her. She'll be fine."

And she was, following like a pet dog behind her mistress, across the meadow, through the corral and shed and thence to the back porch. Ethan was beside her then, grasping the stranger by the belt and lifting him to his shoulder. He headed for the porch, Debra ahead of him, opening the back door and leading him into the parlor.

Ethan lowered the limp form onto the sofa and straightened his legs, placing a firm cushion beneath the injured calf. Beside him, Debra felt for a pulse in the man's throat, then bent to place her ear against his chest.

"His heart sounds strong, but I'll need to make a poultice to draw any poison still in his body from the wound," she said. Straightening, she went to the kitchen and Ethan heard her footsteps as she crossed to the pantry. For a moment he waited, and then watched as she came back into the parlor, a wooden box in her hands.

"It's my mother's salves and potions," she told him. "Watch him for a few minutes, while I get hot water and ready a poultice to put on his leg."

Ethan nodded, his gaze firmly on the face of the man before him. Even in his unconscious state, his features were stern, his mouth taut as if he would not speak unnecessarily, his chin firm and his jaw a harsh line. His face was that of a man whose business was danger, a man who was to be respected, perhaps feared.

Dark hair fell against his forehead, a long scar rode the line of his brow, coming perilously close to one eye, and Ethan wondered at the knife that had almost taken his vision. Another scar stretched from his ear to the top level of his cheekbone, a remnant of some battle in the past. The man had been familiar with guns and knives in the past, and he bore the proof of it. A man who rode alone, who perhaps lived by the gun.

Debra reappeared, carrying a basin of water that steamed, proclaiming it hot and her speed in placing it on the floor by the sofa told him her hands felt the heat from it. And yet she did not pause, but dipped a white cloth into its depths and squeezed the water from it, then placed it on his leg.

"The heat will draw the wound," she said. "I'll prepare the poultice, but in the meantime, the heat alone will help."

He nodded, knowing that she was capable of all she said, that her skills included the healing arts. He felt no surprise at the revelation, for she had the look of a healer, her hands deft as she worked, her eyes touching the still form before her with a canny understanding. An old piece of fabric, probably part of a sheet, was spread on the floor and she opened her wooden box, sorting through its contents until she found a container, a pouch that had a drawstring at the top.

Opening it, she allowed a handful of its contents to spill upon the fabric, then closed the pouch and returned it to the box. With a quick movement, she scooped water from the pan and moistened the dry powder, mixing it into a paste with her index finger.

When she seemed satisfied with the results, she folded the material over it and turned it, so that it was completely covered with a double layer of fabric. Lifting it to the stranger's leg, she placed it upon his wound, removing her original dressing to soak in the water.

"There. I can do no more for a while," she said quietly. "The poultice will draw the poison from his body. I fear it had a chance to do much damage before you were able to suction it out."

"Sometimes we have no way of helping when someone has suffered snakebite," he told her. "That you have the knowledge to help him is a miracle in itself. If I'd been alone, I probably wouldn't even have found him until it was too late, Debra. He will owe you his life if he lives through this."

She smiled, a strangely sad lifting of her lips that touched him, a movement of her features that expressed a fear she did not acknowledge openly.

"You fear that you may have been too late, don't you?" he asked.

"There is always that fear," she told him, bending low to touch the man's forehead. "He will have fever soon, and if his body is strong enough to fight, he may recover. But he may never open his eyes again, and we'll never know why he came here."

"I know why." Ethan's words were dark, his expression bleak.

"Yes." Debra spoke but a single word, an admission of his knowledge, a knowledge she shared. "He is here for you, Ethan. He has sought you out."

"I won't run."

She smiled at him, and he was touched by the sadness in her eyes. "What will be, will be," she whispered. "We can only try to heal him, bring him back to the living."

She turned to Ethan then and buried her face against his chest, her arms reaching to enclose him in her embrace. They stood together, there in the parlor, and he felt the deep, tearing sobs she could not conceal from him. He only held her close, his arms supporting her, his head lowered to press his lips against the crown of her head, his own mind traveling at tremendous speed as he thought of what this stranger might bring into their lives.

CHAPTER NINE

IN THREE DAYS' TIME, Debra knew that the man would live, pronounced him in a whisper to be on the road to health and then shook her head in a way that revealed her turmoil. That she had healed a man who might be set on taking Ethan from her was a possibility she could not ignore. She bent over him on the sofa, her awareness of the stranger's identity firm. Some inner knowledge told her that he was a man set on bringing Ethan back to the place he had fled.

She knelt by the sofa, wiping the strong face before her, waiting for a sign that he had regained consciousness, secure in the knowledge that he would live. His eyelids fluttered and opened and she met his gaze without hesitation. Blue eyes held hers, a harsh voice spoke in slurred tones, and she did not flinch from him as his hand lifted to touch her shoulder, his fingers tightening on her flesh.

"You're the woman he married, aren't you?" the stranger asked.

Debra only nodded and then asked the questions

she had held within for three days. "What is your full name? Should I fear you?"

He attempted a smile, and succeeded only in twisting his mouth into an expression that hovered on the edge of pain. "I think you hold the upper hand, Mrs. Tyler. If it weren't for you and your doctoring skills, I would be lying out there in the tall grass, my body moldering in the heat of the day." As if it caused pain to speak, he inhaled deeply, wincing at the effort.

"Your name?" She would not be put off by his words of praise.

"Jay Sinclair. You don't know me, Mrs. Tyler."

"I know more than you realize," she said tightly, her voice on the very verge of trembling.

"How can that be?" His voice was softer, his speech slurring a bit, as if he were weary, perhaps on the verge of losing his strength. And then his eyes focused more directly on her face and his expression changed, holding a knowledge she recognized.

"You have the sight, haven't you? I've heard of native women who were able to discern things without explanation." He lay back, relaxing again, his eyes still capturing her with his knowing gaze. "You knew I was coming for him, didn't you?"

"Not that. Only that there was something to fear, that some event would change our lives."

"Yet you healed me, anyway? You knew I was a danger to him, and still you gave me the benefit of your skills?"

"I could do no less," she murmured, tearing her gaze from his, looking beyond him, as if she saw a future that threatened her.

"You could have left me to die. A woman without mercy would have ignored my plight, a man without honor might have left me to fight my own demons."

"You have said it, the truth of the matter. Ethan Tyler is an honorable man." She spoke the words as an accolade, telling him of Ethan's character in those few words. "You will do him the favor of listening to him before you plan his punishment."

"I don't have the ability to plan his future," Jay told her. "I can only return him to those who are seeking him."

"And if you find he is not what you've been led to believe? What then?"

"I took a commission, I have a duty to complete it." His jaw firmed as he spoke and she thought he was a warrior in his own estimation. He would fight for what he believed to be the right.

And then he softened. Before her eyes, he changed, his brow furrowing, his eyes resting on her with a look of compassion. "Before I take him away, I will listen to him, and my senses will discern if he speaks the truth."

"Are you a man of my blood?" she asked, her curiosity aroused by his words.

"No, I have no blood of your people in me, only the parentage of good, honest people who sought to do right by all those they came in contact with. My sister and her husband, the man who has been my brother, almost my father, for all of my growing-up years, taught me to listen well before I act, to know whether or not I'm in the right, not to set myself up as judge over any man."

She bowed her head, as a sign of honor for the words he spoke. "I can ask no more of you, Jay Sinclair. You will know the truth when you hear it, and you will know my husband for a man of courage and honor."

"Will you tell him who I am?" His eyes were pinning her where she knelt beside him. "Do you think he is aware that I'm the man sent to find him?"

"Ethan Tyler is a man of many skills. He has the ability to look within another and see that which is good. Perhaps he will find you as such." She could not know how Ethan would react to the knowledge that Jay had been sent to find him. The fear of his anger was ever present, for he had been unjustly accused and the thought of facing a judge who would be prejudiced against him would not ride him well.

From the back of the house, she heard the kitchen door open, heard the heavy footsteps of her husband and shot a look of warning at the man on the sofa.

"I will speak with him." Rising, she went to where Ethan was, envisioning him as he carried the milk pail and the pan of eggs from the shed, completing his chores for the morning.

Debra seemed to be disturbed, he thought, her eyes dark with a worry he recognized. "Is our guest all right? Are there problems?"

She shook her head. "He's better today, and the problems are none that cannot be solved." She went to him and lifted her face for his kiss. "I missed you this morning, Ethan. You got out the door before I arose."

"I heard something out back. Our guest's horse showed up and I cleaned and fed him. You were sleeping soundly, love. I let you stay warm in the covers, even though I was tempted to stay with you for a while longer." His voice lowered a bit as he leaned closer to her. "I'm not fond of having a guest in the house. It cramps my style, I fear. Your fingers covered my lips more than once last night, and I had to hush you with my mouth when you found your pleasure."

He loved the blush that crept over her cheeks. That she could still be embarrassed by his words after the months of their marriage was a joy to him. Debra was still an innocent, still a woman without the full knowledge of her own worth. She was generous in her loving, fully devoted to his pleasure, and yet there were avenues they had not explored, places he had not taken her. Lest she recoil from his touch, lest she feel less than the joy he wanted her to know in their bed, he was slow in bringing her to a place in which she might surrender herself to him in every way.

The time would come. He was a patient man, and she was a willing woman. There were places to visit during their hours together that would bring great pleasure to them both, and he had not chosen yet to introduce her to some of the skills he owned. With what he had of her, with the joys he'd found in her tender body, he was more than satisfied. The future held great promise, and he cherished the woman he held in his arms.

"Ethan." He knew she had something to tell him, some news to relate that held her apart in some way. And so he nodded and muttered an indistinct sound, urging her to speak.

"I know who the man is. He told me his name. Jay Sinclair."

"He's a bounty hunter." The knowledge had been his almost from the first, from the moment he'd seen him unconscious in the field. He'd felt the menace that exuded from the still, silent figure before him. And yet, he'd been compelled to give him aid, to help him in his struggle to live. And if Debra had not possessed the healing arts of her people, the man might have died.

"You knew already?" Debra sounded surprised, as though she had only just found that knowledge as a certainty for herself but moments ago. "He told me he was sent to find you, Ethan. I told him he must listen to you, and not judge you without cause."

"Ah, sweetheart. We hold the upper hand here,

you know. He is unknown to the townsfolk, although he must have found us by asking questions somewhere. But no one else knows he is here, and his life is in our hands for now."

"You won't harm him, anymore than I would," she said firmly. "We both respect life too much to take another's breath from his body without due cause."

"And you don't believe that his taking me away from here to face a judge isn't due cause?"

"No. For you are a man innocent of that which hangs over your head. Your crime was in loving your wife and son more than your good sense. You acted out of a wounded and broken heart, and no man who has known the love of a family can condemn you for what you did."

His smile was tender as he dropped a kiss on her nose and squeezed her tight. "But that you were to be my judge, Debra Nightsong. I would have no fear of the future if you were to pass judgment on me. But as it is, I'll eventually have to face a man of the law, a man who will only look at facts, not the reasons behind my act."

"I won't let him take you away from me," she whispered, holding him tightly against the peril to come.

"Some things cannot be changed. We have a set path to walk and nothing can deter us from it." He levered her away from himself and turned her toward the parlor door. "Let's go in and talk to Jay Sinclair and see how reasonable a man he is."

He waited for them, his head on a pillow, his blue eyes sharp with knowledge and his hands empty of weapons as they neared the sofa. "Will I leave here alive?" he asked, and Ethan could only admire his bravery in the face of impossible odds.

"I am not a killer," he told Jay. "Nor is my wife. We would not have brought you into our home otherwise. Your horse is being fed and cared for in our barn. Debra has fought to keep you alive and I have supported her."

Jay's eyes were warm as they focused on the man before him. "I know all of that. She brings to mind my sister somehow, although there is no physical resemblance. Rachel is tiny, with hair like many shades, like honey and sunshine combined. But they are both women of strength."

"You speak with the tongue of a man who has known love in his life," Debra said. "You talk of a sister who is much loved."

"She saved my life. Myself and my brother were the most important things to her for some time. Our parents died and we were left alone with a sister older, but not much larger than we were. She protected us and cared for us."

"And what of the husband you spoke of?" Debra obviously knew more about this man than he'd known, Ethan thought.

"His name is Cord McPherson and he has a ranch in Kansas, a place where I grew into a man. He is my brother, not of blood, but of love."

"Strange words for a man to speak," Debra said thoughtfully. "Is he a good man to your sister?"

"He's filled with love for all who live in his shadow," Jay said. "And if I sound sentimental, so be it. He gave us a home and raised us to be men of worth. My brother and I owe him much."

"And why did you leave there? Was there a misunderstanding?"

"No, it was time for me to choose my own way. I went east and found a man who had been working as a bounty hunter for years, a man who I could admire. There's money to be found in chasing down those who have escaped the law."

"How much am I worth?" Ethan asked, his mouth sober as he asked the query that haunted him.

"More than you can imagine. The man who was killed had brothers who are determined to see you hang, Tyler."

"And you're determined to take me back to Ohio to them."

Jay nodded. "Your wife tells me that you are a man who has been misjudged. Will you tell me about it?"

Ethan pulled a wooden chair closer and sat near the sofa. "Debra," he said quietly, "will you get me some coffee? And perhaps something for Mr. Sinclair."

"A piece of bread, if you don't mind," Jay said, as if he were feeling hunger spasms, something that had not occurred in the last days.

"Yes, of course." Without argument, as if she knew that the two men needed this time alone, she left the room, and Ethan heard her footsteps against the wooden floor, knew the moment she put the coffeepot on the hottest spot on the range to heat the coffee. She went into the pantry, then back to the sink, where she washed quickly, and he turned to the man on the sofa lest she return too swiftly.

"I'll tell you what happened, Sinclair. No frills, only the bare facts. You can make your own judgment."

The next few minutes were spent with Ethan recounting details of his years with his wife, the birth of his son, the devastation he knew upon returning to his home to find their bodies, already rigid in death.

"He killed them, after he'd attacked my wife and taken her with no care for her pain. She bled, not only from the bullet wounds in her head, but from her body, where he'd harmed her beyond reason. My son was killed, a two-year-old boy, with his future ahead of him. He was too young to be a witness, and his death was without reason."

"You found the man?"

"I found him. He lived but a mile away, a man without morals or good character. He couldn't run fast enough or hide from me with success. I found him and he bragged about killing them, holding a gun on me as he told of their begging, of my son's crying at his mother's distress. I ignored his gun, tackled him before he could fire a shot, and I killed him."

Ethan's head bent and hot tears fell as he recalled the day of his revenge. There was no shame in the grief he showed to this stranger, for the shame belonged to the man whose filth had touched his family and left its mark on all of them.

"I don't expect you to believe me," Ethan said slowly. "I know you have heard another story or you wouldn't be here now."

As he spoke, Debra came into the room, a tray in her hand, two coffee cups on it, and a plate holding several slices of buttered bread. She looked from one to the other of the men and her eyes held sadness such as Ethan had never seen.

"Here you go, love," she said, handing him the coffee he'd requested. She placed the tray on a table by the sofa and took the plate to Jay, placing it beside him.

His mouth formed the words of thanks, and he struggled to sit up, the better to eat the food she'd prepared. "Is that other cup for me?" he asked after taking several bites of her bread, chewing, then swallowing them with obvious enjoyment.

She took it to him, careful not to spill the hot liquid on him. "I did not put cream or sugar in it," she said.

"I take it black. Thank you." He lifted it to his mouth and sipped carefully, acknowledging its temperature. "Umm…good coffee, Mrs. Tyler."

"I think you will be able to join us at the table for dinner today. I'm going to make soup. It will help you to heal."

"Thank you, again." His eyes met hers and Ethan knew a moment of doubt as he saw the empathy between the two. There seemed to be a bond there that he had not felt before.

Jay looked at him then. "Your wife is a staunch champion, Tyler. She is determined that you are a man misjudged."

"And how do you feel about that?" Ethan watched him, saw the beginning of trust in the stance, the attitude of the man before him. Yet he waited for an answer, held his breath as Jay Sinclair seemed to sort through his thoughts.

"I suspect you've convinced me of the truth of your story. I feel good vibrations coming from you, Tyler. I think your wife has you pegged right, you're an honorable man. I'll have to think about this."

Ethan bowed his head, his mind offering thanks for the open mind of the man who had heard his plea. Sinclair was at his mercy, but the man apparently knew no fear, obviously recognized that he was safe here, that his life was not in peril.

"We'll still have to go back, you know," Jay said quietly. "You need to face the judge and perhaps find those who will testify for you. Do you have friends back east?"

"Oh, yes." There were those who knew him well, who might be easily persuaded to speak in his behalf. "I can't leave Debra alone here," he said, looking up to catch her gaze.

Peel off seal and place inside...

LIFT
HERE

An Important Message from the Editors

Dear Reader,

Because you've chosen to read one of our fine novels, we'd like to say **"thank you!"** And, as a **special** way to thank you, we're offering to send you **two more** of the books you love so well plus **2 exciting Mystery Gifts** – absolutely FREE!

Please enjoy them with our compliments...

Pam Powers

EC3-RS-07

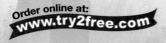

The Reader Service – Here's How it Works:

Accepting your 2 free books and 2 free gifts places you under no obligation to buy anything. You may keep the books and gifts and return the shipping statement marked "cancel". If you do not cancel, about a month later we'll send you 3 additional books and bill you just $5.49 each in the U.S. or $5.99 each in Canada, plus 25¢ shipping & handling per book and applicable taxes if any.* That's the complete price and – compared to cover prices starting from $6.99 each in the U.S. and $8.50 each in Canada – it's quite a bargain! You may cancel at any time, but if you choose to continue, every month we'll send you 3 more books, which you may either purchase at the discount price or return to us and cancel your subscription.

*Terms and prices subject to change without notice. Sales tax applicable in N.Y. Canadian residents will be charged applicable provincial taxes and GST. All orders subject to approval. Books received may vary. Credit or debit balances in a customer's account(s) may be offset by any other outstanding balance owed by or to the customer. Please allow 4 to 6 weeks for delivery.

"I was alone before you arrived. I'll be safe for a while without you. I have the dog now, and I haven't forgotten how to shoot my gun."

"We'll speak of it another day. I'm not in any shape to travel now and I won't be for a week or so."

"At least a week or so," Debra told him firmly. "You've come very near to dying, Mr. Sinclair."

THE WEEK PASSED QUICKLY, with Ethan finding much to do before he could leave Debra on her own. He spoke of her neighbor, and she was not pleased to have him beg the man's protection over her while he was gone.

"I'm able to be alone, Ethan. I told you, I can care for things myself."

"The hay must be cut, and we need to get more oats from the livery stable. I can't leave you with things undone."

"All right. We'll take care of those things first. I'm anxious to have you gone, so that you will be back sooner. I don't want to face the winter alone, and the sooner you leave, the quicker you will return."

"If I do return." For the first time, he spoke the fear that had ridden him since the knowledge of Jay Sinclair's identity had been spoken aloud.

"You will return to me, Ethan Tyler." Fierce and angry, her words were a threat, one he cherished, for only death would keep him from her.

THE DAYS OF Jay Sinclair's recovery were slower
than they'd anticipated, and Ethan went to the hay
field with Debra to use her scythe on the hay that
stood tall, ready for harvest. He swung the tool with
vigor, his muscles strong from the work he'd done
in the past months. Where they would put the hay he
cut, he didn't know, for the hayloft was heavy already with the first cutting months ago. But Debra
had said they must cut it and rake it to dry in the sun,
and he would not dispute her knowledge of such
matters.

She raked it beneath the hot summer sun, leaving
it in rows that she turned daily, until the hay was dry
enough to harvest. And slowly the nights gave way
to the first chill of autumn and they slept with a quilt
over them, the window open to the darkness, their
bodies together beneath the coverings, sharing their
warmth. Debra's neighbor, Sam Shane, came to
check the readiness of the hay field, and Ethan told
him of his decision, that the hay was worth more than
a side of beef.

Without argument, Sam agreed, for as Debra said,
he was a fair man, and recognized Ethan's words as
truth. They settled on a price, the neighbor brought
his crew of men to cut the rest of the crop and Debra
and Ethan took their share into the barn. They loaded
as much as they could into the loft, the rest they
piled in two empty stalls. The need for a larger barn
was upon them, and Ethan chafed at the thought of

leaving the farm with so much undone, but knew he had no choice.

He could either leave Debra for a matter of weeks, or take another life. It would not be a difficult thing for no one else was aware of the presence of Jay Sinclair in their house. But he could not live with himself, thinking of the man's death as if it were already a fact, and he dismissed the idea, knowing it was not worthy of him or of Debra.

And so he did what he could to ready her place for the autumn months to come, aware that she would be working harder than ever, with the extra mares to feed and clean up after, with five stalls to shovel out every day. The thought of her wheeling the manure into the corral made him flinch, for although she was strong, she seemed of late to be not herself.

Whether she was ailing or not, she kept up her usual pace, but he saw glimpses of weariness in her eyes by late afternoon, knew that her steps slowed as she went about her work, and his heart was grieved that he must leave her alone to face the hardships of working alone at a task that had kept both of them busy.

He traveled to town and brought back lumber, Jay lending him a hand to unload it in front of the barn, covering it with a tarp against the rain that threatened. If time would permit, he would work at a small chicken house, ridding the shed of the presence of the feisty hens and their leader, a broody hen who was determined to sit on a clutch of eggs.

Debra said it was late in the year for such a thing, but the hen was persistent, and eventually, Debra gave way to her single-mindedness and allowed her to settle her feathers over a clutch of eight eggs. The hen clucked contentedly on her treasure as Ethan gathered eggs from the other nests, and he cast the self-satisfied creature a look of scorn.

"If I had my way, you'd be in a stew pot," he muttered. "Debra doesn't need the tending of a clutch of new chicks to keep her busy. She has enough to do already."

And yet, he knew that she looked forward to the event, to the day the eggs would begin to crack, and the young chicks would make an appearance. She made a bed behind the stove, in case the weather was too cold for them to remain in the shed, and the dog was put into the bedroom at night on a permanent basis.

That part of her planning met with Ethan's approval, for he felt safer with Sport near the bed at night, knew that the lanky, protective dog would be ever vigilant when he was gone. At least Debra would have warning if a stranger should approach the house, and with her shotgun handy, she would be able to protect herself. Fear of strangers had never loomed large on her horizon, for she had been taught as a young girl how to shoot, how to aim for vulnerable parts on a man, and her mother had given her firm instructions that, if she were threatened, she must shoot to maim or kill.

The doors had good locks on them, and the front door had a bar across it, never removed for they did not use that exit from the house, coming and going by the kitchen door. Windows were another matter, for someone could slash the screens, break the window and crawl into the house. When they touched her bedroom door, they would face an angry dog, set to attack, and a woman well armed.

He'd made as many precautions as possible for her safety, but yet, Ethan dreaded the day he would leave. Only the knowledge that his past would forever haunt them did he not return to face the court persuaded him to go. That and the presence of the bounty hunter, the man who owed them his life, and who would, Debra was certain, do his best to protect Ethan from wrongdoers.

And so they left, mounted on two of her mares, using Jay's gelding as a pack animal, Ethan's old horse not considered suitable for the trek. They would lodge the animals in a livery stable when they reached the city of Chicago and go by train from there to Ohio. She worried that her mares might not be fed properly, knowing that they would drop their foals early in the year and she might not have them back in her possession by then.

How long the trip would take was a moot question, Jay said, but he promised Debra that he would be speedy, that he would be sure Ethan was not mistreated. With that she had to be content.

She watched them ride down the lane, waving until they had disappeared down the road toward town, tears running freely as she considered the next weeks and perhaps months without Ethan beside her.

She had not told him of the child she carried, knowing he would not leave her alone if he had that knowledge imparted to him. She bore the burden of her pregnancy alone, although Jay seemed to have some idea of her problem, his brow lifting as he looked askance at her one morning while Ethan was tending to the animals.

She had come from the bedroom and then excused herself abruptly, running back to lean over her slop jar, her stomach almost empty, but bile running from her mouth. She'd heard of the morning times being difficult for women when they carried a child, and now she was a prime example of the problem.

Keeping her condition from Ethan had not been easy, for she knew he would rejoice in the news, but his leaving would be an issue with him, and she would not put him in the position of leaving her alone, knowing that she would likely bear a child in the spring.

And so she held her secret close, only telling Jay that he must not let Ethan know she had not felt well on that day. He'd promised and she trusted his word, knowing he liked his prisoner more than a bounty hunter had a right to. It was a strange situation they were caught up in, with Ethan depending on Jay for his very life, knowing that he was wanted, that the law would be after him, given the opportunity.

And so she depended on Jay to protect her love, keeping him safe and helping him to return to her.

Yet she mourned his leaving, and for three days, she only did the necessary chores, working sluggishly at the churning, the egg gathering and such. Only showing a spark of interest as the broody hen showed signs of chicks beneath her one frosty morning in October. Bits and pieces of eggshell scattered on the edges of her nest alerted Debra to the fact and she lifted the hen carefully, lulling her with soft words and gentle movements.

Seven chicks huddled in the depths of the nest, the eighth egg apparently not fertile and she tossed it into the field, for it should have been hatched by now. The rooster had gone to sleep on the job, she decided, not tending his harem as he should. She carried the chicks to the house in the depths of her apron, holding them close, lest they fall to the ground. They were warm in the box she'd prepared behind the stove and she watched them, enjoying their antics as they explored the four corners of their new home.

Exhausted by their travels from the shed to the house and lulled by the heat of the woodstove, they slept, a small golden huddle in the center of the box.

The broody hen was unhappy with her loss, but Debra knew that a few visits from the resident rooster would solve her problem and she would be allowed to nest again.

From the back of the house, she heard a horse whinny and ran with fright to the window, fearful that one of her mares had somehow gotten out of the shed through the front door and was loose. The sight of her neighbor astride his plow horse was welcome and she opened the door.

"Good morning, Mr. Shane," she called out. "What can I do for you?"

"My wife sent me," he answered. "Our cat had kittens awhile back and they're big enough to be out on their own. Anna thought you might like one, maybe raise it to be a barn cat."

Debra stepped out onto the porch, her eyes eager as they scanned his bulky form for the promised kitten. And was delighted when he held up two, one in each hand, for her approval.

"Which one would you like?" His grin recognized her pleasure in the gift and she was stunned by the choice. That she'd be given a kitten was a joy in itself, but that she would be allowed to choose between two of them was an added delight.

"I don't know. They're both so cute." One was spotted, black and white, with a black speck on its nose, the other a calico, marked with gray, orange and black on a white coat. Both were tiny, claws outstretched as the man handed them down to her. She cuddled them against her bosom, looking down into the blue eyes that met her own with fearless bravado.

"There's nothing so cute as a kitten, is there?" she asked Mr. Shane, and was met with a laugh of pure enjoyment.

"Well, when you have a tabby that deposits a litter faithfully, twice a year in your barn, they get a little wearisome," he told her.

"Is there any chance I could have them both?" Debra asked hopefully. "I'd love to have the pair of them. I'll take good care of them. Tell your wife my Jersey gives more milk than I know what to do with, and they'll be well fed."

"I doubt she was worried about their well-being when she sent them here. And she had a suspicion you'd want them both. You're welcome to them, missy. The calico is a female, of course, and I haven't checked out the spotted one. If it's a male, you'll have a population problem of your own in another year." He laughed heartily at his own joke and Debra joined him as the kittens decided to climb the front of her dress.

"I'll be ever so thankful for them," she said sincerely. "Tell your wife to stop by sometime when she has a chance. She can see how well they're doing here."

Samuel Shane lifted a hand in farewell and turned

his horse away from the porch, riding back down the lane to a break in the trees that lined either side of the road he traveled. He headed off, cross-country to where his farm lay, just beyond the wooded area that marked the boundary of Debra's land.

She carried her treasure into the kitchen and in the depths of the pantry, found a box for them to sleep in. An old towel provided a warm bed and they curled up together, their eyes closing almost immediately.

The room was becoming crowded with her assortment of animals, and she sat beside the kittens' box watching them, even as she heard the soft chirping of the baby chicks who had wakened behind the stove.

For the first time since Ethan's departure, she felt her heart lift with a semblance of happiness.

CHAPTER TEN

THE WEATHER TURNED cold suddenly, as though the winds came out of the icy legends of the north country. As a child, she'd been told of the gigantic piles of ice that sent their fingers of cold south to bring misery on her people yearly. She'd hated the long months of winter, dreaded the short days and long nights, when staying warm had become the uppermost thought on all their minds.

Here on the farm, she had the stove to give warmth. In a tent made of deerskin, she'd huddled with her mother over a fire that never seemed to produce enough heat to keep the chill from their bones.

There was much to be thankful for, Debra decided, even though the source of her joy was miles away and she had not heard any news from that front. She planned a trip to town as soon as the cold spell eased, hoping to find a letter at the post office that would give her news of his journey.

In the meantime, she trudged back and forth to the shed, caring for her animals, gathering the eggs she would take to town with her, milking the cow and throwing much of the skim to the earth, since she could not use it all. The cream was churned into butter and even now many pounds of it awaited her trip to town. She wrapped each loaf of butter in a length of cheesecloth, as her mother had taught her, and stored it in the fruit cellar, keeping it cold.

That night she dreamed again of Ethan. His appearance in her sleep was not uncommon, but when he sat beside her bed and spoke of his love for her, she felt she could almost feel his weight on the mattress, hear his words as if they were alive in the room, and her heart was comforted by his presence. His parting kiss was warm and sweet and she awoke with a smile, her body alert and awake to his.

She thought of it often, this latest dream that had seemed so real, and in her inmost heart, knew it to be but a manifestation of their love. And was comforted by the knowledge.

The mares were growing larger by the day, her own golden mare seeming to be adding weight by leaps and bounds. It would not be long until her time was near, and Debra watched her closely, knowing her foal would be large, judging from the size of her. The mares taken by the two men on their trip east would no doubt drop their foals before they returned, and whether or not they could make the journey, returning to the Dakota Territory with the animals in tow was not a question she could answer.

The first snow fell in November, but it was a storm that left the ground blanketed by several inches of the white stuff, and Debra gamely shoveled a path to the shed, then carried in wood for the stove, noting that she was past the halfway mark already in the store Ethan had prepared for her use. Unless there was a break in the weather, she would have enough wood until the first of January, and no longer.

Her own condition would make it impossible for her to chop more, for her balance was becoming a problem. She felt constantly pulled forward by the weight of the child that grew within her, and her clothing was becoming tighter by the day.

She had begun to wear Ethan's trousers for comfort's sake, and frequently donned his flannel shirts to stay warm. The faint aroma of his scent in the fabric soothed her fears and brought back memories of his presence that comforted her. By wrapping herself in his clothing, she felt a kinship with him, no matter that hundreds of miles separated them.

One morning in December, the sun seemed especially bright, glittering off the piles of snow she'd tossed to either side of the path to the shed, and she made a decision to set off for town, lest her store of eggs and butter be spoiled and no good for trade.

The mares they used for pulling the wagon stood easily in the harness and she loaded her goods into the back, then dressed in her warmest clothing before she climbed to the high seat and took up the reins. The wagon moved slowly, for the snow had not been breached in the lane, and the wagon was heavy for the horses to pull through the several inches of the white stuff that lay in their path.

It took longer than she had planned, the road only becoming traveled halfway to town, with the tracks of others who had made this trek in the past day or so. By the time she arrived at the general store, she was exhausted, for the mental strain of driving her team past the perils of the road had worn her out. More than one set of wheels had furrowed the snow and the results of carelessness had overturned at least one wagon as it traveled down the town road.

Debra tied her horses to the hitching rail in front of the store and carried in the first of her baskets. Mr. Anderson took pity on her weariness as she shoved the door open and approached the counter with a full load of eggs, and bade her stay indoors while he made his way to the wagon to carry in the butter.

Julia came from the back room to greet her. "How are you?" Julia asked, greeting her with a hug. "I've been worried about you. We saw Ethan and his friend ride through town and he stopped to let me know he had urgent business in the east and you were alone out there. If the weather hadn't turned cold so early this year, I'd have ridden out to see you, but I kept hoping you'd make a trip into town."

"I've been busy with the animals, and staying warm. The weather is the worst for this time of year that I can remember," Debra said, cuddling in the depths of her coat as she fought the chills that possessed her.

"Have you been ill?" Julia frowned at her distress and pulled her hat and scarf from her, unbuttoning her coat, so that the heat of the store might warm her.

"No, just weary." And wasn't that a lie, Debra thought, for her misery had more to do with the absence of Ethan than the bad weather or her aches and pains.

"You look as if you've gained…" Julia's words trailed off as she cast a measuring eye over Debra's body. And then her eyes brightened as another thought seemed to occur to her.

"Are you in the family way?" she whispered. "Does Ethan know? Will he be back in time for the birth?"

"Yes, I'm going to have Ethan's child and no, he doesn't know about it. I couldn't let him travel with that worry nagging at him. As to when he will return, I don't know. His business back east was necessary, and I don't know how long it will take."

"You poor child." Julia's consoling words brought a wide grin to Debra's mouth and made her laugh for the first time in weeks. She was far from being a child, and she felt no need of sympathy for her plight, for carrying Ethan's child was the pinnacle of her life to this point.

"I'm doing well," she assured Julia. "I feel tired sometimes, but the baby is growing and seems to be flourishing. At least he's going to be a big one, if my calculations are right. I think he'll be born early in the spring. That will give me time to help when my mares foal after the first of the year, and hopefully I'll have another clutch of chicks running around by then."

"You're raising chicks, too?" Julia asked. "Won't they freeze?"

"I kept them in the house for a couple of weeks after Ethan left, and then put them back with the hens. The second batch is doing well. I only lost one, and he was sickly from the first. My father would have killed him early on, but I didn't have the heart to do so."

"You have to be harsh sometimes in this world to be kind," Julia said firmly. "I've heard my daddy say that more than once."

"Well, I'm doing just fine out there. If we don't get any huge storms, I'll winter over without any problems. Ethan left me with a woodshed full of chopped logs and I've enough to last me for another month or so, I think. Then I may have to ask my neighbor's boy to chop wood for me."

"I'll ride out to see you when I have a day off work here," Julia told her. "I can bring back your eggs and butter for you, and if you'll tell me what you might need from the store over the next little while, I'll bring it with me."

"You're a good friend, Julia. I would look forward to that. I'll make a list and leave it with you."

"Let's go sit by to the stove and talk awhile," Julia suggested, leading Debra to a pair of rocking chairs that were pulled near the heat.

They spoke of Christmas, a time which Debra had not ever been much aware of. Julia told her of the church services that would be open to everyone, the celebration of the Christian holiday, and Debra felt an urge to see for the first time the pageantry of the season.

Ethan had spoken but little of his mother's faith, but she knew he prayed to the God of his heritage, and she admired him for the beliefs he held dear. Perhaps she could manage to make the trip to town for this event, and even stay overnight at the hotel. Maybe make a holiday of it, a celebration of her own. If she milked the cow before she left home late in the afternoon and planned to return by noon the next day, it might not be too long for the Jersey to wait for attention. She vowed silently to consider the idea.

The door of the store opened, the bell announcing a patron, and Julia rose quickly, then settled back down as the postmaster entered and looked about with curious eyes.

"I thought I saw you come past the post office, ma'am," he said, directing his words at Debra. "You have a letter from Chicago. Thought it might be important, so I brought it over."

Debra rose with haste and approached the man. "I thank you so much," she said, reaching for the envelope that bore her name. *Debra Nightsong Tyler.* The words were written clearly above the address. *General Delivery, Holly Hill, Dakota Territory.*

She had never seen Ethan's handwriting, except on a grocery list or two, but she would have recognized it anywhere. It was strong, as he was, definite loops defining his strokes, and pride written in the letters that formed her name. *Debra Nightsong Tyler.* She held the envelope to her breast and then lifted it to her lips, uncaring of the scrutiny dealt her by the man in front of her.

"I'm glad to see you looking pleased, ma'am," the postmaster said. "I figured it was important, so I hurried over with it."

Debra inclined her head with regard for the man's good intentions. "I thank you again, sir." His actions spoke of respect directed toward her and her appreciation was real. Not often was she accorded any measure of esteem from members of the white race, and when the occasion occurred, she was willing to be beholden for the act.

Sitting again by the stove with Julia, she held the envelope, blessed with the knowledge that Ethan's hands had held it thus, that his eyes had rested on the letters that spelled out her name, that he had sent it with his own name written boldly, giving her the respect of calling her his wife in such a manner.

It was obviously known in town that she was married to him, but receiving mail with her name designated as Tyler gave her a sense of pride she had not felt until now. He had claimed her in this way, and she was pleased that he had done so.

"Aren't you going to open it?" Julia asked, leaning forward, obviously torn by curiosity as to the letter's contents.

"Yes, I will," Debra answered, reveling in this proof of Ethan's concern for her. She slid one finger beneath the flap of the envelope and opened it carefully, not wanting to tear it in any way that might damage the contents.

A single folded sheet of paper was within and she drew it forth and opened it with care. She had learned as a child to read and write the white man's language and so it was a simple matter to read Ethan's words to her.

My love, he began, and her heart lurched within her at the reminder of who she was. *His love, his wife, the woman he had married.* He wrote that the journey had been without undue hardship, that the mares were stabled in Chicago and that they would be given the proper care while he and Jay went on to the city where their business would take place. He would write to her again as soon as possible, and when things had been settled, he would return to her.

She read that much of it aloud to Julia, recognizing that Ethan wrote of nothing that would reveal his reason for going east, knowing that she would understand that of which he wrote, but leaving nothing for anyone else to speculate about.

And then her voice faded as her eyes took in the rest of his message.

I dreamed of you again last night, so real it seemed you were in my arms, and your lips were on mine. I sat by you and spoke with you. It has been one of many dreams, and they have served to give me strength for this journey.

Her breath caught in her throat as she read and she was lost for long moments in the knowledge that they had somehow communicated though miles of space separated them.

She was torn from her thoughts then. "How long do you think he'll be gone?" Julia asked. "Where is he now?"

"He wrote this two weeks ago," Debra said. "It must have gotten lost somewhere after he sent it out. He's probably already taken care of his business by now." She folded the letter and placed it inside the front of her shirt, beneath her chemise, next to her skin. It was a warm entity there, and she thought perhaps his love soaked through the written lines, directly into her heart.

"I'm hoping he'll be back for the delivery of the foals here. Maybe they can bring my mares back on the train. They won't be in any shape to be ridden unless they've already delivered by then. And that's the only way the foals can travel, for I'd think the long walk home would be too much for them to bear."

"I hate to think of you alone out there on the farm, Debra." Julia bit at her lip as she spoke her words, and Debra sent her a reassuring glance.

"I'll be fine, once the weather breaks. We usually have a warm spell in January, and maybe the mares will deliver then and I won't have to spend time out in the cold with them. Of course, I'll have to feed and water them afterward, but they can stay in the shed awhile. Perhaps I'll ask my neighbor to help me with shoveling out the stalls, once my strength is taken up with carrying my child. He has a boy, George, half-grown already, who might be persuaded to come a lend a hand."

"Why don't you stop by there on your way home today?" Julia asked. "I'd think he would be happy to help you out. Isn't he the one who shares your hay crop with you?"

Debra nodded. "Yes, he's been most kind since Ethan came to be with me. He hired him on and sold him a horse as part of his wage. Ethan seemed to think he was a good man."

The sun had shone for a good part of the day, but now it hid behind lowering clouds and Debra roused herself from the lethargy produced by the warm fire, and stood from her chair, searching out the coat she had removed earlier. "I need to be on my way," she said. "If you'll load up my supplies, I'll take them out to the wagon and head for home."

"My father will carry them out for you. I'll go in the back and find a couple of boxes to put things in and ask him for his help."

Debra thanked her and followed her to the counter, where Julia sorted through small items and found all the necessary bits and pieces Debra had included on the lined paper she'd brought with her. Cheese, a bag of salt, pork sausage and pickles from the barrel, for she'd developed a taste for the salty things. A piece of oilcloth to replace the one currently on the kitchen table, heavy stockings for herself, and of course, a sack of coffee. An assortment of canned goods were taken from the shelves, the current supply somewhat limited because of the weather and the off-and-on schedule of the trains from the east.

Within a half hour, they had packed up her things, Mr. Anderson had carried them out to the wagon, and Julia had said her goodbyes in a teary voice. She hugged Debra close and spoke of the next visit she would make.

"Don't let it be so long 'til next time," she begged. "I worry about you out there all alone."

"I'm not alone. I have a half-grown pup and two kittens to keep me company. And if I don't get home in a hurry, they will have left puddles on the floor and perhaps even worse tokens of their bad temper, after being cooped up all day in the house."

Julia laughed as Debra had meant for her to, and the small talk about her animals eased her path to the door and onto the wagon. With a wave of her hand, Debra turned her team to the road heading west and left the outskirts of town within a few minutes.

She knew her horses would relish the feed awaiting them in the shed and felt a pang of guilt that she had sat by the fire for so long, leaving the faithful animals to bear the cold while they waited for her return. Yet, she could not regret one moment of her time with Julia, or the thrill of the letter she'd placed beneath her clothing, next to her heart. She would sleep easier tonight, knowing that Ethan thought of her, and had sent his love to her via the written word. Knowing that somehow, through the unseen boundaries of the human heart and mind, they had somehow communicated.

That part of the letter she had not read aloud, for it was meant for her eyes only, and not to be shared with another. He'd written words of soft assurance, citing the joy she gave him, the memory of her presence keeping him warm at night. It was a love letter, a phrase she'd heard spoken, but never thought to know of, firsthand.

Now she possessed such a thing, a treasure she would cherish, and reread over and over during the dark nights to come when Ethan was so far away.

Perhaps she might dream again, and share that dream with the man she had married. Her mother had said that such a thing was possible, and Debra prayed fervently that it would come to pass again in the nights she spent alone.

She made a stop at the farm where the Shane family lived, and spoke to Anna, who came out to the porch to greet her. With the assurance of the boy's, George's, help in the next day or so, Debra turned her team and left for home. Anna had asked her to alight and have coffee first, but the night was falling quickly, the darkness promising to be full before Debra arrived home and she was anxious to have her team under the shelter of the shed roof and herself in the house, where hopefully the fire would still be smouldering.

She put the horses in their stalls, gave all the animals lush amounts of hay and feed, then approached her cow for milking. The animal greeted her with a soft lowing sound, and munched contentedly at her fresh hay while Debra took her milk from her. The bucket was heavy and she walked with care toward the house, knowing that a slip on the icy pathway could be a tragedy. She couldn't afford any broken bones or even an assortment of bruises, for being alone was enough danger in itself without an injury to lay her up.

She'd forgotten to feed the chickens, and she deposited her first load from the wagon on the table, then accompanied by the dog and two cats, she went out again into the yard, heading for the chickens, stopping in to break the ice on their water before she gave them their feed.

The eggs would wait until morning, she decided, and would be welcome for her breakfast, since she'd taken every blessed egg she had to town. She couldn't complain, for her credit at the store still held good and she could buy many more boxes of supplies with the money due her there.

The kitchen was dark as she entered, but in a moment, she had lit the lantern, hung it high over the table and added wood to the stove, catching the heat against her body as it flared to life and the flames provided heat for the room.

She might just sleep out here tonight, she thought, for her bedroom was cold, the stove not being replenished all day. For now, she must find food for her supper, and with the supplies she'd brought home with her and the fresh bread she'd baked only yesterday, she had her repast already in mind.

Slices of cheese, a bit of pork sausage fried up in her skillet and bread toasted in the oven made up her meal and she sat down with her back to the stove while she ate. The letter inside her chemise rustled at her every movement, and she took it out to place it on the table before her. Halfway through her meal, she opened it again, and the words met her eyes, familiar now, the soft sentiments Ethan had put to paper warming her more than did the stove behind her.

She cleaned up her plate and the cup she'd used for coffee heated from the morning, and pushed the table to one side of the room, against the back door. Dragging quilts and her pillow from the bed, she made a pallet on the kitchen floor and removed her boots before she lay down for the night. The dog curled up against her feet and she praised him with words that delighted him, enjoying his heat and the comforting weight of his body.

The kittens found beds upon her person, the calico lying at the top of her head, warming her scalp and purring noisily. The small black-and-white male lay against her breast as she curled on her side, his tongue reaching to touch her fingers as she petted him and whispered her pleasure in him and his littermate. She was certain he was a male, having done a thorough investigation of his private parts, and recognizing that they were different than those of the calico.

The thought that they might present her with a litter of kittens next year was a pleasurable one, and with the image of four or five tiny kittens curled in her lap, she went to sleep, for the first time since Ethan had left knowing true contentment as she awaited his return.

Again she dreamed, this time aware that Ethan came in the door and lay beside her on the quilt, his arm over her, holding her close. His whispers were like magic to her ear, words of love and assurances that he would return to her. Again, his kisses were warm on her flesh, his hands possessive of her body and she savored the blessing she had been granted of his presence with her in this way. It seemed to remain a part of her throughout the next day as she fed her animals and cleaned the house. As though he had truly visited her in the night, the memory of his kisses stayed with her and sent a semblance of peace to her lonely heart.

THE NEXT DAYS were but a reminder that winter was harsh in this part of the country, for the snow fell in amounts measured better by feet than inches. She struggled daily to find her way to the shed, the shovel barely able to deal with the piles of snow that blocked her way. She found Ethan's old boots and stuffed them with socks, wearing them as protection against the snow and cold.

George arrived, and cheerfully began the chore of cleaning the stalls. Debra had done what she could on a daily basis, but her strength was not sufficient to complete the job, and it took almost a full day for George to empty all the soiled straw and replace it with clean. The pile in the corral was huge by the time he finished, and Debra fixed him a meal of hot soup and corn bread before he left for home.

He was a tall boy, rangy and rawboned, but a likeable lad, much like his father, she found. They spoke of the coming year, of the foals she would have in her pasture, and he told her of his father's own stock, of the cows who would drop calves in the spring. He offered to bring her a piece of pork, perhaps a roast or two to vary her menu, for she was limited by the meat supply in the smokehouse.

In return, she sent him home with a batch of cinnamon rolls and fresh bread for his mother, that lady having spent her time of late in bed with a bad cold. A Mason jar full of the soup they ate for supper was wrapped and sent along, in case his mother might enjoy the sturdy broth and find it to be soothing to a stomach torn by coughing and a body weary from the results of her illness.

With a promise to return in two days' time, George left before dark and headed for home, a trip that might take fifteen minutes on horseback in the summer, but now, in the dead of winter, with snow swirling about his pathway, would no doubt take a full hour of his time.

It had been a good day, Debra decided, spent with a young man who was both friendly and knowledgeable about the subject of farming and the care of animals. She yearned for the evenings spent with Ethan, remembering the times they had shared, sitting together in the quiet of the night, no words being spoken, only the silence of companionship surrounding them. After the conversation she'd enjoyed with George, she felt more alone than ever tonight, she decided, and her heart yearned for the husband whose presence she craved.

She lay on the floor again, having decided that

sleeping alone was not preferable to sharing her blankets with two cats and a dog, and was comforted by their bodies pressed close to her. It was after she had stretched and yawned and almost sunk into the depths of sleep that she felt a small movement within her and wakened fully, as she awaited a repetition of the sensation.

It came again, as if somewhere deep inside her belly, a small hand or foot, or perhaps a tiny mite of a body turned against her and provided her with the knowledge that she was not truly alone. She'd felt some small reminders of life within her before, but now the movement seemed to have a purpose, as if her child turned over or pushed with minute power against the confines of its temporary home.

"Did you feel it, Ethan? Can you know, wherever you are right now, that our child moves within me?" She spoke aloud and sensed the presence of his love within her, wishing that she had told him of the baby he had placed within her womb, a child of their love. And yet, though he would no doubt still be here with her, the need for his freedom of blame from the charges against him in Ohio was of vital importance, and she could not rue his absence from her. For his spirit seemed near and she cherished the sense of communion she held to her heart.

She felt tears of joy touch her cheeks as she dwelt on the kinship of the child she carried and the man she loved. This child might be a small replica of

Ethan perhaps, or maybe a girl child who would have dark hair and eyes like her own.

She was past the middle of her pregnancy, by the calculations she had worked with, the memory of the times of her monthly issue blurred by the passing of time. Even knowing of the baby before Ethan left, she had not shown signs of the growth of a child until the past weeks. Now her waist had thickened and the rounding of her belly was obvious to anyone with eyes to see.

She felt as if she'd been chosen for this marvelous task, that of bringing Ethan's child into the world, and rejoiced that she would have this news for him upon his return. Her hope that Jay would not give away her secret still reigned, for she trusted the man to keep his word. Why she felt so strongly about Jay Sinclair was a puzzle to her, for she had no other proof of his honesty than the man himself. And yet she recognized with a deeply felt knowledge that he was a good man, that the brother and sister he spoke of were people of great worth, and he was to be trusted.

His memories of home and his growing-up years had been shared with her gladly and she hoped he would do Ethan the honor of giving to him his childhood as he remembered it. She wished she might meet his brother, Henry; his sister, Rachel; and the man she had married, Cord McPherson—people who seemed to be of fine quality. But most of all, she hoped for the influence of Jay in the hearing before a judge, and prayed that his words would be taken into account, as he helped Ethan prove his innocence of guile and murder. For killing a man who had attacked his family surely could not be considered murder, but a form of justice, whether delivered by the victim's family or the court, itself.

The days passed slowly, George coming on a regular basis to help with the chores she could no longer work at with any semblance of efficiency. Twice, Julia came out from town, driving her father's sleigh, wrapped warmly in robes and a heavy coat, delighted with the friendship they shared.

She brought another letter, and Debra rejoiced in the words Ethan wrote, words of his love, small snippets of his time with Jay, the news that things had gone well in the court hearing. It seemed that he had friends who had been more than willing to speak in his defense, and she offered them her thanks, unbidden, knowing they would never hear the words from her mouth, and yet hoping they might somehow have recognized that Ethan's wife was deeply thankful for their loyalty to the man.

And then he wrote words that filled her heart with joy.

I dreamed of you again last night. You slept on the kitchen floor and I was there with you. My arms held you and my lips touched yours. Have

you had a child visiting there in the farm-
house? You spoke to me as if there were one
there in my dream with us. I know it was only
in my mind, but it was as real to me as the
paper in my hand right now, as real as the love
I feel for you, even though we are miles apart.

She smiled and wiped her tears, her hands trembling at the reading of his words.

Accompanying the letter were the supplies Debra had indicated would be needed, and Julia was faithful in her friendship, carrying Debra's eggs and butter back to town and crediting the proper amount to Debra's page in her father's black book. Her visits were welcome, and Debra cooked meals she knew would appeal to the other woman, sending home bread and rolls and coffee cake on occasion to be shared with Julia's family.

The horses in the barn grew round and heavy with their foals, and Debra watched them closely for signs of impending birth, knowing that sometimes the babies were born before their time, and would need special care. She took extra quilts to the shed, carried an extra lantern out there for heat and light when the time should come and in all ways prepared as best she could for the occasion of birth.

She mourned daily the time she might have spent with Ethan, sharing the wonder of her pregnancy with him, dealing with the frustration of an empty house and empty arms, yet, aware that his trip was one of necessity, should they have any sort of future together.

CHAPTER ELEVEN

IT WAS THE SECOND WEEK of February when Debra went to milk the cow and found her mare in labor. The horse whinnied when she came in the door, welcomed her into her stall, pushing her nose against her breast asking for attention in the only way she knew to do. Debra soothed her as best she could and finished her chores, taking the milk back to the house.

She poured coffee into a jar and took it with her, buttered bread and wrapped it in a towel, included a generous slice of cheese, enough to sustain her until the next day. Should the mare not deliver by morning, she would have to go to her neighbor and ask for help. But the mare seemed to know what she was doing, and by the middle of the night, it seemed birth was imminent.

Debra sat on the clean straw she'd forked into the box stall and spoke softly to the animal she dealt with. The animal's long neck was the recipient of comfort from Debra's stroking fingers, the forehead received the scratching of her nails and she praised the mare profusely as she labored to bring forth the foal she had carried for almost eleven months.

Dawn brought with it the arrival of a tiny colt, dark with the moisture from his mother's body, spindle-legged as he attempted to stand and equipped with a voracious hunger he slaked with the milk from her bag.

Debra watched in wonder as the mare tended her foal, wept as she shared the joy of motherhood with the dumb animal and admired the product of the long hours of labor. The lantern had warmed the shed, and the colt's coat dried to a pale hue, fulfilling Debra's hopes for its light color. Daylight brought bright sunshine with it, perhaps a cessation of the snow that had plagued them for months, and she was pleased. She could only hope that the weather would break, for they had not had the long-awaited January thaw, which was expected weeks ago.

Another one of the mares looked to be considering her upcoming motherhood in a serious manner. Debra planned to move her own mare to another place in the shed to allow the next candidate for motherhood the large stall in which to deliver her foal.

George arrived before noon and helped her tear down a partition between two stalls, making a larger place for the mare to inhabit with her colt, and the knowledge that she had done what she could to prepare for the event was comforting to her. George shoveled out the stalls, replaced the straw with clean bedding and filled the mangers to overflowing with hay from the loft.

He stayed for supper and Debra fried a chicken, one of her young roosters seeming to be a good choice for the skillet. She killed it, dressed it out and washed it thoroughly before she took it in the house to cook. A pan of stuffing in the oven used up her old bread from the last baking, and she peeled potatoes that were only slightly wrinkled from the fruit cellar. A quart of green beans completed the meal and George declared that her fried chicken was a match for that of his mother.

Debra preened with the praise he offered, and sent him home, laden with fresh bread and cinnamon buns for their breakfast in the morning. She sent a note to his mother offering to help in any way she could, with the family's mending or perhaps sewing new curtains for the springtime to come, when many of the wives sewed curtains and made rugs for their floors to welcome the warm weather.

She'd asked Julia to bring her a dozen yards of percale in a yellow-and-white check to make curtains for her own kitchen, and sat in the evenings with her hand sewing. She found herself speaking aloud to the babe within her body as she told him of his father. She made much of the love she had given with a glad heart to the man who had shared with her the creation of this tiny creature she awaited.

She wanted her child to know, even now, before it

took its first breath, that it was conceived in love, that its parents would ever tend to its growth and development as did the birds in their nests and the animals of the fields and forests. She thought of names they might give their child, yearning all the while for the man who had given her this gift, this babe she carried.

The second mare gave birth one night a week or so after her mare's colt was born, and again, Debra spent the night in the barn, staying in the stall with the new mother, helping as best she could in the delivery. She might as well have stayed in the house, she decided afterward, for the mother seemed to know exactly what to do, and when the tiny filly was born and the afterbirth right behind it, the mare took over the task of caring for her infant as if she were an old hand at the job.

One mare stood in the last stall, still round with a foal showing no signs of imminent birth, and Debra fretted that there might be a problem with either mare or foal. She checked daily for progress, and yet the mare only languished in her stall, seeming to be growing by leaps and bounds, yet showing no signs of delivering her burden.

Debra asked George if he would speak to his father about the delay, and the boy brought back news that his father said to be patient, that the mare would foal when she was good and ready, and no amount of fretting and stewing would help.

And perhaps the man was right, Debra thought,

resolving to put the matter to the back of her mind until some signs should appear. She tended the two foals already born, even let them out into the corral one day when the sun was bright and the weather unusually warm. Their mothers looked after them, followed them closely and seemed relieved when she put them back in their stalls.

It seemed that the mares had all chosen to deliver their burdens during the long hours of the night, for when Debra went to the shed one night almost a week later, near the end of February, she found the last mare down in the stall, laboring heavily. With rapid movements, she milked her cow and set the milk aside, knowing it would no doubt be poured out on the snow in the morning in order to fill the pail anew at daybreak.

Then she went to the stall where the mare labored, great groans emerging from the animal's throat, her head thrashing back and forth as she sought to deliver the foal she carried. Debra's knowledge of such things was limited, but she went to the mare's side and investigated the progress as well as she could. She found a single hoof emerging and knew that the problem was beyond her ability to salvage, unless she were to do as common sense dictated. She had heard of such complicated deliveries and knew of the danger inherent in these things.

Yet she felt she must do what she could for the mare, else she would lose her to the pains of labor, for the death of the foal would surely also mean the death of the mare. She remembered her father assisting at the delivery of a calf that had not been born in the usual manner, coming bottom first. He had lain on the ground by the cow, his arm inside her body, trying vainly to turn the calf in order to give it safe passage through the mother's birth canal.

It had not worked, for both cow and calf died that day, and her father had rued the fact that he did not have the knowledge necessary for the task he'd undertaken.

So now, faced with a similar circumstance, she prepared herself for helping the mare in her struggles. Vaguely, she recalled her father greasing his arm to more easily enter the animal's body, and she hastened to the house, bringing back a bucket of lard with her.

She liberally covered her hand and arm with the greasy stuff, then forced her way into the opening where the tiny hoof could be seen protruding. She pushed the hoof before her hand, her entire arm almost enclosed in the creature's body before she came to the pouch that held the tiny foal. Pushing the sharp hoof inside the bag, she reached past the softer parts of the fragile animal until she found the second foot. With a sigh of relief and the knowledge of pain the whole length of her arm brought, she possessed the small, sharply formed part in her hand, then drew the twin legs out of the mare's body.

She felt the urge to cry as the foal was delivered

after long minutes of the horse heaving and twisting frantically in the stall. So great was her joy at the task she'd taken on and completed, she lifted her face and spoke words she'd almost forgotten, a prayer from her days in the village with her mother.

Then, in a movement she had not foreseen, as she released the foal's feet and tried to lift herself from the floor, the mare rolled toward her. She found herself pinned against the side of the stall, her body almost crushed by the heavy weight of the animal she had worked so hard to save, and she cried out in pain, then stifled the sound lest she frighten the mare with her distress.

The foal rose to his feet, trembling on spindly legs and nosing his mother's form. With a tremendous effort, the mare rose from the floor of the stall, and Debra was released from the weight of the animal's body. She rolled to the doorway and pulled herself up on the gate that swung in the opening.

"SOMETHING IS WRONG with Debra." Ethan halted his mount in the middle of the street, in the small Ohio town, his heart beating double time, his mind filled with a dreadful knowledge that frightened him.

"How do you know?" Jay spoke quietly from his saddle just feet away, his eyes ever alert to the nuances of Ethan's words.

"She was in my mind, she cried out in pain. Something is wrong, Jay. And I'm not there to care for her."

Jay's mouth hardened and he frowned. "Surely there will be someone nearby during the day. She won't be alone for long. Your neighbor may ride by, or a friend from town."

Ethan's eyes closed and from somewhere deep within himself, he caught sight of the storekeeper's daughter, Julia, lowering herself from a wagon, walking toward the barn and speaking aloud just inside the door. His sigh was deep and filled with thanksgiving, for the disquiet in his heart stilled as he realized that Debra was no longer alone. In some unknown way, he had been given a glimpse across space, to where his wife was even now being cared for, and he was comforted by the knowledge that she had again somehow reached out to him. That her vision, that gift from her heritage, had once more come into play. For there was no other way in which he could know the things that dwelt in his heart.

DEBRA HURT FROM HEAD TO TOE, aware that she had hit her head on the side of the stall, and more aware that her body was going to be bruised from the fall she had taken and the weight of the animal who had rolled against her in the midst of her own pain and anguish.

It was still early in the day, not near noon as far as she could figure, and the cow was sadly lowing her song of distress at not being milked, when Debra stood finally at the opening of the stall and watched as the small colt nursed at his mother's bag, his head tilted at an awkward angle, his mouth suckling the live-giving flow.

A sound from the yard alerted her to someone's arrival and she lifted thankful eyes to the shed door that opened a few minutes later. Julia stepped inside, squinting in the dim light, and called her name.

"Debra. Where are you? Are you all right?" She was frightened, as if she were shaken by the discovery of an empty house, and her words trembled as she called out her greeting.

"I'm here, Julia," she answered, amazed at how feeble her own voice sounded. She was bone weary, and hurting in every joint she owned. Fear for the child she carried was uppermost in her mind, for if she were to deliver now, the baby would be too small for survival, and she had only the promise of this child to keep her sane until Ethan should return to her.

The next half hour was a maze of fear and pain, as Julia helped her into the house and put her to bed. She brought hot water from the stove and washed her, cleaning the lard from her arm and hand, brushing the straw from her hair, putting her into the voluminous nightgown she had worn during the winter months. And indeed she needed its warmth, for she trembled in the aftermath of her accidental injury.

Julia made tea and fixed a scrambled egg for Debra, once she had raided the chickens' nests, and then vowed to go for help.

"I'm not having labor pains," Debra said anxiously. "It won't do any good for the doctor to come out here."

But Julia would not be deterred, and by noon, she was on her way back to town to find the local doctor, determined that he should come to Debra's farm and check out her physical condition.

The good doctor did as he was asked. In fact, as he said to Debra, Julia had demanded that he make haste and call at the farm. Julia accompanied him and introduced him to the woman who awaited his care.

"This is Doc Harrison," she told Debra. "He delivered me twenty years ago and my mother said he did a good job." She laughed as if she would relieve Debra's anxiety, and it seemed to work, for the doctor proved to be a kindly man, with hands that offered comfort.

He examined her minutely, and Debra was stunned by the procedure, such a thing unknown to her. His declaration that she was safe and sound, that her experience had not seemed to harm the baby she carried, came as almost a miracle to her and she rejoiced in the news. Julia was as happy to hear the declaration as she, and together they shared a cup of tea, once the kindly doctor had left to return to town.

He'd told Debra to stay close to her bed for a week or so, to keep things quiet, and not encourage any sudden onset of labor. She agreed to do as he asked, all the time knowing that she must do her chores and tend her animals whether she was pregnant or not. But Julia told her she would come back in a day or so and make sure she was all right. Debra told her that George would no doubt be by to help with the chores within a few hours, if Julia would but stop by the neighboring farm and let them know of the events of the day.

So it was that Julia smiled and agreed to all her friend asked of her, her heart obviously lightened by the knowledge that, in spite of her aches and pains, Debra was alive and as well as could be expected. Julia left before dark, a pot of tea steeping on the kitchen table, and let the dog and cats out for a run before she closed them in the house for the night.

Debra dreamed again of Ethan that night, his words a blur in her memory, but his presence was clear and vital in her heart. He'd held her in his arms and whispered his love for her in her ear, and then, as the rooster crowed his salute to the sunrise, Ethan's presence left her and she was alone in the big bed, still warmed from his kisses and caresses.

Telling another of her dreams was not to be considered, for they were private and deeply cherished moments to be held close to her heart. Someone else might think she hallucinated or perhaps imagined in some way the events that had come to pass, but Debra knew with a deep sense of the unknown that such things were possible, that her own mother had had knowledge of things to be, or images of the past in her mind. The gift she held fast was to be kept inviolate, a private thing, a blessing to cherish.

Julia's arrival the next morning was not a surprise to Debra, for she'd known how concerned her friend was with her condition, and though she had only promised to come back in a day or so, her return so quickly was but a proof of their friendship. In the kitchen, Debra made a pot of coffee and wondered just how long she dared wait to milk the cow, hoping against hope that George would arrive in time to take on the task. Whether or not her neighbors knew of her plight was a mystery, but perhaps Julia could solve that query, she thought, watching as her friend approached the back porch, and then came into the house.

"What are you doing out of bed?" she asked sharply, and then smiled. "You seem to be feeling all right, don't you?"

"I'm a bit creaky in my joints," Debra admitted, unwilling to tell anyone how badly her back ached and how stiff her muscles had been upon arising. Breakfast, followed by a nap, was a mighty appealing idea to her as she lifted her skillet and put it on the front of the stove.

"If you'd share some eggs with me, I'll fix them," she offered, nodding at the pantry where Debra had put the results of yesterday's laying.

Julia shook her head. "I'll get the eggs and fry them up or else scramble them, whichever you like, but you're going to sit down and put your feet up while I do it. Then, after we eat, I'll gather the eggs and even try my hand at milking the cow, if you think she'll cooperate with me to that extent. I expected George to be here before now. I stopped last evening and let Mr. Shane know that you'd been hurt. He said he'd send his boy over to take care of things."

The news that relief was on its way was comforting, and seeking the nearest chair in which to deposit her feeble self seemed to be a fine idea to Debra. She sat as bid, watching as Julia took over the breakfast chores, cracked four eggs into a heavy bowl and whipped them to a froth with a fork. Obviously used to such preparations, she found the butter, put a scoop into the skillet and proceeded to cook the eggs.

"Do you want any meat with these?" she asked, and looked relieved when Debra shook her head.

"Just bread and butter, I think," was the reply, and Julia waved a hand in her direction as she would have arisen to get the bread from the cupboard.

Bringing it to the table, she asked where Debra kept her knife and then sliced off four heavy chunks. "Shall I put these in the oven to toast, or even warm up a little?" she asked, awaiting instructions.

Debra simply shrugged and sank wearily back into the chair. It seemed she would get toast for breakfast, for the oven door closed on the bread and Julia dished up the eggs onto two plates before she sought out the silverware, and found a jar of jam in the pantry. The butter plate sat on the table and Debra lifted the lid, awaiting the return of the bread, once it was toasted to Julia's specifications.

She hadn't long to wait, and indeed in a less time than she could have imagined, they were sitting together, the coffee poured; the toast buttered, covered with jam; and the eggs ready to eat.

She hadn't thought she was hungry, but the smell of the delicious food banished that thought and she ate everything on the plate before her. Julia watched her like a hawk might watch a hapless chicken, noting every bite she took and finally sitting back, sighing with relief as Julia ate her own food.

"I was worried about you," Julia said after a few moments. "Thought I'd better come out and be here in case you have a visitor."

"No one but the hope of George coming this morning," Debra said, wondering at her friend's concern.

"Well, there was a man in the store late yesterday afternoon, asking about you," Julia said. "My father didn't recognize him, but he said he looked to be a full-blooded member of the tribe north of here. Isn't that where your mother's people live?"

Dread struck Debra. Why would someone be looking for her? She didn't know anyone from the village, and surely they'd been happy to see the backside of her over three years ago when she'd left the village and began her life on the farm.

"What did your father tell him?"

"He said you had a farm outside of town, and you were married. The man didn't ask directions but nodded and left the store.

"I don't feel good about leaving you here alone today," Julia said. "But I need to be back at the store by noon. It's my day to work while my father helps my mother out at home." She rose and cleared the table, poured hot water from the reservoir into Debra's dishpan, added soap and then washed the few dishes they'd used.

"I'll be fine," Debra said, not worried overmuch, since the doors were solid and well locked and she had the shotgun always handy. "When George comes he can take care of the stock and let the horses out for an hour or so."

"And who will let them back into the barn afterward?" Julia asked, her hands on her hips as she defied Debra on the matter. "You shouldn't be going out there alone, and you know it."

"I'll go out with George and stay with him while he tends things and then come back in the house when he goes home."

Reluctantly, Julia agreed, but remembering her promise, went out to the shed to feed the chickens and gather the eggs. She came in a half hour later, laden with another panful of eggs but admitted defeat when it came to the cow.

"That cow wouldn't let me near her. She tried to kick me twice and I gave up. Now what shall we do?"

"George will be here soon and I'll let him milk her," Debra said readily. "You leave, so you won't be late. I don't want your father angry with you, or he might not allow you to come back."

"No chance of that happening," Julia said, obviously aware of her place in the general scheme of things at home. "I'll be out the day after tomorrow. If you need me before then, tell George to listen up for the sound of your gun and you can fire it off if you have a problem."

"Sounds like a good plan to me," Debra said, knowing that Julia needed to be on the road. She watched as her friend made ready to leave and waved a hand at her as she drove her buggy down the lane.

The bed beckoned her and she made her way to the bedroom, sitting thankfully on the edge of the mattress before she rolled to the center of the bed and pulled the quilt up over her shoulder.

"MISS DEBRA, I've milked the cow for you and put the horses out in the pasture. Miss Debra, can you hear me?"

Outside her bedroom window, she made out the voice of her neighbor and Debra rolled from the bed and opened the window. George stood there, a worried look on his face.

"What shall I do with the milk?" he asked. "I'll wait for a half hour or so before I let the horses back in the barn, if that's all right."

"I'll open the back door," she told him, "and you can bring the milk in for me. Put it in the pantry, please."

Thankful for the young man who seemed intent on his neighborliness, she pulled on her robe and went to the back door, opening the lock and swinging it wide.

The sun had come out in its full splendor and the snow looked to be melting at a fast pace, the yard looking muddy and not fit to traverse. George brought in the pail of milk and placed it in the pantry, and told Debra he would let the horses back in the barn and secure them before he left.

She thanked him profusely for his help and he gave her regards from his mother, telling of the pleasure they'd had eating the cinnamon rolls she'd sent home a few days before.

Neighbors were a fine thing to have, Debra decided, an hour later, when the boy had taken his leave and waved a friendly hand at her, while she watched from the window.

It was still an hour from noon, she thought, looking up at the bright sunlight, and she decided to take an hour's respite before she thought about churning butter. It was a task that must be done or she would lose her cream, and throwing away the topmost of the last two days' milking was not to be considered. Bad enough that she'd had to lose the whole bucketful the night the horse had mashed her against the stall.

She'd barely found herself a comfortable place on the mattress when she heard the sound of a rider approaching. Not that the horse whinnied or that its hooves threw stones in the yard, but the change in the silence alerted her. Rolling to her side, she looked out the window and saw a man, mounted on a dark pony with a blanket of white spots on its hind quarters. He rode without a saddle, just a rope in his hands as he guided the horse with the touch of his knees.

It was a familiar sight to her, having seen men of her mother's people ride in that way for the years that she lived in the village. Their methods had been instrumental in the training of her own mare, for she searched her memory for their skill when she caught up the mare and made of her first a pet, and then an able riding horse.

Now she watched as the man with skin darker than her own leapt from his horse and left the rope hanging to the ground. She knew the animal would not move until the rope was picked up and the man mounted his horse again.

He made his way to the porch and she heard a rap on her back door. A feeling of apprehension assailed her, yet she did not fear the visitor, but wondered at his purpose for being here. She pulled her robe on again and went into the kitchen, facing him as he stood outside the window closest to the door.

He looked at her without any trace of anger, nor did fear mark his features. He was tall, lean of build, indeed very close to the size of Ethan, she thought. His hair was long, held by a tie around his head, his eyes were dark—almost black, she thought—and his face was handsome. He was probably several years older than herself, his nose a sharp blade that gave him a harsh look. He was a stalwart brave, and she was surprised as she designated him as such.

But a brave he surely was, no doubt a member of her mother's people, and she would not turn him away or insult him with a show of force. Her shotgun and Ethan's rifle both sat in the corner, but she left them there and unlocked the door, aware that he had moved from the window and was now standing on the other side of her door.

She opened it, looked at him through the screen of the second door and spoke a greeting she'd thought long gone from her memory. It was in the native tongue, even though the thought in her mind was in English, the language of her father.

The man on the porch answered her greeting, and then added words of his own. "I am from your mother's village," he said, his words showing his presence in the white man's school, yet the hesitation in his speech gave proof that English was not his first language of choice.

"I thought as much," Debra said, opening the screen door to allow him entry. He accepted the offer and stepped across the threshold, keeping his distance from her, his quick gaze lighting on the guns in the corner.

"Do you feel the need of a weapon?" he asked, a smile touching his lips.

"No. Are you laughing at me, here alone?"

He shook his head. "No, for if you wanted to, you could have shot me and no one would have blamed you for killing a stray member of the tribe, an Indian who probably was set on causing you trouble or hurting you."

"And do you intend either? What do you want?" She knew she was abrupt, but the fear of a man in her house without Ethan's presence did not set well with her.

"Only to introduce myself to you. You are my half sister, Debra Nightsong. My mother was the woman who bore you when I was a boy of seven. She came back to the village with you, but my father's family would not let me approach her. They kept me with them when he died, and I never knew her as my mother. Not in my memory, at least, for it was during my earliest years when she left to live with your father, here on this place of his."

CHAPTER TWELVE

"YOU'RE MY BROTHER?" It seemed impossible, yet in his eyes Debra saw a glimpse of the woman who had loved her so well, for so long. His chin was rounded as hers had been, and he had about him a reminder of a young man, for he'd been almost of age then, years ago, when she'd first gone to the village with her mother.

"Will you sit in my house?" she asked, remembering some of the words that were used when a visitor arrived. "I have food if you are hungry, brother of mine."

"So easily you believe me, Debra Nightsong," he said with a laugh. "Are you so ready to take in a stranger?"

She shook her head. "You are not a stranger, for you are Gray Wolf, my brother."

"How did you know what our mother named me?" he asked, sitting in a chair and watching as she began to fix him some food. She found soup left from the day before and put it to heat on the stove, then turned to slice bread before she turned back to him.

"She told me of your name when I saw you. Just

once, before your people kept you from our sight. Before she died, she told me you were almost a man, that if I ever needed you I should find you and ask for your help."

"Was she so sure of me, so certain that our blood would run true, that I was man enough to come to you if I felt you were in need?"

Debra shot him a telling look and laughed aloud. "She was right, wasn't she? I think you'd have a hard time denying her trust in you. For whatever reason, you're here now, and if I have ever needed you in my life, it is at this moment. How did you find me?"

His lips narrowed as he chose the words he would say to her. "I saw you in my sleep, sister. You were injured, lying in a stall with a horse, and I awoke, knowing that you were in need of my help. I know of your father's holdings here for our mother made no secret of where she had lived with your father."

Debra lifted her brow, her heart beating heavily as she considered his words. "You have our mother's gift, then, Gray Wolf. She could see things that had happened or sometimes the future events that were to be."

"And you?" he asked, his dark eyes searching deeply into hers, as if he could recognize that part of her that was inherited from their mother, a heritage neither of them could deny.

"I see things sometimes," she admitted. "I don't know why it happens, but when it does, I am always thankful for the gift my mother gave me. Some say it isn't right, that we shouldn't be able to see what is yet to come, but my gift has only come into being when I saw a need before me, or when danger was lurking. I find no wrong in it, for I think it is from a higher being than either you or I, and I will not argue what I've been given." That she had felt Ethan's presence with her over the past weeks was a secret she would keep to herself, not to be shared with another, no matter that her brother would understand.

"The shaman disliked our mother," Gray Wolf said bitterly. "It was because of him that I was kept from her. He told my father's people that she was a witch, and I should not be exposed to her power."

Debra denied the words of the man considered as a leader among her mother's people. "She was no witch, only a woman who had the gift of healing and the ability to see into the heart of men and women. She knew you were a good boy and would grow to manhood with decency and pride, no matter your upbringing with those who held you from her. She was a woman to be honored."

His head bent as he thought on her words. "I'm pleased that she thought well of me, Debra. I honor her memory, for I can recall some small bits of my time with her. She held me close and sang to me and told me stories of brave men and of my father, who loved her as an honorable man loves his mate."

"She was fortunate, our mother." Debra thought for

a moment before she spoke, as if she would not damage the memory of one man in order to make another look more fit for the position in her mother's heart.

"My father was a good man, too. He took her from her people, but he married her in a white man's ceremony and lived here with her happily. I was born in the bedroom upstairs, and my mother told me later of the years we spent with the man who fathered me. He was a man of peace, a good man also, standing between my mother and the white man's world. He kept her safe, took good care of me and my mind holds only happy memories of him."

"We've been fortunate, sister. Our mother was able to instill in us the good that surrounded her, and leave us both with memories that will sustain us into the future."

Debra bowed her head as she allowed his words to sink into her being. Her brother was a wise man, a man who had a heart bent on helping her, and she could only be grateful for his presence here.

"How long will you stay with me?" she asked. "I have an extra bedroom for you."

He shook his head. "I will sleep in the building with the animals. I'd rather be in the woods, but the weather is cool enough yet that I find it easier on my bones to stay where it is warmer. The heat from horses will keep me comfortable during the night hours."

"I have blankets for you to use," she told him.

"There is much hay in the loft and the heat rises to that level."

They ate together, Gray Wolf giving her praise for the food she'd cooked, telling her of his hunger during the past days while he searched for her.

"I asked for directions in town, and the men looked at me scornfully, as thought my skin was not as fine as theirs, as if the blood flowing in my veins was impure. I spoke to an old man on a bench outside the store and he talked of a white man married to a native woman years ago, and of the farm they lived on, a farm that was in the family of the white man. He said the daughter of that union had returned and was there now. That she had found a husband who was not of her race, and yet was, for she was a blend of two people who differed in their beginnings."

"Did he point you in the right direction, then?" she asked, smiling at the words the old man had spoken.

Gray Wolf laughed. "He waved his hand down the road, and sent me on my way. I think he knew somehow who I was, for he seemed to feel that I was no threat to you. And he was right. I'm your blood brother, Debra, and I will never bring harm to you."

She felt tears well up in her eyes, yet did not give way to the weakness, for she would not shed salty drops when her heart was singing with joy for the gift she had been given. "I know that, Gray Wolf. I trust you as I trust the man I married. He will be your brother one day, also."

"Will he return soon? Have you heard where he is?"

"He sent met a letter, telling me that he'd left my mares in a city named Chicago, and he was going east from there to face a judge who has sought him out for a crime. A crime he is not guilty of."

"Yet he went there of his own will? To face a judge who could have put him to death? Or sent him to prison? How did this come to be?"

She began the tale of Ethan's first marriage, of the woman and son he'd loved so well, and told Gray Wolf of their deaths and the subsequent death of their killer. It was a story that made him frown and then a look of anger took him in its grip as she spoke of the man who had taunted Ethan with the death of his family.

"He had the right to kill the man," Gray Wolf said with pride. "He would have been less than a man had he not avenged the deaths of his family members."

"The white man's world is different than ours, my brother. They speak of things like trials and justice and judges who make decisions that are not always the right ones."

"They make things more difficult than they need to be," he said scathingly. "True justice is wrought when the right prevails and the cruel men of this world are sent to their maker without hesitation."

She sighed deeply. "I miss him terribly, Gray

Wolf. He's a good husband, and he has left me with a child in my belly."

Her brother smiled. "I noticed that right away. It is too late to try to hide it, my sister. You will bear a son before very long."

"Another two months or so. But my hope is that Ethan will return before then."

"And until he does, I will be here. I'll protect you and tend to your farm in whatever way you want me to. Nothing else is calling to me now. Only the need I felt for you in my dreams. I am here to answer that need, Debra Nightsong. My mother would have wanted it so, and I will do the work you aren't able to tend to, until your child is born or until your mate returns."

"I don't want to lose you from my life, Gray Wolf. Don't speak of leaving when you've only just arrived. Just stay with me, and when Ethan comes back, you can grow to know him as a brother. He is worthy of the name."

"Your love for him colors his memory in your mind, sister." He teased her and she responded quickly.

"He is all I've said, and more. His honor is without question, and he is strong and intelligent. A man to be proud of."

Gray Wolf ducked his head, hiding the smile he could not contain. "You are a proud woman, a staunch champion of your mate, and I admire you for that."

He finished up the soup she'd heated for him, ate

the bread and pushed back from the table. "What chores do you have for me to accomplish today? I must earn my food."

"Anything I have is yours. Everything here is available to you, for you are my brother." She bowed her head to him in a gesture of submission and he rose, coming around the table to where she sat.

"I am honored to be a part of your life for this time. I will go to your shed and see to the animals there, and take your horses out to the pasture to where the grass is beginning to show green sprouts above the earth."

"I need a new coop built for my chickens. Have you the skills for that sort of work?"

He nodded. "I earned money while I was in school, working to pay my way, building homes in a town north of the village. That was three years ago, but I haven't forgotten the skills I knew then. Putting up a coop for chickens is but a task of perhaps three or four days. Do you have wood to build it with?"

"Out in front of the shed is a load from the lumber mill in town. It was covered with a tarp against the weather when Ethan and Jay left. They'd brought it to work with but couldn't do so before they had to leave. If you want to do something with it I can help you."

"A woman does not work in that way when she is with child," Gray Wolf said firmly. "You can supervise me and tell me what to do. And trust me, sister of mine, that position is not one I have given to any woman before this day."

She couldn't help the smile that lit her face, for her brother looked chagrined at his admission. "I'll go in and clean up the kitchen and perhaps we can find time before nightfall to lay out the lines of the new building." Excitement sang in her as she thought of the next few days and what Gray Wolf's presence here would mean to her.

THE NEXT MORNING was sunny and the winds died down, so that the warmth lingered, offering a day that was pleasant and filled with promise. The early arrivals of the bird kingdom made their presence known, two robins worrying a worm between them in her garden area, mourning doves cooing in the trees near the smokehouse. It was a day meant for looking ahead, of happiness to be, and Debra took it as a gift, relishing each moment she spent in the sunshine.

Gray Wolf carried wood from in front of the shed to the place where they had marked out the size of the chicken coop she wanted. She had fourteen chickens now, too many for cooping them up in the shed with the other animals, and today they ran loose, ranging over the yard and beneath the trees in her orchard. She'd scattered their feed before the shed and they returned to it, pecking hurriedly at bits and pieces, before scattering out over the open area again, clucking and chortling quietly among themselves.

The horses were in the pasture, the new foals running together as if they played a game known only to themselves, their mothers watching from beneath the trees. Even the cow shared the pasture, for she stood with her head low to the ground, seeming to prefer the fresh grass to the hay she'd left behind in her manger.

It was a day in which to celebrate, Debra decided, to rejoice in the life that thrived in this place, both that of her brother and herself and the child who was to be. Beneath her dress, the baby kicked strongly, letting her know of his presence, for surely she carried a son, giving her a thrill she had found nowhere else in her world, for this was the supreme joy in life. That of being the vessel in which a new life was formed and allowed to begin its existence, sheltered by his mother's body.

She looked up to find Gray Wolf's eyes upon her, his smile a blessing she accepted gladly, knowing that he shared with her the joy of their meeting, here at this time and in this place. As though he'd been sent as a messenger, a living being to tell her that she was protected, that Ethan's fears for her were in vain. For who better could she have by her side than the brother she had craved so long to know?

He dug now, forming the lines for a foundation for her chicken coop. Deeper holes dotted the line he made, there where the four-foot-long posts would stand, upon which he would erect the new outbuilding. He worked quickly, with assurance, and she found herself thankful for the labor he had done to prepare himself for this.

"How long did you work at the building trade while you went to school?" she asked, wanting to know as much as she could of this brother so newly restored to her.

"For almost three years. There was a crew of men, formed mostly by the young men at school, all of us eager to get a weekly wage, in order to pay our way and get an education."

"How did you happen to go there?"

"I left of my own accord, when I'd learned all I could at the white man's school near the village. My people were not in favor of me leaving, said I would become as a man with a pale face if I left my own village to live with the white man."

"And did you?" she asked, thinking that he was as far from the men in Holly Hill as any she'd ever seen. He was tall and straight, an honorable brave of his people, and she admired his skills, given so gladly on her behalf.

"You see what I am, sister. I can be no other. I am a man of our people, and yet there is about me a bit of the men I worked with, the ones who paid my wage. They told me I was a good worker, that if I needed a job again, I could come to them and be taken on as a man in their employ."

"Is that a possibility?"

"Not while you need me here," he said with a

quick glance at her, his dark eyes making the words a vow she'd been given. "I'll stay until your man returns, and even longer if he needs me."

As he spoke, he finished with one of the holes he had dug, then carried a post to it, dropping it to its depths and measuring it with his gaze. "I'll need seven more like that to hold the building," he told her, and set about with the task he had set for himself. Digging and measuring, carrying the posts to where they would stand, and then when they were all in place and at the right height, he filled in the dirt around each.

"That's the way Ethan made the corral fence," she said. "You work in the same way he does."

"Ahh, he is a good worker, too, then," he said with a smile.

"Yes." She could say no more, for her memory had been prompted to return to that day last summer when he'd begun the task of fencing in her pasture. Recalling the joy of working with him, the pleasure she'd found in his company, she fought the tears that would have overflowed her eyes.

"Have you a memory that brings you pain?" Gray Wolf asked, his gaze upon her.

"No. Just the opposite," she told him, smiling as she attempted to assure him of her well-being. "I was remembering Ethan and the work he did for me. He is strong, Gray Wolf, a man you will admire."

"If he has made you happy, if his feelings for you are true, I will admire him. He has given you a child, and if he cannot return to you for some reason unknown to us, you will always have a part of him in your life."

"Yes." The impact of what he told her sank in as she stood watching him. That Ethan might not return had not even entered her mind, for she had faith in his mission, faith in the man who had gone with him to accomplish this thing, this ridding Ethan of blame.

The posts stood straight now, almost two feet above the ground, ready for him to continue the framing of the coop. He took longer pieces of wood, squared off lengths that would measure from one end of his building to the other, placed them atop the posts and nailed them into place. Upon that framework, he began to build upright, forming walls and leaving space for a door both front and back, and a runway for the chickens to leave and enter their new home.

"We'll put fencing out here and make a yard for them," he told her, pointing to the far side of the skeleton. "I'll be ready for it inside of two days. Will we be able to take the wagon to town and get some from the mill? Or the hardware store?"

"I have money for anything we need," she told him, recalling the cache Ethan had left for her beneath his small clothes in the dresser. "Ethan did not leave me without coin to purchase what I require."

"He took care of you? He provided for you?"

"Always. I have earned my supplies for years with

eggs and butter from my animals. And now my flock of chickens is twice the size and the eggs are in good supply. I'll have several broody hens setting on eggs in the spring, and my coop will be full."

"You will have chicken in your canning jars then," he said, his eyes showing his liking for that idea.

"We can have chicken in a pot for dinner if you like."

"You are a good cook? Our mother taught you well?"

"I learned much of what I know by myself, but I remember a lot of the things she cooked for my father when I was but very young. She showed me how to make biscuits when I was less than ten years old. And baking a batch was my chore in the mornings while she helped my father with chores. I could make corn bread, and most anything she cooked found its way into my memory. I liked working in the kitchen with her. My father said I would make some man a good woman someday, and my mother put her hand on my shoulder and told him not to be impatient. That I would be but a girl for a long time to come."

"And how old are you now?" he asked. "This will be my twenty-sixth summer, if my memory is right, but I'm not sure how many years of age I was when my mother left the village."

"I was born here, nineteen years ago," she told him. "I was twelve when my mother took me back to our people and sixteen when she died. It was a hard four years for me, for I didn't belong there, and they made sure I knew it. It hurt my mother that I was not accepted."

"Do they welcome you now in Holly Hill? Or just take your money and look at your back with hatred?"

"The people are not cruel to me, neither do they welcome me with open hands. The girl whose father owns the general store is a friend of mine, Julia Anderson by name. She comes to see me when she can, and always treats me as a sister."

"I would like to meet this woman," he said, stepping back to look closely at the work he had completed. One wall was over his head already, the other three standing over four feet from the ground.

"You've done this quickly," she said. "I didn't think it would come together so well. Perhaps we should go to town in the morning and get the fencing so it will be ready for you when you've completed the roof and are ready to begin the yard."

As she spoke, she caught sight of a lone rider coming across the meadow and she lifted her hand over her eyes, shading her vision to better see the visitor. "It's George, the boy from the next farm," she told Gray Wolf. "He comes to help me when he thinks I need a hand. His father is a good man, and the boy has taken on the ways of the man."

"What does he do for you?" Gray Wolf asked, standing erect as George rode closer.

"Whatever I need to have done. Milking, shoveling out the manure with the used straw and filling the stalls with fresh. He feeds or brings the horses in and out of the pasture."

"It's a good thing to have a neighbor to depend on," he said, obviously prepared to like the young man, who dismounted and walked to join them.

"George, this is my brother, Gray Wolf." She extended her brother the courtesy of being presented to the boy before them.

George offered his hand and Gray Wolf took it solemnly, shaking it as the boy obviously expected him to. "I'm pleased to meet you, sir," the youth said politely. "I stopped by to see if your sister needed anything. My pa told me I should make a point of checking on her every day or so."

"You are a good neighbor." With a nod of his head, Gray Wolf accepted the boy's words, and gave him his approval.

"Would you like to help me with my chore here for an hour or so? Or are your parents expecting you to return more quickly?"

"No. I can stay as long as you need me," George said, looking over the building project they had undertaken. "Will this be for the chickens?"

"You figured that out in a hurry," Debra told him. "Gray Wolf has worked with this sort of thing before, and he won't let me help. He thinks that a woman who is with child should not do physical labor such as this."

"My pa would agree with him. When my mother had my sisters and brothers, he made her stay close to the house and he wouldn't let her climb into the loft or handle the horses. She milked the cow, but that was because she'd always done it, and the cow likes her better than the rest of us."

"I milk, too, usually," Debra said, knowing that the boy knew well her schedule and the work she was capable of, so many times had he come to lend a hand. "I've been thankful for all the work you've done for me, George. Tell your mother that she has a son to be proud of."

"She'll be happy to hear you said that," the boy said, flushing a bit at the words of praise she offered him.

"I need to go in the house to begin supper," Debra told the two young men, and her brother waved a hand of dismissal as he turned back to his work, George beside him, apparently awaiting orders.

She left them, certain that they would work well together, happy that Gray Wolf had a companion to share the rest of the afternoon's work with.

She went into the kitchen and filled a pot with hot water from the reservoir, placing it on the stove to heat. Three chunks of wood from the wood box promised to build the fire to a greater heat and she waited for the water to boil as she prepared a chicken for supper.

While she waited, she went into the fruit cellar

and found potatoes and carrots for cooking. Her potato supply would hold out well, she thought, for she'd had Ethan carry several bushels to the cellar last fall, before he left. A sack of onions hung from the supports and she took several up with her when she climbed the stairs, her dress front filled with the results of her scavenging the cellar.

She watched the building progress as she peeled potatoes and prepared the meal. Washing the chicken and flouring the pieces before she heated lard in her skillet took but a few minutes, and soon she was listening to the sizzle of the meat in her pan.

The roof was being formed by the time the men came in to eat, and the long boards showed the shape of things to come.

"Do you have roofing material?" Gray Wolf asked as he sat down to eat.

"We'll have to get some in town," she told him. And then turned to George. "Do you think you could go in with us tomorrow and pick up supplies?" she asked. "Will your father be able to spare you for a few hours?"

"We've got most everything done for the week," George said. "I spent the whole day yesterday putting up new clotheslines for my mother, and we even carried out the rugs and threw them over the lines to air. I don't have a lot to do tomorrow. Once the chores are finished I should be free for anything you need."

Gray Wolf nodded his agreement with the plan and they ate in silence, both of the men hungry from the work they'd accomplished. The chicken disappeared quickly, the potatoes and gravy, the carrots and peas soon but a memory. Even the biscuits she'd put together just before they ate met a similar fate. Buttered and piled with strawberry jam, George declared them as good as dessert. And so they were.

He left when they'd finished eating, taking home the last loaf of her bread, and Debra faced baking a fresh batch in the morning. There would be time to set it to rise before they went to town, and if she hurried and churned butter now, she could take along a good basketful with her. Six nice-sized loaves of butter sat in the pantry from her last churning, and she had a good number of eggs to pack in the basket, too.

The dog sounded a last farewell bark as George rode off and Debra fixed a pan of leftover gravy, using bits of the chicken she'd put aside. The kittens were happy with fresh milk and chunks of bread soaked in it, and before long the three animals were nicely rounding out from their meal.

"I'm surprised you keep animals in the house," Gray Wolf said, watching as she played with the kittens on the floor. She sat before the stove and the two soft creatures climbed over her legs and into her lap, or the little bit of lap she still had. One of them climbed up over the rounding of her belly and sat atop the lump that moved beneath him.

He shifted, looked down at her skirt, a perplexed look on his tiny face. Debra laughed at the sight, and picked him up to hold him next to her face. "I enjoy them. They're good company for me."

"I thought you might have them in the barn."

"They'll be out there soon enough, when the weather warms up and the mice begin to run the aisle and the loft. They'll not need any food from the house then."

"Where does the dog go at night?" Gray Wolf asked. "I don't see him in the barn or out back anywhere."

"He sleeps in my room. If someone were to come close, he would rouse me and my gun is handy. I'm better equipped than you know to take care of myself, brother."

"Did your husband teach you to shoot?"

"No, my father did, when I was but a child. He said I would need to know how to load and unload a gun and how to hit what I aimed for. He was right."

"And have you used your gun often?"

"I ate a lot of rabbits the first summer I was here alone. They liked my garden and I kept them away with my shotgun. Once I'd killed a dozen or so, they began to stay away."

Gray Wolf laughed at her words. "You are an independent woman. I can see that. I'm surprised you let your Ethan stay here with you."

"I had no choice at first," she told him. "He

caught me unaware one night when I returned home from town, and he would not leave. We came to terms before long, and he's been here ever since."

"Tell me about it," Gray Wolf said, and she knew he would persist until she had made him aware of all that had gone on.

"All right, I will," she said, and settled down to speak of her relationship with Ethan, knowing that Gray Wolf would learn of his brother in this way.

CHAPTER THIRTEEN

THEY SET OFF FOR town early in the morning, as soon as breakfast was finished and the chores had been done. Debra was torn between wearing one of Ethan's shirts, which would hide her enlarging belly somewhat, and donning a dress that did nothing to conceal the baby she carried.

Deciding to let anyone who cared know about the child she would deliver in a few weeks, she wore her dress and carried herself proudly. Bearing Ethan's child was not a thing to be ashamed of, and if there were any sly glances turned their way as brother and sister entered the general store, she ignored them.

Julia greeted her profusely, was introduced to her brother and directed several long glances his way. Debra took another long look herself, seeing almost immediately what was so intriguing about him to Julia's eyes. He was a handsome man, unlike many others of the village; he had a straight nose, a firm chin and eyes that were set apart and held an intelligent expression. He was tall, another difference between him and others she'd seen when she lived with her mother among the people of the tribe. Many of the men had been short, heavy and without the handsome looks of Gray Wolf.

But then, her mother had been a beautiful woman, and Debra did not embellish that memory, but was as honest as she could be as she recalled her mother's fine features and slender body. Hair that hung past her hips when she let it down, and brown eyes that burned with love as she looked at her daughter and husband were memories that hung as clear as the sun in the sky in the gallery of Debra's mind.

Many things from the past were there, but the things she held dear all seemed to encompass her mother and the man who had fathered her and loved her so well. Now there was the brother she had been sent, and for whatever powers had put him in her life, she was thankful.

He stood before the counter, his expression solemn as she gave her list to Julia, and spoke of the things she would buy. Her butter was duly examined and found to be of the best quality, and Debra was pleased by the words Julia spoke.

"We'll have this sold by the end of the day," she said. "Your butter and eggs are always in demand, Debra. You keep your milk clean of insects and bits of hay and such. Some folks don't care what they have floating around in their cream, and as a result it gets churned up in the butter. And your eggs are always clean. Nothing worse than a dirty egg to turn a lady from town away from buying them."

"I always wipe my eggs with a damp cloth. There is no shame in bringing in dirt from the coop, but it is not to be heard of that it remain on the eggs until they are used. My mother always gave me the task of wiping them clean."

Julia laughed at her words. "I've learned so many little odds and ends from you, Debra. When you live in town, as we do, you don't know all the ins and outs of farming and the care of livestock and the food they provide. Your parents taught you well— it's no wonder you manage to make a success of your farm."

"But only with help," Debra told her. "My brother has done much to lend a hand now that I don't have Ethan there to do the heavy work. We've just completed a chicken coop, all but the fencing, and we'll pick that up today."

Julia bent closer and her words were low, a warning of what might occur. "The man who bought out the hardware store is not the same sort of gentleman you've been used to dealing with, Debra. He has a particular hatred for the natives, and often refuses to sell to them. Watch your step."

Well warned, Debra nodded and walked from Julia, giving her an opportunity to put together her order while she looked at the counters full of merchandise that was offered for sale. Gray Wolf stayed near the growing pile of stores they would take back to the farm, exchanging a few words with Julia.

Aware of Mr. Anderson's presence near the back room, Debra watched and listened as the older man kept a close eye on the native who spoke to his daughter. He was not known for his friendliness to those of mixed blood, and Debra feared for the insults he might toss in Gray Wolf's direction. Noting the proud stance of her brother, she knew he would not take to any sort of insult, and would not accept such as his due.

Julia was friendly, piling up the lard tin, cans of fruit and bags of flour and sugar, speaking briefly of the lack of salt and spices that sometimes were in short supply. Gray Wolf listened, nodded and gave his attention to her, but in no way asked for attention to be drawn to himself. In fact, were it not for her familiarity with him, Debra might have missed the interest he displayed in the young woman before him.

They loaded up their supplies in boxes provided by Mr. Anderson, and Gray Wolf carried them to the wagon and then helped Debra onto the high seat. She waved at Julia, who stood by the door watching them leave, and noted Gray Wolf's last glance in the direction of the slender figure behind the wavy glass of the door.

"She is a beautiful girl," Debra said as the wagon moved slowly down the street at her direction. The hardware store was a fairly new building, just beyond the bank and the sheriff's office. It sat apart from the rest of the stores, with a fenced-in area on one side and around the back to accommodate the outdoor materials for sale.

As Gray Wolf stopped the team in front of the hardware establishment, he turned to his sister. "The woman is not a girl, my sister. She is a woman, full grown and past the age of having a man of her own. Do the men in this town have poor eyesight, that they have not attempted to claim her in marriage?"

"She's been courted by several, but none of them have come up to her father's standards," Debra told him. "And none of them have really appealed to Julia, herself. She is looking for a man who will treat her well, one who will respect her."

"I shouldn't think that would be a difficult task, either for a man to comply with her needs or for her to find such a candidate. Surely a man would be foolish not to be kind to his woman. A woman thrives on such attention from a man, so far as I can tell. I have watched men of our people who were kind and those who were cruel or sometimes just thoughtless, and the men who treat their women well are always the happiest."

"My mother always said that it was the mark of a man that he did not use his strength against a woman, and that he care for her needs and tend to her as he would a flower growing, so that he might one day have full advantage of the scent of the blossoms she bore and the healthy fruit she produced."

"And did your father understand her needs?"

"He was her happiness," Debra said softly, "As Ethan is mine."

In mere moments she'd been lifted from the wagon and they had entered the hardware store, where the scent of paint and oil was strong. "Each store has its own aroma, have you noticed?" she asked Gray Wolf. "The emporium smells of spices and fabric and the wood-burning stove, and this place smells of the metal objects that men make use of." She looked around her at the gleaming walls.

"And of the fresh paint the new owner has just put on his walls." She looked at bins of nails and arrangements of hammers and small tools that hung from the walls, walking toward the counter at the back where a gentleman watched them, waiting for their approach.

She let Gray Wolf take the lead, as was his due in this thing, for though she might speak first in the emporium, where their purchases were mainly those that would be in her kitchen, this was a different thing altogether. Men respected other men who knew what was needed for outdoor projects and for the building of sheds and barns.

She was not without knowledge herself, for her father had taught her much of the use of hammer and saw, and she was able to pound nails with a credible skill and was capable of chopping wood with her hatchet. But, in this case, she knew little of fencing and the building of such an enclosure.

"I'm putting up a chicken yard," Gray Wolf said,

his tones assured and his words polite. "I'll need enough chicken wire to fence in the area. Perhaps forty-five feet in length."

The man behind the counter looked his fill at the tall man who had addressed him, and his lip curled a bit as he lifted an eyebrow and shrugged.

"I'm not usually in the habit of dealing with half-breeds and never with men such as you. You'll have to go somewhere else to get your fencing I think."

Debra stepped up behind Gray Wolf. "This is the only place in town that sells chicken wire. What seems to be the problem, sir?"

"I just told you. I don't deal with natives."

"You've sold supplies to my husband, and he's married to a woman of the people you disdain."

"You're married to a white man, lady, and this here fella is not your husband. I don't know about anyone else in town, but I'd think you're courtin' trouble hangin' around with this man. Your husband has gone off to who knows where and the next thing you're takin' up with another man."

"My dealings have nothing to do with you," she said boldly. "This man is building a chicken yard for me and we need wire for the fence."

"This man is living with you, Nightsong. I don't sell to such as him."

"You can sell it to me, then," she said stiffly, fear rising within her as she saw Gray Wolf's stern visage become even more angry.

"Go on over to the mill. See if Hogan over there will sell you fencing. He's got a supply on hand." With those words, the new owner of the hardware store turned his back and walked away, and Gray Wolf made a quick move in the man's direction. Debra laid her hand on her brother's arm, and got his attention, shaking her head quickly, knowing he was close to doing physical damage to the man.

He hesitated, looking down at her, his eyes dark with fury. Then, as if he bowed to her greater knowledge of the situation, he nodded and turned with her to leave the store.

The short walk to the wagon was made in silence, and then Debra spoke as he lifted her to the seat. "He's not worth arguing with, and it is his choice whether or not he sells to us. We'll speak to Mr. Hogan at the mill and see what he says."

"I don't have to like it," Gray Wolf said bitterly. "How do you stand the knowledge that you are looked down on by the people in this town?"

"Not all of them are like that man. Some are very kind, others are ignorant, and it is my choice whether or not I will allow them to make me angry. I choose to deal with those who are fair and sell at fair prices. The man at the mill is one of those. Wait and see."

Gray Wolf joined her on the seat and picked up the reins, setting the horse in motion as they rode the short distance to the mill where the noisy saw was even now cutting lengths of board from large logs.

They walked around the side of the big building where Mr. Hogan worked his saw, and stood watching as he completed his cut.

He turned to them and waved a hand at Debra. "What can I do for you?"

"We need wire for the chicken yard my brother is building for me," she said. "The new owner at the hardware store refused to sell to us, and we wondered if you have the materials we need."

"I'd think so. And if I don't, I'll buy some of him at the wholesale price and sell it to you." He spoke with assurance, his glance at Gray Wolf short, but not unkind.

"My brother says we need forty-five feet of fencing. Can we get it now?"

Mr. Hogan nodded. "I'll figure it out, and have my boy measure it for you. I have that much and more here on hand. It shouldn't be much more than three dollars or so."

"I have cash with me," Debra said, and opened the reticule she carried.

Mr. Hogan waved a hand in her direction. "We'll get to that part in a few minutes. Why don't you come with me, young man," he said, looking at Gray Wolf. "We'll go out back and speak with my boy."

Gray Wolf touched Debra's shoulder and his look at her was one of warning. "Stay here until I return. Don't go out front without me."

She nodded, uncertain of what he spoke, but

trusted his advice as good. If he wanted her to stay where she was, she would do as he asked. The place she waited was shady, her position sheltered between two buildings, the mill on one side of her; the small building on the other side of her was a storage area. She was only twenty feet or so from the front of the store, where the wagon was waiting, and she could see the passersby from her vantage point.

The sound of two men speaking reached her ears, and she recognized the voice of the man from the hardware store as one of them. "We don't need that sort of trash hereabouts," he said harshly. "Someone needs to do something about it. Those people up yonder at that native village can go elsewhere for their goods. We've got enough business with the white folks buying from us."

"I heard he's living with that half-breed out at the old Thornley farm." The second voice was younger, harsher, and his words were unkind, Debra decided. The urge to walk toward the road and confront the second man was strong within her, but she obeyed Gray Wolf's dictate and stayed where she was.

"We'd do well to clean out that mess. Thornley was a good sort. He don't deserve to have that woman bringin' in her men to his place and making a mockery of our way of life."

Again she stiffened at the unkind words the men spoke, knowing them to be lies, yet unable to defend herself. Her father had left her the farm, free and clear, and it was legally hers to do with as she pleased. If she wanted her brother there with her in Ethan's absence, it was her own business. Yet, she knew that her people were hated and sometimes feared by the ignorant few among the townspeople, and those were the sort she steered clear of.

Now she felt at risk, and knew that her brother was likely to be the target of some act of hatred. She stood close to the wall of the mill and wished desperately for Ethan's presence with her, even as she acknowledged the fact that he was not likely to return for some time. She was on her own, and the thought was frightening beyond measure.

Sheridan Falls, Ohio

THE APPOINTMENT was set for morning, when the circuit judge would arrive in town. For today and tonight, Ethan and Jay were sleeping out of doors, a scant half mile from town, rolled in their blankets before a fire. They'd found sustenance at a boarding house where the owner welcomed them without hesitation. She'd offered them rooms there, but neither of the men felt the need of a roof over their heads.

They'd managed to spend their time well, traveling by train from Chicago, where their horses were lodged, to this town, where Jay had been told to bring his quarry. Now they waited, their time of uncertainty almost at an end. The lawyer Jay had consulted had agreed to appear in court with them, spending long hours with Ethan, hearing his story and then making inquiries in town, where the killings were still spoken of.

"I'm worried about Debra." Not for the first time, Ethan spoke his feelings aloud. He'd been quiet for several days, his mind on the woman who waited for him, wondering if she were able to take care of the stock without his help, wishing he could see her and hold her close. The fact was, he missed her in a way he hadn't thought possible. She had become so much a part of him during their months together, that now he felt incomplete without her presence. Even the comfort of his dreams of her were not enough to keep his thoughts from the danger and perils she might face by being alone on the farm. In the dark hours of the night, he had sometimes marveled at the strength of her presence with him, had almost been able to catch the scent of her body, the sweet, clean smell of her hair. He knew, in a way he had no knowledge of, that she was well, that she was not alone. Yet he could not sense the face or form of the one who was with her, yet knew that it was so, and was comforted by the fact of his knowing.

As if he sensed Ethan's thoughts, Jay spoke of Debra. "She's a strong woman. She'll be able to tend things. I'll warrant she did all right by herself before you got there, and she'll no doubt keep everything in good order until you return."

"I know her strengths, but I know that she is only

accepted in town on sufferance. There are those who don't accept the color of her skin, and those who would like to get their hands on her farm. I've left her unprotected, and if it weren't for the fact that I know I must clear up these things in my past, I'd be on my way home right now."

"Once you're cleared, we'll be leaving in a few days," Jay assured him. "I don't doubt but what the lawyer will be able to set things to rights."

"You have more faith than I do. There are those in town who remember me well, and those who will give me a good word in court. But the fact remains that I had no witnesses to my wife and son's deaths. It remains as my word against the killer. And I won't lie about it. I shot the man dead and I'd do it again if the need arose."

"Rest easy, my friend," Jay told him. "Think about the woman who waits for you."

"I've been thinking of her. She wasn't well when I left, and I'm concerned that she might have been sickening from some sort of disease."

Jay laughed and drew Ethan's attention in a way that appeared deliberate, Ethan decided. "I don't find it to be a humorous situation," he said, his anger flaring.

"I don't think you need to worry at this thing a bit. She wasn't sickly, only acting like a woman who is thinking of her future and trying to cope with changes in her body."

Ethan sat up and poked the fire that glowed in the

darkness of the clearing where they had camped. "And what is that supposed to mean? What the hell are you talking about?"

"Use your head, Ethan. She was doing her best to keep it from you, but any man with a particle of intuition could see that she is going to have a child."

Ethan felt as though someone had hit him over the head with a two-by-four. He was silent as his mind ranged over the last few days before his departure from the farm. Debra had not been ill during the afternoons and evenings, only during the early hours of the day, when she'd been pale and languid, as if... He felt a pang of guilt strike him, at the knowledge that he hadn't recognized her problem.

"I didn't know," he said dully. "I wouldn't have left if I'd known."

"She knew that, too. She wouldn't keep you there with those sorts of ties, Ethan. If you'd guessed at her condition, you would have fought me to stay with her, and she knew that it was the right time for you to face the charges against you. I suspect she was more than aware that I would help you all I could to become free of the ties that held you."

"You knew and you didn't tell me. I can't forgive you for that," Ethan said dully. "I left her alone when she needed me most, and for that I can't forgive myself."

"Stop the foolishness, man. We have a job to do tomorrow. If the people the lawyer and I have lined up all agree to testify for you, and there's no reason why they won't, you'll be free of all charges and the judge will let you go. Do you think Debra would want you worrying about her instead of thinking about becoming a free man?'

Ethan shook his head, his mind filled with the memories of his woman, of the slim body that must by now be filling with his child, for if she were indeed to be expecting an event of that kind, she would be well past the halfway mark by now. And how could a woman in that condition keep up with the livestock and all that winter on the plains brought. A woman alone. Yet not alone.

Holly Hill, The Dakota Territory

WITH THE HELP of Mr. Hogan, they had purchased the fencing needed, and returned to the farm. Debra worried about the conversation she had been privy to while Gray Wolf and Mr. Hogan had settled on the proper fencing and she had paid for it with gold coins from Ethan's stash of money. They traveled back to the farm in silence, for it seemed Gray Wolf sensed her troubled thoughts.

He was right, but at the forefront of Debra's thoughts were the chores she'd left half-done in her house. She cooked a quick meal while Gray Wolf unloaded the wagon, and when he'd finished up his chores, he carried in her supplies to the pantry. The meal she'd put together was but leftovers in fact, but nourishing nevertheless. For she'd used yesterday's roast and potatoes, added carrots and onions and managed to concoct a stew that simmered on the stove, the gravy smelling rich and inviting. At the last minute she'd run to the fruit cellar and found apples in her stores, then fixed an apple tart to please her brother's sweet tooth.

When Gray Wolf came in the house, it was almost dark and she lit a lantern over the table as she readied his meal.

She had not told Gray Wolf of the men in town and their harsh words regarding his presence here, and knew that he must be informed, so that he would be aware of the possibility of danger. And yet, she dreaded his knowing of such hatred running rampant in town. But there was no point in waiting longer, she thought, and when they had finished eating, she told him, as closely as she could remember, all the things that had been said.

He listened and nodded, not seeming surprised by her words. "It is ever the situation when there are two races struggling to live in the same place. One day, perhaps, our people will be welcome in the white man's villages, but for now, we must prove our right to live in their midst. And there is often trouble when the two races are blended in a woman or man such as you, Debra. There are those who cannot understand that men are men and women are women, no matter what their race. The idea that two such people can find love and a life together is never accepted by some. And even if a half-breed finds a measure of acceptance, a man such as me is still an outcast."

"It's not fair," she said bitterly. "But then, my mother told me once that life was never promised to be a fair situation for any of us. I thought she was just speaking words that did not apply to me. Not until I came back here and faced the world of the white man on my own did I understand what she meant."

"We must be careful," Gray Wolf said quietly. "Even the woman, Julia, in town will be under watch, for her father knew that I found her to be attractive. He watched me closely while we were in the emporium, and kept a close eye on me."

Debra smiled and shot him a teasing look. "She thought you were handsome. She did not say the words aloud to me, but when you weren't looking, she gave me a nod and glanced your way. And when she did not know I watched, her brows rose as though she admired you. Julia is not a woman to scorn skin such as yours, or mine for that matter. I found that Ethan did not even pay any mind to our differences, only admired me for what I was and the abilities I possess."

"He must be a man among men," Gray Wolf said. "For he has made you a happy woman, and you have soft eyes when you speak of him. I think you are proud to carry his son."

"You are right in thinking that, and I'm proud to be his wife. I only hope he doesn't find his own people turning against him because of me."

"Ha! Do you think he would care?"

"No. Probably not. But I wouldn't want him to be scorned. He deserves better than that." She was quiet for a moment, her gaze turning to the window where the darkness had fallen and the night had settled around the house.

"We will go to bed early," she said. "And I would feel safer if you were to stay in the house tonight, my brother."

"Is your concern for your safety or mine?" he asked and she gave him a long look that spoke the fears she held in her heart.

"For both of us, but mainly for you. For if those two men I heard speaking on the sidewalk in town spread their ideas around, it could mean real danger for you."

"And don't you think I will bring that danger close to you by staying inside your house? I can't do that, Debra, for it would mark me a coward. I will stay in the barn and keep watch over you and your farm. Until your husband returns, I will be here to stand in his stead."

She knew there was no use in arguing the point with him and bowed her head in submission to his greater knowledge. If he was determined to face danger from the barn, he must have found a way to protect himself. And with that thought, she asked his plans.

"Do you have a gun? Ethan has a rifle here, and I have my shotgun. I'd feel better if you took one out to the barn with you. I want you prepared in case of attack."

"I don't fear attack. I have weapons of my own, and they are hidden where they won't be found. Don't fear for my safety, sister, for I learned at a young age to defend myself."

She nodded, unwilling to gainsay his plans. "I'll keep the dog inside with me then," she told him. "Unless you want him in the barn to sound an alarm should there be visitors in the night."

"I'll be safe," he assured her, and in few minutes had finished his meal and cleared his plate and cup from the table. From the yard, she heard a horse and then steps on the porch, and watched as Gray Wolf went to the window to look out.

"We have visitors," he said. "I think it is young George and his father. And it looks as though they come bearing a gift for you."

"A gift?" She stood and went to the door, opening it wide and stepping out onto the porch. "Welcome," she told the two men who approached.

"I had an idea you might need something besides a pair of kittens to eat your leftovers around here," Mr. Shane said cheerfully. "I brought a young pig for you to fatten up, and another dog to keep things in order out back."

He motioned to the pig George carried, a young

shoat who didn't look old enough to be gone from his mother in her estimation.

"Can the piglet eat on his own?" she asked, even now looking past George to where a half-grown dog stood in the shadow of the porch, looking around himself as if taking stock of his surroundings.

"He'll eat all the leftover milk you have," Mr. Shane told her, "and any scraps of food. You can give him ears of dried corn in a few weeks, and he'll thrive with the milk from your Jersey." He motioned to the other part of his gift and introduced the mutt, who perked up noticeably as if he knew he was the center of attention.

"The dog here is just a bonus, only a mutt, but I thought you might need one to be in the barn at night to keep your brother company."

Debra looked at her neighbor in surprise. "Have you heard rumors that might make you think my brother is not safe in the barn alone at night?" she asked, and noted the look Sam Shane exchanged with Gray Wolf.

"I think your brother is a man of great strength," her neighbor said, "but I think he could use a little backup in the form of a watchdog. If he doesn't mind sharing his space with the animal. Butch is a good dog, but we have almost more than we can feed, with two litters already produced from our females. He's already proved himself, for he's been a little too busy with my females this year. I think he'll hang around so long as you feed him and keep him happy."

"As long as he gets along with Sport, he's welcome. And they're both probably young enough not to be set in their ways yet," Debra said, pleased at the thought of another dog to keep strangers at bay.

"Well, my wife sent me to let you know that you have only to shoot off your rifle twice in a row and me and George will come a'runnin' to help if you need us."

She was stunned by his words of support and she smiled her thanks. Gray Wolf spoke from his place by the window.

"I thank you for your friendship, both on behalf of myself and my sister. It is good to have neighbors who are willing to help."

"Well, you've been good to my boy, giving him work and sending him home without empty hands when he comes here," Sam said. "My wife and I have been talking about it and decided it was time we did something to show our appreciation for you. My woman wants to come by to talk with you, Mrs. Tyler. She wants to know if you'd show her how you make those cinnamon rolls. She said hers aren't nearly as tasty."

"I'd be happy to keep you supplied with some until she picks up on the making of them," she told him. "Send her over and we'll spend a day in the kitchen."

"She says she's not much of a hand for baking.

Her meals are good, but she hasn't had much to do with sweet things, and our boy here likes pies and is right fond of your cinnamon rolls, ma'am."

"Well, we'll see what we can do," Debra said. "And I'd be most happy to have company anytime she wants to visit."

Gray Wolf left the kitchen to step outside, walking from the porch with Sam Shane, and Debra closed the door, knowing that their talk was not meant for her ears. The thought of her neighbor accepting Gray Wolf was enough to warm her heart, she decided, and she wrapped one of the fresh loaves of bread for the visitors to take home to Anna Shane.

CHAPTER FOURTEEN

THE NIGHT SEEMED overlong to Debra, lying awake, her gaze seeking the window for hours, awaiting the gray light of dawn on the horizon. There was nothing to be heard from the barn, no growling or barking from Sport, who slept undisturbed next to her bed, and she finally arose, aggravated with her inability to lose herself in slumber.

The sun was aglow on the horizon when she let Sport and the two cats out into the yard, where the dog investigated the scents that drew him, and the cats merely did their morning duties, then returned to be let in for breakfast.

Debra spilled the cream from the top of last night's milk into her churn, then gave a big bowl of the milk left to the two felines who wrapped themselves around her ankles as she worked. They stuck their noses in the morning's offering and set to with a will. She set aside the rest of the skim for the piglet, wondering where Gray Wolf had put the little fella for the night.

It seemed that an empty stall had provided a bed for the little creature, for Gray Wolf was full of plans at the breakfast table for a pen to be built to contain the animal. In the meantime, the skim milk and a few crusts from breakfast were taken out to the barn and a blue speckled pan served as a breakfast tray for the pig, in the stall where he had cuddled up in the loose straw.

A small structure that resembled a doghouse soon appeared outside the barn, with Gray Wolf nailing on the final boards that would provide a roof.

"Will this do for a pigsty?" he asked her, grinning widely as she approached from the house. "I'd thought we could turn it into a doghouse for the mutt when the pig outgrows it."

"And where will it go in the meantime?"

"I'm going to build a small enclosure at the side of the shed. It won't take long and it'll give the pig a place to dig in the mud when it rains. He doesn't need a lot of space, but it can't be too close to the house, for if my memory serves me, these animals can create a lot of odor."

"That's a polite way of putting it," Debra said with a laugh. "I suspect that's why I've never been fond of raising them. I enjoy eating the bacon and the chops, but smelling the odor of their leavings turns my stomach, and right now, I can't afford any more of that than I'm coping with already."

He shot her a measuring glance. "Are you still suffering with the early time of sickness that comes on with women when they carry a child?"

"No, with me it's anytime I smell something that doesn't hit me right. I stopped tossing up my breakfast months ago, now I just get puny when I smell certain things. And somehow I have the notion that a pigpen might qualify as one of those things."

"Maybe I'd better put him out back, beyond the shed. How about beneath a tree in the pasture."

"I'll help you," she offered. "I'll hold your nails and keep the boards in place while you hammer them together. You'd be amazed at how much I can do to help."

"You've convinced me. We'll haul this little coop out there and build a sty around it. In fact, you might want to think about raising a hog every summer. It'll give you a tidy bit of meat for your smokehouse."

"I haven't even used it as a smokehouse since I came back here. My father used to smoke hams and bacon every year, now that I think about it. I just store things there and sometimes let the milk sit overnight until the cream rises and I can dump it in the churn."

"Didn't I see the churn out in the kitchen earlier? Are you making butter today? I'd think you'd do better to tend to that rather than helping with this project."

"I've got your number," she said, realizing his ploy. "You think it's hard work for me to be out here hauling your lumber and helping with the pigpen, don't you?"

"You're going to have a child, Debra. My nephew, in fact. I don't want your man to be after me when he returns and finds you exhausted from the work I've forced you to do."

"Ha! Fat chance of that. He knows me better than you think. And he's well aware that I ran this whole shebang on my own for three years, before he showed up."

Gray Wolf walked to where she stood and put his arm across her shoulders, an act that was out of the ordinary for him, for he did not show his feelings easily. "You're my sister, the last link I have with my mother, and I cherish you, Debra. I want to turn you over to Ethan when he arrives, looking whole and hearty and healthy. And if directing your path will make that possible, that's what I'll do. Now go in the house and make your butter, and then come back out to see how I'm doing. You can put in your two cents' worth then."

She shook her head, as if she wondered at his words. "It seems I'm to be at the mercy of a man all my life. Do this and do that, don't work too hard, sit down and rest, and on and on."

He laughed at her pose, her hands in her apron pockets, her jaw tilted upward in defiance, and yet there was about his chuckle a sense of tenderness, as if he would approve of her wayward disposition.

"All right, you win. Come on out with me and pick up a shovel. Dig holes and hammer nails and spend your strength on the work that is beneath you. Your Ethan would tell you to sit and watch, wouldn't he? And you expect me to do any less?"

"Ethan would scold me and send me into the house, and perhaps even make me lie down for a rest. He frets over me, even though he tries not to let me see his worry when he thinks I'll overdo and wear myself out. He says I need a man to take care of me, and I'm just ornery enough to argue that point."

"Well, you have two men to tend to you, even though one of them is not with us. But mind my words, sister, he will be back and you must be as I said, healthy and in a fit condition or I will bear the brunt of his anger. He would expect me to care for you as he would."

She waved an impatient hand at him. "Go on and build your pigpen. Take the doghouse with you and just remember that it will be your job to scrub it clean when the pig outgrows it, or it won't be fit for the dog to sleep in."

His grin told her she had not won the battle, and she watched as he carried the small building he'd put together so quickly, taking it through the shed and past the corral into the pasture. It was good to have him here, handling the things she would find cumbersome. For even though she hated to admit it, her pregnancy was wearing on her, and she was weary already, with the day not even half done.

IT WAS PAST NOON when she heard a buggy roll past the back porch, and when she went to the door, she found Julia climbing down from the seat, clutching a letter in her hand.

"Hi, there," her friend called out. "I knew you'd want to see this right away, so I asked my father to watch the store by himself so I could bring it out to you. The postmaster got it from the morning train."

Debra's hands trembled as they touched the envelope, its front soiled by the fingerprints of those who had handled it, but managing to look most precious to her eyes. She slid her finger beneath the flap and tore it open, careful not to disturb the missive it contained. She turned it over, noting the handwriting that spelled out her name, recognizing the quick, slashing letters, admiring the name they spelled. *Mrs. Ethan Tyler.*

"It's from Ethan," she said, her voice whispering his name as if it were a prayer.

"Open it. Quickly," Julia said, dancing impatiently as Debra lingered over the thrill of holding in her hands a link to the man she missed so desperately.

The single sheet of paper contained a brief message, but one that was welcome, for he told of returning to Chicago to find two fillies in the barn with the mares. He was bringing them on a train, knowing that the fillies were too small and weak to walk the distance home. The trial had gone well, he wrote, and he had been absolved of all blame in the circumstances of the death. The people in town had spoken in his behalf, and the judge had dismissed the charges.

He would be arriving with Jay very soon, and upon reading those words aloud in Julia's hearing, she burst into tears. Julia held her close, her arms closing around her with all the comfort she seemed capable of, and Debra relaxed against her, her sobs coming to a halt very quickly.

"I have nothing to cry about. I never cry," she said, as if furious with herself at the lack of control she'd presented in the face of such good news, her statement seeming to fill Julia with amusement, with tears and sobs painting a picture to the contrary.

"What's wrong?" The masculine voice that spoke was harsh with concern, and Julia seemed stunned by the approach of the man behind her.

She grabbed Debra even tighter and held her as if she would protect her from harm. And then seemed to realize that there was no threat to be found in the tall man who had only concern for Debra, making him seem abrupt and angry.

"She got a letter from Ethan."

"And is he not well? Is there a serious problem? Has he been kept there?" Gray Wolf shot his questions rapidly at Julia, his frown impressive, his worry apparent.

"No, it doesn't seem to be the case. He's coming home and the two mares they rode to Chicago have dropped their foals. Debra has two new fillies to add to her herd."

Gray Wolf shook his head. "I do not understand

women. These are three things to be thankful for, and instead, my sister cries on your shoulder as if some great tragedy has struck."

"She cried because she's happy," Julia said quietly. "Something a man cannot be expected to understand."

"Well, that gives me an excuse then, I suppose. For I am a man. And glad of it."

"Yes, you are." Julia's gaze touched upon his face, then slid down his length as if she would verify that fact.

Debra looked up at her brother, and thought that crimson flame touched his cheeks, for he seemed to be suffering under Julia's frank admiration of him. "And we are women," Debra said staunchly. "Julia understands my tears, although they are not really tears, but an expression of my joy."

Gray Wolf shook his head. "I hope your Ethan will be here soon, for I think that having his child has made you into a dim-witted female. He must cope with you, for I cannot." With a final sigh, he turned from them and made his way back to the shed and the task he had left so precipitously in order to find out what had caused the hullabaloo.

Julia and Debra collapsed together in a spate of laughter that threatened to bring tears flowing down their cheeks. As she caught her breath finally, Debra tugged her friend toward the house. "Come inside and I'll make tea. I'm almost finished with the dinner I've cooked for Gray Wolf, and you can join us."

Julia took her arm gladly and together they climbed

the step to the porch. "What are we having?" she asked, obviously willing to share the meal, whatever it might be.

"Soup. I had a Mason jar full of beef I canned when Mr. Shane gave me a good big chunk of the last steer he butchered, and I just added vegetables and a quart of tomatoes to it. There are biscuits left from breakfast, and I'm sure we'll find enough to hold us over 'til suppertime."

"Sounds good to me. My mother has gone to the church today for a quilting bee and my father isn't much of a cook. He got interrupted halfway through anyway when I asked him to come into the store and watch things so I could leave. Maybe I'll take him home some soup with me."

"He would be welcome to a share of it," Debra said, pleased to have Julia's company today, for she felt a celebration was in order, with Ethan's return almost upon them.

Julia put bowls and plates on the table, and found silverware in the drawer. She paused in her task to mention something that obviously had been troubling her. "There is talk in town of you living with another man while your husband is gone. My father told several of the men that Gray Wolf is your brother, but the general opinion seems to be running against him. I fear there will be trouble if Ethan does not show up very soon."

Debra turned to her from where she was taking

the biscuits from the warming oven. "I overheard some men talking in town when we were there yesterday, and I feared then for Gray Wolf's safety. Mr. Shane came last night and brought us another dog, one to sleep in the barn with my brother, a dog to sound an alarm if there should be unwelcome visitors."

"My father fears that the younger men who have little to do will take it upon themselves to start a fuss. They are always looking for something to meddle in, and he is worried that you are out here alone."

Debra felt a pang of fear touch her as she considered the harm that could be done to her brother, and her thoughts were troubled. "What do you think will happen?"

Julia shook her head. "I don't know. In fact I don't even like to consider what mischief they might plot. But I think you'd better be on the lookout for problems."

Gray Wolf's arrival at the back door halted their conversation and they sat down together to eat the simple fare Debra had provided. True to her promise, she filled a jar with soup and readied it to send with her friend as she prepared to leave.

"My father will appreciate it," Julia told her, hugging her tightly as she readied herself for the trip back to town. She walked out to the buggy and Gray Wolf appeared from the barn, speaking to her softly as he helped her to the seat. With a simple wave of his hand, he sent her on her way, and then turned to Debra.

"I'll need your help for a while, putting up the boards. You can hold them while I nail them in place," he said. "I think your feeble strength will be sufficient for the task."

She snapped the dish towel she held in his direction and he winced, as if he feared her retaliation for his words, then laughed as he reached for her. "You do not frighten me, little sister. I have faced bears and wild wolves, and you offer me no more harm than they."

His hands held her waist and he smiled his approval at her. "I like your friend," he said.

It was a simple utterance and yet, Debra felt the deeper meaning it conveyed, for her brother was not given to words of approval such as those he spoke of Julia. "She has been a good friend to you, hasn't she?" he asked, and yet it was not a query but a statement of fact, and Debra only nodded her agreement.

They stood thusly on the porch, and only the approaching sound of horses brought their attention back from to where they were. From across the side pasture, a band of men rode up beside the house and around to the back porch, several guns in evidence.

"What do you want?" Debra asked loudly, her voice filled with an anger she seldom displayed. "There's nothing for you here."

"We came out to protect your husband's interests, ma'am," one of the group said, and another laughed heartily at his cohort's words.

"My husband's interests don't need protecting," she answered stoutly, and then found herself behind Gray Wolf's back as he moved to stand before her, protecting her symbolically with his body.

"What do you want here on my sister's land?" he asked harshly. "You are trespassing."

"And who are you, a dirty Indian, to tell us where we can go or not go?' one of the men called out. "You're the reason we're here. You've come in here and made yourself at home in the house of a white man, as if you have a right to take over his property."

"This is my brother," Debra called out, anger vibrant in each syllable she spoke.

"That's a fancy tale you've concocted to put everyone in the dark," the man who seemed to be the ringleader of the group charged, his voice filled with nasty allusions that sickened Debra to the depths of her soul.

"Leave my farm," she said loudly. "You don't have any right here."

"We have the right to defend a man who trusted you to behave yourself. He should have known better than to leave you alone here. It sure didn't take you long to find a dirty Indian to take up with, did it?"

Debra backed from Gray Wolf and darted into the house, grabbing up Ethan's rifle and turning it toward the door. It was kept loaded and she knew how to shoot it, although she felt more comfortable with the shotgun. And now, she burst through the door again and showed the men gathered in her yard the proof of her anger.

With a sudden move, she pointed it in the air and shot off two quick bullets, then faced the suddenly silent group before her. "Will you leave peacefully, or must I begin to pick you off, one at a time?"

"Your puny gun against seven men?" the leader asked with scorn painting each word.

"I'll take out two of you before you can aim at me," she told them, and then was stunned when a shot from the back of the tightly knit group hit the wall of the house beside her.

With a shout of fury, Gray Wolf was off the porch, his tall figure almost enclosed by the men, who clustered their horses around him. He'd pulled the gunman from his horse and then laid him low with a solid punch to his jaw before the man behind him used his pistol as a club and hit the side of Gray Wolf's head with a mighty blow.

Without a sound, he collapsed on the ground and with a howl of madness, two of the men left their horses to pick him up and hold him as a target for ready fists.

A rope appeared as if by magic, and they dragged Gray Wolf into the orchard, seeking out a tree to suit their purpose. From the porch, Debra could only watch, fearful of hitting her brother should she let loose another shot. Again, she fired two bullets into the air, hoping against hope that the sound would be heard in time at the neighboring farm. Surely she would receive help from that direction, she prayed.

The rope was tossed over a limb and held taut as a loop was formed at the other end and placed over Gray Wolf's head. He was unconscious, limp in their hold and Debra screamed her fury and fear aloud, Sport running from the house as she cried out her anger. The dog barked and snarled, heading for the men, who were totally out of control. One of them aimed his pistol at the dog and fired a single shot. Sport went down without a whimper, and blood flowed from the hole in his chest.

Debra's anger knew no bounds and she screamed out words of rage, a wrath she could not contain spewing from her, the sight of her dog's body maddening her almost beyond reason.

"Let my brother go. Turn him loose, you bastards."

Two of the men tossed the lifeless-looking body of Gray Wolf atop a horse and she felt a panic she had not known before this time strike her. They would hang him, and with no reason. It was more than she could bear, and she watched as one of the men lifted his hand, preparatory to striking the horse and send him bolting, leaving Gray Wolf to dangle at the end of the rope they'd brought with them for just this moment.

She fired now into their midst, aiming for the man who would so readily kill her brother with a slap of his hand. Better that her brother be wounded as he sat astride the horse, than that she not attempt to halt this brazen display of hatred.

The man she aimed at slumped to the ground, a victim of her shot. She fired again and the group scattered, one of the men howling with pain, yet able to draw his gun, one of several aimed in her direction. Their shots went wild and she crouched behind the upright post at the corner of the porch, half-hidden by the structure itself as the dust kicked up before the porch as the bullets ricocheted across the dirt.

Another rifle cracked from beyond the orchard, and the leader of the gang let out a snarling oath, and jerked with the force of a bullet striking his body. He turned in the direction of the new attack, along with his cohorts, all of them eager to face the guns that threatened their mission.

Without hesitation, the two men from beyond her property line rode hard through the orchard, firing their guns in rapid sequence at the men who were trapped between Debra's offensive rifle and their own attack. Another man went down, then a second rifle bullet, apparently coming from the gun George held, found its mark and a fourth man fell to the ground. Seeming without fear, Samuel Shane rode to where Gray Wolf sat, still astride a mare, hanging over the horse's mane, unable to help himself.

With a quick snap of his wrist, he took the rope from the unconscious man's neck and tossed it to the ground, then steadied Debra's brother across his own saddle with a strong arm, as he looked around at the carnage he and his son had created. Including the man Debra had shot, there were four bodies on the ground, three men standing and a tidy group of horses milling about as if they were confused by the melee.

Their reins dangled to the ground, but they were ranch-trained cow ponies, raised to stand where they were left, and well disciplined enough to obey the silent command of the reins that tied them to the ground.

Debra screamed aloud, her fright overcoming her relief at the rescue Sam and his son had effected. She ran from the porch through the yard and to the orchard, stopping only when she reached the inert form of her brother, now slumped over the saddle Sam sat upon. She reached up to touch the dark head, the long hair that flowed in the breeze, and the tears of anguish were hot, flooding her eyes and spilling onto her cheeks.

"He's alive, ma'am," George said. "Just knocked out. Somebody must have slammed him a good one."

"Several some ones," Debra said bitterly, touching the reddened areas that promised to be bruises before many hours had passed. "Take him to the house, will you, please?"

"Yeah. My son can keep these fellas rounded up while I cart your brother inside for you."

Indeed, George looked to be anxious to prove his

mettle as he scanned the three men still on their feet, his shotgun aiming at them without hesitation.

"If one of 'em moves, I'll take every last one down, Pa," he said, his eyes gleaming with a look of anger that Debra thought must be a trait among men.

She followed as Sam walked his horse to the back porch, slid from the animal's back and lifted Gray Wolf over his shoulder to carry him into the house.

"Where do you want him, Mrs. Tyler?"

She opened the screen door and let him walk past her. "Into my bedroom. I'll go pull back the quilt." And so saying, she ran ahead into the room she shared with Ethan, and made ready the bed for her brother.

With gentle movements she would not have expected from him, her neighbor placed Gray Wolf on the bed and then backed from the room. "I'm gonna take that bunch to town, ma'am, and send back a wagon for the bodies. You just stay here in the house 'til someone comes out to see to it."

"Yes, I will." Debra could not force herself to argue, indeed did not have the strength to do more than rinse a cloth in her basin and wash the dirt from her brother's face. He muttered low words of anger beneath his breath, and she bent low over him, speaking softly, phrases of praise for his bravery, thanksgiving for his rescue and words of joy that his life had been saved by Sam's quick answer to her cry for help.

CHAPTER FIFTEEN

IT WAS LATE AFTERNOON before the undertaker's carriage from town arrived, and Debra heard the sound of the new dog from the barn raising a ruckus announcing the visitors. It brought back the death of her pup, and she felt a pang of guilt that Sport had met so bad an end to his short life, and she had not been able to halt the danger to the animal.

The carriage drew up near her watering trough and the gentleman who ran the undertaker's parlor stepped down, another man at his heels. "We heard there was some business out here for us," Harley Madison said. He was known to Debra, but only as a passerby on the street and she knew his name from reading it on a sign in front of his establishment.

"Thank you for coming, Mr. Madison. I fear there is a job awaiting you in my orchard, beneath those peach trees out there." Pointing at the scene of recent violence, she caught sight of Sport, lying in the dirt, unattended.

"I think we'll use your shovel to bury this little fella, too," Mr. Madison said, sending her a glance of pity. "You've had quite a day out here, haven't you, Mrs. Tyler?"

"I'd just as soon never see another like it," Debra answered, thinking of the young men who had met their deaths on her land.

"Young fellas didn't have their heads screwed on right," Mr. Madison said. "There's a big hullabaloo in town, you can bet your bonnet on it. There's folks stormin' around like the end of the world has come to Holly Hill. Things sure enough got out of hand, and you wonder where these young'uns got their ideas of what's right and wrong in this world. Dirty shame when law-abiding folks like you and yours have to face a bunch of hooligans and fight to protect their lives."

"If we hadn't had help from my neighbor, I doubt we'd be alive to tell the tale," she told him, thinking once more of George and Sam and their part in this day.

"Samuel Shane is a fine man, and he's made it known all over town that you were the victim in this whole thing. Not a word against you from anyone, especially not the families of those men out there," he said, pointing at the orchard where his work awaited him. "There's a lot of shame attached to it when men attack a woman, especially without due cause. Hell, their behavior would have been wrong if they'd had any reason at all on their side. Just goes against the grain for men to turn on womenfolk, thataway."

With a simple salute and doffing of his hat, he headed for the orchard, his helper climbing back into the carriage to follow his path. Together they would rid her land of the men who had bled upon the soil and lost their lives for such foolish reasons. She could not find it in her heart to wish the dead men good thoughts on their final journey to the hereafter, for she doubted they would receive a welcome that would be pleasing to them on the other side of life.

Debra went back into the house, and as she walked across the kitchen, heard her name called in a voice that was fast gaining strength. From the bedroom, Gray Wolf was awake and aware, and unless she was mightily mistaken, he was about to emerge on the scene.

As she reached the bedroom door, she caught sight of him, staggering toward her, and she leapt to his side, holding him erect but barely, his weight too great for her to hold.

"Are you all right?" he muttered, his grip on her firm, his arm warm across her shoulder. "I felt strong when I rose from your bed, Debra, but somewhere in my journey across the room, I found I had no bones in my legs."

She laughed shortly and helped him back to the bed. "Stay here, my brother, while I look you over and make certain that you only bear bruises, and no other damage."

"Who was outside with you? Did those men return or was it your neighbor?"

"The man from town who tends to the dead. They have peculiar ways of saying farewell to those who find their final resting place, and it involves much weeping and wailing by their women and singing of songs and speaking of words that they think will help those who breathe no longer to gain paradise. I much prefer my mother's way of simple burial and the remembering of the dead in silence."

"Is that how your father was tended upon his death?" he asked, touching her hand with a gesture she appreciated.

"She dug his grave beyond the orchard and buried him beneath the ground as the white man buries his dead. The same man who married them came out and spoke over his grave. He was already in his grave, for my mother had placed him in a blanket and taken him out there ahead of time. I was but a child, and she did not let me know that she had buried him until it was finished."

"Does he have a gravestone or a marker of some sort?"

Debra shook her head. "She told me that among her people a man who knows he will die goes out into the forest beyond his village and lies down to die. If a man dies without knowing it will happen, the people carry him to a place where they have built a platform and he is placed on it. Some of our people burn it, others just let him be taken by the earth in a natural way."

"Would you want your father to have a marker on his grave? Do you think he would want it to be done that way?"

"I believe he would be willing to be buried any way my mother chose. It is the custom among the white men to mark their graves, and perhaps it would be good to have that done for him, but I wouldn't know how to go about such a thing."

Gray Wolf seemed lost in thought for a moment, and then he spoke his thoughts. "I have seen the place near a church where the burial field is, and there are stone markers on some graves and wooden markers on others. Sometimes a cross, as an emblem of belief, sometimes just a piece of wood with carving on it."

"What would I put on such a marker, if one were made for him? His name? Perhaps the time when he died?"

Gray Wolf nodded. "I think his name and the date of his birth and death. That is how I have seen it done."

She was silent, thinking of all the time that had passed since the time of the spotted fever, the disease that had taken her father from them. "I know the year, and the month, but I don't remember the date, for I was very sick that summer. Many people died of the fever, but my mother was able to nurse me through it."

"I'll make a marker for him, Debra. It won't matter how old he was or the date of his death. It will be enough that it has his name carved on it and the year he died. Then, sometime in the future, when he has grandchildren, they will be able to stand by his side and think of his memory."

She thought of the years to come, of the family she would have with Ethan, and her words were a promise to the brother who had come to mean so much to her. "My children will know of him, and if there is a marker for his grave, I will take them there when they are old enough to understand who he was, and I will tell them stories of how he taught me the ways of life that would be important to me. I will tell them of my brother, who cared about me, and who worked hard to help me when there was no one else who cared. When I was alone and needed a strong arm to lean on. I will tell them of how my brother made the marker for the grave of my father, how he made certain that his death would be remembered and his memory cherished."

"He surely deserves to be remembered, and what I do to honor him is in the manner of his people. Because our fathers are of different races means nothing, my sister. I owe it to you to help you in the preserving of his memory, so that his life will not have ended without the honor due him living on into the future.

"This will be done, by both you and me, tending his resting place. Perhaps I will feel well enough later on today. You could come to the shed with me and we'll look for a piece of wood to use. This would be a good day to remember him and make a memorial for your children to hold dear."

She smiled at him, sitting beside him on the bed. "I'm not sure you feel well enough to do all of that yet today, brother, but if not now, then tomorrow we could do this thing."

Gray Wolf sat up, edging to the side of the mattress. "I think I would feel better if I had some food. Perhaps some bread and milk."

"I can do better than that," Debra told him with a laugh. "There is food aplenty in the pantry and you need more than bread, although that will be good if you wrap it around an egg or two."

"I will eat eggs if you prepare them for me. If I have your arm to lean on, I will go to the kitchen and watch while you cook for me."

She stood and lent her strong arm as he rose and steadied himself. With his arm across her shoulders, and hers around her waist, they went to the kitchen and she settled him in a chair.

"I think I should boil them for you. If I crack the shells and let them slide into boiling water they will cook but not have grease on them from the skillet. I think that may settle well on your stomach."

He sent an appreciative look her way and agreed. "I'll eat them on bread or alone, whatever you want. When someone is willing to prepare my food, I don't cause a fuss over the way it is cooked. I learned very young to eat what is put before me."

They laughed as they spoke together of the food they had eaten as children, of the difference in their way of life in that long-ago time.

"I didn't understand why my mother no longer had a cookstove with an oven, after we returned to the village," Debra said. "I wanted her to bake the pies and bread rolls she once made for me and my father, and she could not explain why the ways of cooking and eating were so different between the races."

"I learned much when I went to school in the north country," Gray Wolf told her. "I was again the different one, with only a few of my people ever given the opportunity to attend a school such as the one where I lived. The fathers who dwelt in the church there made it possible for some of us to learn from their books. Alone I could not have learned as I did, for there was no money for such a thing. Our people eked out a living, and luxuries were unknown to them.

"I was chosen to learn more, to be educated as the white man educates his sons, and I felt that the sun shone with brilliance upon me, for the opportunities I was given."

"You are a man of higher learning, Gray Wolf, and yet you know so much of our people, and you use both parts of your heritage to make your path smoother in this life." Debra felt a sense of pride that this brother of hers should be pleased to live in her home and work to help her survive. There were men who would not labor so hard or care so much, and she was grateful for his presence.

The afternoon found them in the shed, sorting through the bits and pieces of lumber left over from all the building projects Ethan had completed. One piece of planking was deemed appropriate for use, and Ethan pulled it from the stack where it had been lying, holding it up to the light to better see the grain of the wood.

"We will sand it down and let the hidden beauty come forth," he said. "There are lines and circles from the tree that provided this wood that must be coaxed out of the depths of this piece."

He worked at the task he had assumed, sanding and cleaning the wood, preparing it for the carving he would do and the finish he would place on its surface. Debra used a piece of chalk and wrote her father's name on the marker, then the month and year of his death below it. Then without thinking, she wrote two more lines, words that would tell of his life.

Husband of Nightbird, She Who Sings, and then beneath it, *Father of Debra, She Who Mourns.*

Gray Wolf read her words and nodded. "I wonder if he would have approved of me, would have been honored by my presence here on his place. I would have been pleased to be his son, also, for my own father was not a kind man. I think this David Thornley was a father to be proud of."

Together they worked to bring a shine to the piece of wood they'd chosen, then Debra watched as Gray Wolf carefully carved out the letters she had chosen to appear. The wood was rounded at the top, formed simply, the bottom of it squared off to sit evenly in the place they would dig for it to rest.

THE LATE EVENING SOUNDS spilled from the doors of the saloon as the two men climbed down from the late train from the east. It had been held up on its journey by a piece of track that had been torn from its place by some unknown culprit, and the arrival that was to have been in early afternoon had been postponed to late evening.

Ethan and Jay led their horses from the platform at the station, the two foals trailing behind, secured by lengths of rope. Saddled for the first time in months, the mares were skittish, looking back at their progeny, then nosing the men who led them on ground that was solid beneath their hooves. As if they felt more at home, they soon ceased flicking their ears and tossing their heads and followed placidly, as if they sensed a familiarity about their surroundings.

Past the doors of the saloon, that place where men who were alone and sought company congregated in the evenings, down toward the hotel and sheriff's office, the men led their mounts, not choosing to ride through town, lest the mares protest at the weight they had not borne for so long a time.

Walking past the hotel, they were hailed by a man who walked to the edge of the boardwalk and waved them down. "Ain't you that fella that married the squaw out the other side of town?" the man asked, his voice raucous, his manner insolent.

Ethan stiffened at the insult tossed so casually at his wife and halted the progress of the mare he led. "I'm Ethan Tyler, and yes, I'm married to Debra Nightsong," he said, his voice a dark warning, if the man had the sense to recognize it.

"You got you a rival, is what I hear," the stranger said mockingly. "I heard those native women liked to have men comin' and goin', and it looks like yours ain't any different than the rest of them."

"What are you talking about?" Ethan stopped directly in front of the man, who had obviously had too much to drink. "How do you know who I am, and what right do you have to insult my woman?"

"You shouldn'ta left her alone, my friend." The drunk wove his way to a bench in front of the hotel and slumped to its surface. "Your woman found her a man while you was gone, a fella who looks to be a brave from her tribe."

Ethan stood silent, disbelieving of the words coming from the man's mouth, yet there was in him an anger he could not keep silent. "Have you seen her? Or this man you speak of?"

From the shadows beneath the porch, the man waved his hands and laughed loudly. "Ever'body's seen her, and him, too. They come to town, just as pretty as you please, buyin' at the emporium and trying to spend their money at the hardware store. Fella at the hardware store chased them on and told 'em to go to the mill for their supplies. Wouldn't have any truck with 'em."

Jay reached from to touch Ethan's arm. "Don't listen to this derelict, Ethan. He's drunker than a skunk, probably doesn't know what he's talking about."

Ethan cut him a dark look. "We'll soon find out, won't we? Get mounted, Jay. We've got a little riding to do. It'll have to be slow with the foals trying to keep up, but it shouldn't take us long to get to Debra's place."

With the strength of men who had walked many miles and whose muscles were honed by the harsh road they had traveled they mounted their mares and tugged the foals into walking once more.

With the drunken laughter of the sot left behind, they rode slowly from the edge of town, down the road that led west. The pain that vied with anger in the breast of the man who rode in the lead was painful, bringing him to a resolution to deal with whatever he found in an expedient manner.

If a man dared live in his place with Debra, he

would kill him. And this time, he did not care if he should be given leniency, as he had just weeks ago in the courtroom in Ohio. For if Debra had betrayed him, he would wish to die himself, and flee the pain of her perfidy. His heart seemed to lodge in his throat as he rode, his hands trembled on the reins, and it was all he could do not to whip his mare into a frenzy, and ride ahead with no thought for the foal who followed.

The road had never seemed so long, the night had never been so dark, and his thoughts were darker than the overwhelming depths of midnight that surrounded him. The woman he had left behind had been his salvation, the one bright star in the night of his despair, and that she could turn her back on his love and betray him with another man was unthinkable.

"Ethan. You're gettin' way ahead of yourself," Jay said quietly, riding beside him. "You got only the word of some old reprobate telling you a story that promises to be a pack of lies, and already you're plotting murder."

Ethan laughed, a harsh, unlovely sound. "What are you talking about?" he jeered, yet knew in his heart that Jay had pegged him right.

"Debra is a woman of honor, and well you know it," Jay reminded him. "She is carrying your child, and she's been grieving for your absence all these long months. Will you go there now and insult her with a greater blow than that of the drunk who told you these lies?"

"Are you certain they're lies?" Ethan asked bitterly. "I've been gone a long time, and women get weary being alone, without a man to depend on."

"Don't you have any faith in the woman you married? I thought I knew you, Ethan Tyler, but you are proving to be a man with his head screwed on crooked."

"Insulting me won't make her betrayal any easier to bear," Ethan said harshly. "If she's done nothing to be ashamed of, I'll know, and I'll ask her forgiveness for my doubts. But if she's taken another man into my bed, I'll kill them both."

"That's where you're wrong, Ethan, for I won't let you do it. You'll take your gun out of your holster and put it in your saddlebag before we arrive at the farm."

"And who will make me do that?" His tone was scornful as he turned to face Jay.

"If I have to knock you off that horse, I will," Jay said. "This is stupid, Ethan. You know that Debra is an honorable woman, and if you can't remember her strength and the honesty of her very life, you are a stupid man. She deserves better than this. If you ride up and make unjust accusations against her, you'll ruin your marriage and your future with her."

Ethan rubbed his hand over his brow, his weariness catching up with him. He ached in every muscle, his mind had been tormented for so long with the pain of death visiting his loved ones. The remembrance of his child lying in a pool of blood was but a part of the agony he lived with, and he found himself almost unable to think of things that lived now in the present.

The picture he saw when he closed his eyes was not that of Debra, but the man he had killed. The man whose death had been deemed appropriate when measured against the robbery of both the wife and son of another human being.

Yet now he forced himself to recall the words spoken that had so readily condemned the woman he had taken as his wife. Surely it was not possible that the woman who had given herself to him so sweetly, so freely, could be guilty of betraying him with another. He vowed silently to hold back his anger, to give her every chance to defend herself, before assailing her with his doubts.

The man beside him was silent now, as though he had done all he could to steady Ethan's emotions, said all he could say to defend Debra's integrity. And yet, Ethan knew he waited for the gun to be put into his saddlebag, and he could not deny Jay the right to demand this of him. With deft movements, he pulled his pistol from its holster and reached behind him, locating the fastening on his bag and opening it with one hand. The gun was placed inside and the latch closed.

"That's showing a bit more sense," Jay told him, and Ethan only nodded, not sure if his friend could see the movement of his head in the dark.

"We're almost at the lane leading to your place," Jay said. "Are you all right? Have you set aside your anger sufficiently to face Debra without flying off the handle?"

"My mind is calm," Ethan told him. "I'll not jump all over her."

"That's all I ask, then." Without another word, they rode up the lane to the house, where a light glowed inside the kitchen.

The heavy interior door stood open, and through the screen of the outer portal, Ethan could see Debra sitting in a chair by the table. Hidden from his full view by the table before her, only her upper body was exposed to him, and he watched as she bent toward the man who sat at the head of the table, her hand lying in his grasp.

Between them lay some object, large enough to almost cover the width of the wooden piece of furniture, but not deep enough to form a box or container. It seemed to be a slab of wood, and whatever they saw on its surface seemed to hold their interest to the exclusion of all else. With a easy motion, as if she felt free to touch the man beside her, Debra reached and cupped his cheek with her palm, her face turning up to face his.

Inside his chest, deep down, where pain had dwelt

for so long, Ethan felt a piercing, stabbing hurt that drew his lips back in a snarl and pushed an oath from his throat. So easily his wife had given the man beside her a token of her affection, so readily had she smiled into his eyes, her mouth curving in a familiar manner.

The mare he rode whinnied loudly as he rode to the hitching rail, and inside the house, the man beside Debra rose swiftly, moving to stand between her and the door. Jay slid from his horse and tied the reins quickly, then held up a hand in Ethan's direction, perhaps as a warning, he thought.

There was no need, for he was without a weapon, and vowed silently that he would not show his anger until there was a reason he could not doubt. A good reason beyond Debra's familiarity with the man she sat with, the man who even now had been sitting in the chair rightfully belonging to the man of the house.

Ethan's mare was tied beside the other, the two foals left to remain with their dams, and together he and Jay approached the porch.

From inside the house, he heard the stranger speak, his words apparently directed at Debra. "I was foolish to leave the door open. Stay where you are and I'll see who is here."

"Foolish isn't the word for it," Ethan growled, stepping onto the porch, Jay close behind him. They were ranged in front of the screen, and Ethan was not surprised when a gun appeared in the man's hand, taken from his belt in a movement almost too swift to see.

"Who are you?" The words were spoken in a low, harsh voice, and Ethan's temper flared at the challenge.

"The man who lives here," he said, his words filled equally with the gritty sound of challenge he'd heard from the stranger and his own foul-tempered growl.

"Ethan?" From the middle of the kitchen, on the other side of the table, Debra's voice spoke, the sound a breathless word, as if she could not gain strength to speak aloud the syllables of his name.

The man who faced him from his kitchen was, as he'd been warned, a native from perhaps the same tribe Debra hailed from, and Ethan met dark eyes that were focused on his face. "Are you Debra's man? Are you Ethan Tyler?"

"Who wants to know?" He gripped the handle and flung the door wide, stepping into the kitchen, his fury once more apparent. "Who are you?"

"Ethan!" It was the shriek of a woman beside herself with shock, he realized, as Debra rounded the table to step in front of the man she harbored.

She stood before him, her eyes wide, tears flowing, her mouth trembling and her hands reaching for him. He gripped them in his own and held her apart from himself.

"Who is this man you have in our home, Debra. Sitting in my chair, at my table, as if he has a right to be here with you?" He heard the rage color his words, knew the moment his anger had made itself known to her and watched in silence as she shook her head and slumped where she stood. Her head tilted back and for a moment her eyes opened wide and he saw in them a pain such as he had not known her to own until this time. As if she were hurting from some great wound, invisible to an observer.

Only the firm grasp he had on her hands kept her from the floor, and he pulled her against himself, in that moment aware that her form was not as it had been, that she was heavier, her waist larger, her belly distended with the child she carried. He'd known, from what Jay told him, that he should have expected this change in her, but the sight didn't measure up to the expectations he'd held, and his heart seemed to still as he felt the movement of the child she carried, a shifting from beneath her skirt, against his lower belly.

And in that moment, he felt the weight of another man's hands on him, the anger of another man turned in his direction. Like steel manacles, the stranger's fingers clutched at his arms, and the voice that spoke held a threat not unlike that of thunder from the skies.

"Don't hurt her. She is not well. You have frightened her half to death with your noises of anger."

The man was tall, built as might be a chief of his people, his eyes dark with anger of their own, as he sought to defend the woman who was even now unconscious between himself and Ethan. His hands left Ethan's arms, where Ethan sensed bruises would appear before many hours had passed. With gentle care, and a voice that held tenderness, the other man touched Debra carefully, his fingers curving around her shoulder as he spoke her name aloud.

"Debra. I'll get you some water. Hold on, dear heart."

Dear heart. The words of affection bounced from one side of his mind to another as Ethan watched the man turn to the sink, pumping water quickly and bringing back a cupful to press it against Debra's lips.

"Give it to me," Ethan said harshly, taking the cup, holding Debra upright against himself with one hand. He moved carefully with her in his grasp, her feet dragging over the floor, Jay ahead of him to pull a chair from the table. He eased her into a sitting position, but she was limp, and her upper body fell over the wooden shape still lying on the table in front of her.

Ethan knelt beside her, holding her close, feeling the weight of her as she slumped beside him. Jay was there, lifting her head, looking at her face, then turning to Ethan.

"You need to put her on the floor, let her lie flat until we can bring her back to consciousness. Either that or put her head down between her knees."

"That will be quite a trick, for she cannot bend over that way," the native man said with a dry laugh. "She hasn't been able to bend from the waist for some weeks."

Ethan shot him a dark look. "How would you know?" He pulled her gently from the chair and, with Jay helping him, placed her on the floor. A damp cloth appeared and Ethan took it from a darkly tanned hand and placed it on her forehead, then turned to the man who hovered over him.

"How long have you been here?" he asked, and thought of a dozen questions more important that should be asked. *Are you sleeping in my bed? Have you taken my wife from me?* He held his tongue, unable to speak the words that might bring his whole world crashing to a pile of rubble. Before him, the stranger spoke slowly and carefully, his words not flowing freely, as though the words of the white man were a strange language to him. Probably not the language of his childhood.

"I am Gray Wolf, and I am here to watch over my sister."

"Are you? Or are you someone from her mother's village who saw a good place to hang his hat, and only pretended to be Debra's brother?"

"You will believe what you will, white man, but

know that I am a man of honor and I do not harm your woman in any way."

Ethan bent low over the still form on the floor and eased one hand under her neck to lift her head a bit, touching her lips with the cup of water.

"Careful she doesn't choke on it," Jay warned him.

Debra's eyelids fluttered, and opened, revealing dull orbs that seemed to retain the darkness, for they did not focus on the man who knelt beside her. She spoke in a rasping voice, her whisper one of sadness he felt he could not bear.

"Ethan? Have you come back to me? Why are you angry?" The sound of her words trailed away and her eyes closed again, her consciousness fleeing from her.

A sound that might have been a roar of pain or perhaps a groan of sorrow came from his throat and he bent low to touch her forehead with his lips, aching to hold her close and tell her of his love for her. And yet, there was in him a need to know why another man lived in his house, communed with his wife and had apparently taken his place here.

"How did you come to be here?" he asked the man who stood beside him, not looking up lest he loose his anger and cause more pain to the woman he held. One hand touching her was not enough, and he scooped her up from the floor, rising with her to sit on the chair she had so recently vacated. She lay across his lap and he looked down at the rounding of her belly, the tight fit of her dress that reaffirmed the fact of a child within her body, whose birth was not far in the future, beneath her apron.

"We need to get her into bed, I think," Ethan said, and Jay agreed with him readily.

"I'll go turn back her bed and you can carry her in," he said, his look at the third man in the kitchen not without inquiry.

"I will take care of this while you tend to my sister," Gray Wolf said, picking up the piece of wood from the table.

"What is it she was studying when we arrived?" Ethan asked, his attention drawn to the slab on which there were letters carved.

"I have made a marker for the grave of her father," Gray Wolf said. "I am her brother and it was right that I do this for her."

"If she'd asked me, I would have done it," Ethan told him, hurt that such a thing had not been requested of him.

"It is done now," Gray Wolf said. "I'll tend to it and tomorrow I'll put it in its final resting place over the place where her father lies."

"I'll want to speak with you tonight about all these things," Ethan told him. "When Debra is tucked up into bed, I'll want to talk to you at length."

A nod was his answer and Gray Wolf left the kitchen, the marker he'd made carried in his hands.

CHAPTER SIXTEEN

IT WAS LESS THAN an hour later when the three men stood beside the bed where Debra lay, seeming to be asleep now. She had moaned twice, as if something gave her pain, and Ethan knelt to check out her eyes and felt her arms and legs to be certain that she did not suffer an injury he'd missed.

From the foot of the bed, the man claiming to be Debra's brother spoke then, as if he had awaited the knowledge that his sister was indeed asleep and not unconscious. "Debra was injured by a horse out in the barn. She had been spending hours with the horses, and had delivered two foals already. When the third mare was in the throes of labor and the foal was about to be born, the mare thrashed about in her pain and Debra was pushed against the side of the stall and trapped there."

"How did you come to be here? Did you know she was alone?"

Gray Wolf looked discomforted, frowning as he chose his words in reply. "I had a dream of my sister, and I saw her in danger in the shed. She needed me. And I came as quickly as I could."

"Are you a shaman that you saw her in a dream?" Even as he asked the question, Ethan recalled Debra's own knowledge of things to come, of her mother's gift she had spoken of.

"I see things sometimes," Gray Wolf answered, his demeanor stiff, as if uncertain that his words would be believed.

Ethan nodded. "Debra has told me of such things. I am thankful to you for coming to her. I should have hurried to be here, but it is a long way from Chicago, and we were at the mercy of train schedules." He shot a look at Jay that pleaded for words that might free him from the guilt he carried.

Jay spoke, as if he understood the need in Ethan's heart. "You did your best to return, Ethan. Surely Debra will know that. She won't hold you responsible for her danger, or the sickness she has suffered."

"If I'd never come here the first time, she'd have been better off. I interrupted her life and made problems for her where there were none, and now she is carrying my child and my influence over her life will not end. Not for a long time to come."

Gray Wolf spoke softly, his dark eyes burning into Ethan's tortured face. "She loves you, Ethan Tyler. And that is a good thing. She needed someone to care for her, someone she could love and believe in."

"Are you saying she believes in me?" Ethan spoke

the words harshly, thinking of the pain he had caused this woman.

"As she has never believed in anything else in her life. She told me of your past, and her love shines from her eyes, from the depths of her soul, every time she speaks your name. You should feel honored that so good a woman cares for you, Ethan Tyler. Not every man is this world is so blessed, so fortunate as to be the vessel to which a woman's love is given."

Ethan felt the words sink to the depths of his being, knew that Gray Wolf spoke the truth as he saw it, as he knew it, and his knowledge could only have come from the lips of Debra Nightsong. Debra Tyler, the woman who had shared his life for such a short time. Who had given him her belief, her trust.

"I doubted her," Ethan breathed aloud. "I heard the words of the man in town and I allowed doubt to enter my heart."

Gray Wolf looked grim, his features harsh, his mouth set in a hard line that told of his anger. "You have doubted the faithfulness of my mother's daughter, and for that I could take your life."

"No." The single word was given emphasis by the quick movement of Ethan's head. "I feared she had been too long alone, and that she had come to doubt me. The woman I married would not be unfaithful to me. She might seek companionship, but my heart tells me she would not offer betrayal where once she had given her love."

With an abrupt bending of his knee and a weakness he had never known to possess him before, Ethan dropped to the floor beside the bed, leaning forward to touch his forehead to her hand. He felt as if the many miles he had traveled had all come in a single moment to descend on his weary body, and he slumped on the mattress, barely able to move his face against her skin.

With careful movements, he lifted her hand, turning it to expose her palm, and his lips settled there, offering his kiss and the whisper of his love as a vow to the woman who was limp and unresponsive to his touch and his voice. "Let me alone with her," he said, his voice a whispered plea and the closing of the bedroom door told him his message had been heeded and the other two men had gone from the room.

He lifted her, one hand beneath her neck and head, the other under her thighs, and moved her closer to the center of the bed. She was limp in his grasp, her body not responding to his touch, her head falling back against the pillow as he removed the support of his hands and arms.

He took his shoes off, slid his trousers from his hips and stepped out of them when they hit the floor. The mattress welcomed him, and even though it was not a feather tick, it gave beneath his weight, and he blessed the comfort beneath his back, for the nights spent on the trail, and the hard seats on the train had not held any comfort.

Now he anticipated the warmth of Debra's body against his own, the sweet scent of her body next to him, the feel of soft flesh touching his. He slid one arm beneath her neck, easing her to lie on her side, rolling her against him, and his heart quickened within him as he knew once more the blessed joy of holding his wife in his arms.

"Debra." He spoke her name, knowing a depth of pleasure he had not felt in long months away from her side. "My love. Sweetheart." His words were slurred, his voice muffled as he buried his mouth in her hair, in the fragile flesh at her temple. He knew not what phrases passed by his lips, only that he was overcome with the thrill of sharing these moments with her. That even though she did not sense his presence, he still had the joy, the absolute bliss of being with her, here in this bed, where first he had taken her innocence and made her his own.

She stirred against him, and her lips moved against his skin, her mouth touching his throat. A faint sound issued from her, a breath of music he had almost forgotten, the melody of her voice, speaking words he had not heard whispered aloud, but had only cherished in his dreams for the past weeks and months. "Ethan…love…hold me, don't leave me." And then a soft murmur, a song without words, the whisper of his woman's pledge to him. "I love you, my Ethan." It was sweet, a subtle whisper, the sound of her pledge to him.

The sound of his Nightsong.

And yet, in his sleep, in the dreams that filled his mind and tore at his manhood, he saw his wife, his Nightsong, in the arms of another, heard her soft words as she confided her deepest secrets to another, and his body was driven to arousal, with the need to take that which was his. His muscles tightened as he slept, his heart pounding with a beat he could barely contain, and he knew a wrath that filled his soul with black hatred for the fate that had caused a chasm to open between himself and the woman whose desire for him seemed blunted by their time apart.

DEBRA AWOKE TO the raucous crowing of her rooster, his morning call jubilant, as if he had invented the daylight hours, and had called the sun from its travels to shine down on the harem he courted each morning. She smiled, her eyes still closed, the familiar sound a welcome, and the bright sunlight that pressed against her eyelids a joyous warmth. No matter that it might be chilly outdoors—through her bedroom window, she felt the promise of spring.

She rolled to her side and opened her eyes. Rather than the window she'd expected to see, the day breaking in the east, she was faced with the sight of a man, his back to her, his body taking more than his share of the mattress beside her. And though he had not been here in the bed with her for a long time, she knew him as well as she knew her own name. Knew that he was her husband, the father of her child.

He stirred and she stilled, held in place by a fear she could not name. For she had been held in his arms during the long night just past, had whispered her love to him in the darkness. Yet, now she was struck by a sense of dread, for which there seemed to be no reason.

She touched the shoulder that lay just inches from her head, and quickly, as if he had only been waiting for a movement from her, the man who shared her bed jerked and turned to face her, his hands against her shoulders, turning her to her back, then rising over her.

"Ethan." She whispered the name, her eyes drinking in the lines of his face, the violet circles under his eyes, the dark hair that fell over his forehead, then stilling in shock at the harshness of his perusal of her. Her voice faltered, but she whispered the words that hovered within her. "I'd thought for a moment I'd dreamed it. Is it really you, Ethan?"

For long seconds, she forgot to breathe, for an even longer time she could only stare at the face that hovered over her. One hand lifted to touch his jaw, tracing the line of his cheek to where his eyelashes fell in an arc against his face. They rose slowly, and his eyes scanned her face, dark and filled with a judgment she could not read. He looked at her as if he had never seen her before.

"Debra."

It was truly Ethan, for it was his voice that spoke, his lips that formed the shape of her name. She smiled up at him, and vowed that she would not awaken from this dream, that she would hold tightly to the joy of seeing him here, with her, alive and close enough to touch. He blurred before her eyes and she blinked, aware that her tears had tainted the image of him, and she would not have it. Would not relinquish the sight of his dear face.

"I dreamed that you were here. That you had come home," she whispered.

"It was no dream, for I am with you again," he said, his voice low, rasping in her ears. "I came last night with Jay. Don't you remember?"

"You were angry with me," she remembered. "You spoke harshly to my brother, and to me."

"I saw you with him in our kitchen, your heads together, your hands joined on the table. My only thought was that you were in our home with another man," he told her. "I saw you beside him, smiling as you were wont to smile at me and you looked together at something on the tabletop between you. It brought to life a feeling of doubt within me. I didn't know what was happening, only that your life seemed to no longer include me in its midst."

He felt again the burst of unwarranted rage that had burned within him those few hours ago, fueled by the vivid dream that still lived in his mind, and his grip on her shoulders tightened. "You were with another man and my heart was aching with a pain I couldn't hold inside." And if that was the dream he spoke of or the reality of his first glimpse of her those long hours past, he did not know.

He only knew his hands were harsh against her, knew that even through the fabric of her dress, he must be forming bruises to bloom on her flesh, and yet he could not ease the pressure he forced on her. His heart pounded within him, and he bent to kiss her, not a tender message of trust and caring as he'd been wont to offer her, but an almost savage taking of her lips with his own, invading the soft tissues of her mouth with the thrust of his tongue, knowing as he did so, that she did not welcome his advances, that she was shrinking from him.

He lifted his head and heard with dismay the harshness of his tone as he spoke. "Don't pull away from me, Debra. You had kind thoughts and smiles for your brother. You even told Jay of the child you carry, and yet, for me there was nothing, and I learned of our child from another man.

"Now I need the touch of your body against mine, I need the heat of you enclosing me within your softness. I need to own you in a way that will bring peace to my heart." He lifted himself over her, leaning on one elbow as he allowed his hand to run over the rounding of her bosom, dealing with the buttons that formed the front of her dress, opening the fabric wide to reveal the white batiste of her shift beneath.

"You don't know what you're saying, Ethan. I didn't confide in Jay about the baby. He guessed that I carried a child, and I asked him not to tell you, for I knew you would not feel safe in leaving me alone. I would have told you before you left, but it would have changed everything. You'd have felt the need to stay with me, and the greater need was for your name to be cleared."

She struggled to push him from her, but her efforts were in vain, for he was heedless of her words, and his actions more than she could cope with. Almost as if he were trapped in a dream that had captured his mind, his eyes looked at her with memories she shunned.

"Don't do this, Ethan," she whispered. "There are men in the other room. I won't be shamed this way, to have them hear you taking me with only a wall between us."

"They are outside. The door has only just closed behind them. I heard them speaking in the kitchen and they've gone to do the chores and tend the horses."

"I don't want you to touch me this way," she murmured, turning her head to one side as he bent to kiss her again.

"I've been long without your comfort," he said quietly. "I've dreamed of you when I lay on the

ground at night, and when I sat in a courtroom before a judge and wondered if I would ever see you
again. Don't deny me now."

His mouth tightened and his mind again swept
back to the first sight of her the evening before.
"Your eyes were warm for Gray Wolf last night, and
a welcome beamed from them when you saw Jay, but
for me, you had nothing. And I am the man who had
the most right to expect warmth from you. Yet your
brother was the one you hid behind, lest I was a
stranger, come to hurt you."

Anger drove him, a jealous anger that came out
of nowhere, putting harsh strength in his hands. She
was his, and yet she withheld herself from him. His
hands felt large and awkward as he tugged at her
dress, drawing it up her body, exposing her legs and
the undergarment she wore beneath her petticoat.
The material lay wadded at her waist and his fingers
traveled to where her legs clamped together, denying admission to the soft warmth she held captive
between the taut muscles of her thighs.

"You think to keep me from you?" he asked, his
whisper dark and muffled against her throat. "I am
strong, Debra, stronger than the woman I married.
My need is greater than it was on our wedding night,
and I won't be denied now."

He knew the force of his arousal was prominent
against her leg, he could not blame her if she was
angered by his demand, but his long abstinence

hovered over him like a black bird of prey and he could not deny it the release he knew he could find in her soft body.

"Would you harm our child?" she asked, whispering the words. And yet the impact of them was as a sledgehammer against his head. As if she knew she had caught his attention, she pushed at him, attempting to release herself from his grip.

He lifted a bit, looking down at her, knowing his face was taut with the desire he could barely contain, the passion that rode him with harsh spurs. "I will not harm the child, sweetheart. Give to me, soften for me, Debra."

"You have never taken me before without love in your touch," she said sadly. "I feel no caring in your hands now for me…for the woman you promised to cherish the day we were married. For between us now is only the great need of your body that will not listen to my words."

"I told you I would not hurt the child."

"*The child* you speak of is your son," she said quietly, her body unmoving beneath him, but the heavy beat of her heart against the tender flesh of her throat told him of her fear. "I am not a woman who sells her body to the men in town. I'm your wife, Ethan, and I will not let you use me in this way."

He took her lips again in a kiss that bordered on cruelty, his mouth pressing her soft lips open against the teeth she had clamped together, lest he gain entry there. The acrid taste of blood touched his tongue and shamed him.

The hands that had only ever touched her with loving care seemed to have turned into a stranger's grip and he looked down at the woman he loved, watched as his fingers bit into her arms. With a flash of anger that was aimed only at himself, he cried aloud, cursing the jealousy-driven fiend he had become, and his touch upon her softened, his hands rubbing tenderly where only moments ago they had left bruises.

"Debra…" His voice was harsh and broken as he spoke her name and he bent his head to hers, his forehead touching the fine skin of her cheek. "Sweetheart, I'm sorry. I've hurt you, and I'd have sworn it was not in me to do such a thing. Please, Debra, look at me."

She lifted her eyelids, revealing liquid pools that released their content to slide down her cheeks, blinking to subdue the torrent that she could not control. Her chest heaved as a sob tore through her, and her eyes closed again, as if she could not bear to look upon his face.

"Oh, God!" His voice shattered on the prayer he spoke, as if he called upon a greater being to aid him in his plight. "Debra, please don't hide from me. I can't stand it if you hate me now. Not when I need you so badly. Not your body, sweet. Not just the love you've shared with me, but the warmth, the spirit of loving that exists within you. I need to know you'll forgive me for being a brute, for listening to a man who spoke lies about you, for doubting you, even for a moment."

"I have never looked at another man, Ethan. Not in the way you have suggested. I am a woman of honor, and my heart has been yours since the day I agreed to be your wife. It wounds me that you would think otherwise." Her voice faltered and she shook her head in defeat. "I don't know how to reach you."

She swallowed and he knew she battled the tears that would not cease to flow. "Please, Ethan," she said, and he heard the sorrow in her voice, felt against his face the hot salty drops she fought to withhold from his sight.

His groan was low, sounding as though it came from the very depths of his being. "I've made you cry, I've hurt you, and I'm ashamed of my stupid behavior, Debra." He knew she did not cry to soften him. She was too proud for that, too honest to use a woman's guile to make him bend to her will.

His eyes flickered across her face, noting the tightly closed lines of her lips, the harsh line of her jaw, where she had clenched her teeth, and he was struck with anguish, that she should be the object of his anger, ashamed of the force he had used against her. Her eyelids flared open for a moment and then closed, clenched tightly shut, as if she could not bear to see his face. And for that, he could not blame her, for he had used her badly in these few minutes, and the pride he'd thought damaged now seemed to be of little use to him.

The soft rounding of her breasts beneath him was a remembered comfort from other times and he used it now as a cushion for his aching head. He moved carefully in the bed to allow the space for his face to be buried between her breasts. Only the soft fabric of her shift lay between his mouth and the plush surface of her breasts and he ached for the sweet taste of her flesh in his mouth.

"Undo your shift for me," he whispered, and felt a jolt of surprise when her fingers fit themselves beneath his face and she undid the row of buttons that kept him from her rounded curves.

"I will do as you have said, Ethan, for if you take me, I can only hope to blunt your anger before you touch my woman's parts with the thrust of your manhood. I ask you on the grave of my mother, don't be cruel to me."

His heart almost stilled within him at her words, for her voice had assumed a tone he'd never heard before. His wife was asking him for mercy, pleading with him for a cessation of the harsh force he had visited upon her body.

"I won't hurt you, Debra," he vowed. "I only want to kiss your skin, catch the scent of your body and know for this moment that I am here with you."

He flinched at her silence. How had it come to

this? How could he have become so thoughtless—worse than that, how had he turned into a harsh man with no caring in his touch? How had he allowed the taint of jealousy to come between them?

He felt the warmth of her breasts, knew the tempting taste of her skin as his mouth skimmed her throat and drank of the sweetness he found there, and caught the scent of her body, the fresh aroma of woman she exuded.

She had relaxed her legs and he lay pressed against the mound of her womanhood, felt the rounding of her belly against his own as he held himself above her, lest he crush the babe who was protected by his mother's womb. She was soft and warm beneath him and he felt a great rush of shame as he thought of what he had come so close to taking.

Thought of the woman who had given to him everything that she was, and all she possessed, without restraint, for the months of their marriage. He remembered with a surge of guilt the warmth of her loving arms and the wealth of love she had poured out upon his body. And now, he had come within a hair's breadth of hurting her irreparably, had perhaps harmed their marriage beyond mending And his mind rebelled against his foolish pride, the jealousy he had fought.

Jealousy. That besetting sin that had sprung to life in his heart, jealousy directed against his friend: Jay, the man who had risked his own reputation, his career in fact, by defending him in court. And worse yet, the jealousy he'd felt for the brother of his wife, Gray Wolf, whose only sin had been to work in Debra's behalf, who had used hammer and shovel to aid in the upkeep of this place. All while the man who had vowed to love and care for his wife was gone, leaving her alone.

"Ethan." She spoke, her slender body almost buried beneath him in the depths of the mattress, her whisper rose to touch his hearing and he bent his head to her, waiting for the words she would speak.

"I won't turn you away, Ethan. You have been long without the comfort of our marriage bed, and I cannot deny you this thing you need. I know you won't deliberately hurt me or our child, and I won't keep you from what you seek."

Shame swept over him again, as a mighty wind might come from the west and flatten a field of wheat before its power. He bowed before it, knowing that he was the lesser of the two of them, that his pride was out of place, here in the bed where he'd loved his wife and taken all she offered to him. And now, she offered even more, reckoning that her body was his to claim, should he wish it.

She opened her legs wide and her hands touched his hips, drawing him to where the heat of her womanhood beckoned. "There is an opening in my drawers," she said quietly. "You have only to push it open and to one side."

He reached to where she directed him, felt the long slit that ran from her waist in front almost to the same place in back. His fingers traced the heat beneath that opening. He knew that he could, in a simple twist of the buttons on his trousers, have total access to her, and then he stilled his movements.

"Debra…will you…if I leave you now, will you offer yourself to me again, when we have solved the problems we have today?"

She was unmoving beneath him, her hands resting on his hips, her breathing slow, her eyes open and directed at his face. "I am yours, Ethan. My body belongs to you, for when I gave myself to you on the day we were married, I did not leave an opening through which I could crawl, should things not be as I planned. There are few things in this world that are unchanging, but know that this is one of them.

"I am your wife, my body is yours, and you have the right to possess it whenever you feel the need or the desire. Perhaps I was wrong to fight you on this thing, but you frightened me dreadfully."

He kissed her, a soft, undemanding touch of his mouth against hers, knowing that she would understand the message he gave with that simple caress. She opened her lips to him, giving him the soft access he had not demanded, but that she was willing to offer.

He kissed her carefully, tenderly, with a muted passion that was intended only for her pleasure. His mouth brushed against her cheek and his words were low. "Don't move, Debra. I'm going to shift off you, and I don't want to put any more weight on our child."

He did as he'd said, and in turning to his side, took her with him, holding her against his body with arms that were careful of her awkward body, that held her close without binding, and hands that touched her with tenderness.

She burrowed her face against his chest and sighed, long deep breaths that he knew were the aftermath of her tears. A shudder went through her and he held her closer, his need to comfort overriding his aching desire.

"We need to get up, Debra," he said, one hand rising to brush her hair back, tucking it behind her ear, then returning to cup her cheek in his palm. "Can I help you dress? Will you want to change your clothes?"

"Yes, I have a clean dress folded in the drawer," she said, and he rose from the bed, then turned to her and lifted her to stand before him. Her dress hung open and he lifted it, took it from her over her head, then tossed it in the basket she kept next to the dresser.

"Wait a second. I'll get the clothing you need." He pulled open the drawer where she kept her clothing and found the garment lying on top of assorted underclothing. "Shall I bring you a clean petticoat?" he asked.

At the simple shake of her head, he closed the drawer and returned to her, pulling the dress over her head, buttoning the front of it and tugging it to smooth the skirt over her hips. "Let me find your shoes," he said, looking down at her bare feet, and in moments he had found the soft leather slippers she wore in the house and, settling her on the edge of the bed, he slid them on her feet.

She was silent, suffering his ministrations without comment, only offering a half smile as he knelt before her, touching her feet with care and then pulling her to rise before him.

"I'm ready to fix breakfast now," she said. "I'll comb my hair first and wash my hands and face here in my basin. I think there is a good supply of bacon and a plentiful number of eggs to fry. Will you want biscuits, too?"

He felt a rush of thanksgiving as he looked at the woman he'd married, that she could so readily put aside the quarrel they'd suffered through, that she could treat him with the respect due a good husband, when he had so recently been anything but that.

"Debra." He paused, unable to continue, searching for words that would express his shame, his disgust with his behavior, and even as he began to speak, she put her fingers over his mouth.

"No, Ethan. We'll not talk of this now. When we are rested, when things are settled down in our house and I have heard the story of your travels, then we will speak of what has happened between us." She dropped her hand and he snatched it up, bringing it back to his lips to press a kiss there, against her palm.

"Thank you, sweetheart." It was all he could say, his simple words the only message he could extend to her for now, for he feared that his manhood would suffer a tremendous blow should he try to say more, feared the tears that would appear and unman him before her.

She reached for him, her hands touching his face, holding his unshaven jaws between her palms and leaned upward to touch her lips to his, a gentle brush of flesh that sent a message of peace to his heart.

CHAPTER SEVENTEEN

BREAKFAST WAS a silent affair until Debra broke the stillness with a request. They had eaten heartily for a minute or two, and then as Ethan reached for his third biscuit, she touched his hand and asked a boon he could not deny.

"Tell me of your time in the east, Ethan. Tell Gray Wolf and I of the white man's justice and the long train ride you had, and of the birthing of our foals."

She knew that there were two more fillies in the shed, that the stalls were full to overflowing and that even the cow was relegated to standing in the aisle, for her stall had been given over to the golden mare who was, as Gray Wolf said, persnickety, and demanded she be given her own area.

So, as she had asked, Ethan spoke of their journey, Jay adding the bits and pieces that Ethan left out or failed to deem important enough to speak of. As if he knew her need to hear all that was done and each word that had been said, Jay smiled at Debra and spoke of the everyday events she craved hearing.

"The new foals were born in Chicago and we left

them there until our return trip, for we had no way of caring for them in Ohio. We didn't know what lay ahead of us, and thought it would be best to have them housed where they were born. When we reached Chicago on our way home, we picked up the foals and mares and took a train home."

"And what of the time you spent in Ohio?" Debra was happy to hear of the new additions to the barn, but her heart was set on knowing how the results of the trial came about. Ethan smiled at her, as if knowing her thoughts and continued his story.

"There were men there who knew of me, who swore to my good character. Some of them I didn't even remember, but the lawyer who Jay contacted weeks before had done his work well, and the judge seemed to look favorably on me. And then the lawyer brought forth proof of the death of my family. The man I shot had bragged of the shooting to friends of his, and even though they were criminals themselves, they drew the line at the slaying of a child. One of them came forward and told what he knew when the news of my trial was revealed to the newspapers there.

"All that he told was exactly what I had testified about at the beginning of the hearing, and when the final judgment was made, I was declared guilty of manslaughter, but with due cause. The judge let me go."

"He even offered his sympathy for Ethan's loss,"

Jay said, his demeanor rueful, "as if his acknowledgment of the whole mess would make a difference."

"I suspect he meant well," Ethan said, as though he would credit the judge with at least that much good sense.

"Perhaps," Jay agreed. And then shook his head. "What a mess, and what good luck that a man should show up and agree to testify when things looked their worst. I feared that even with the character witnesses, we might have a difficult time showing any proof of Ethan's lack of guilt."

"I couldn't say that I hadn't committed the shooting, and admitting it seemed to make me look like a man with something to hide, given that I had left town and done my best to hide my trail."

"Well, the whole thing's over and done with. And for the first time, I'm happy to lose out on a reward for bringing back a wanted man." Jay grinned at Ethan and slapped him on the shoulder. "I never doubted you, my friend, not once you had told me your story. I don't think you could lie if you had to. You're about as honest as the day is long."

"But now the whole thing is finished and we need not worry any longer?" As if she could hardly believe that the results were so simple, given the worry she'd lived with for so long, Debra looked from one man to the other, her voice perplexed.

Ethan turned to her and his smile was tender. "I'm home for good, sweetheart. There is nothing more to worry about. We can take up our lives and make plans for the future.

"And speaking of the future, I think we need to take a walk to the shed and take a look at the new members of the herd." There were no arguments spoken, for the others were more than happy to set aside the problems of the past and look instead to the time to come. Together they went to the yard and gathered inside the shelter where the horses were installed. The day had become warm enough for the new foals to be outdoors and they opened the door into the corral and turned them loose to romp in the sunshine.

Cleaning the stalls was a chore better shared, Ethan decided, as Gray Wolf began the job and, in minutes, the three men had combined efforts to haul out the used bedding and put clean straw in its place. The mangers were filled readily and the oat barrel raided so that each of the mares could have added feed.

"Are the chickens penned up?" Debra asked as they readied themselves to leave the shed, and Gray Wolf nodded his head.

"They have been cooped up since last evening. We can let them out and spread their feed in the fenced-in yard for them, if you want, Debra."

The hens flocked from the coop into the area provided for them, clucking loudly as they scratched in the dirt as if they might find some trace of feed.

"You've done a good job with this," Ethan said to Gray Wolf. "I don't know what Debra would have done without you being here with her."

"Fortunately, she did not have that worry," her brother said, taking the lid from the barrel of chicken feed to fill the pan for their meal. He shook the pan and the feed rattled in it with a satisfactory sound, luring the hens closer to the fence, before he scattered the feed hither and yon through the wires of the fence, broadcasting it about the yard, so that the hens could peck to their heart's delight and scarf up the meal provided.

"I think our next job will be to build a decent barn for the herd of horses we're harboring in the shed," Ethan said, hugging Debra close to his side as they stood on the outside of the fence watching the clucking hens. "You've helped things considerably by getting the chickens out of the shed, but those horses are falling over each other in there. There just aren't enough stalls to go around and no more space to build any."

"Do the folks hereabouts do any barn raising?" Jay asked. "Back home in Kansas, I remember how the whole community would get together when someone had need of help, and put up a barn in a day or two."

Debra shot a look at Gray Wolf and bit at her lip. "I don't know if we can expect that sort of thing to happen here," she said slowly, choosing her words carefully. "There was a bit of a fuss while you were gone, Ethan. Some of the folks in towns were not pleased with Gray Wolf being here, and we had some trouble with a few of the younger men."

"What sort of trouble?" Ethan's eyes grew hard and he looked down at her with a look that boded ill will for anyone who had done any damage to his wife.

Gray Wolf spoke up and nodded toward the house. "I think this is better spoken of inside, instead of here in the yard. There is much to say, Ethan, and I think my sister has stood long enough for now. Let's find her a place to rest while you hear of the things that happened while you were gone."

ONCE MORE they sat together, Debra and Ethan on the swing, the other two men on the porch, leaning against the tall upright posts that held the roof in place. "Now, tell me what happened?" Ethan demanded, his mind sorting through an assortment of events that might have brought trouble down on Debra during his absence.

Quickly, with a minimum of fuss, Gray Wolf spoke of the men who had come looking for trouble, who had determined to protect Ethan's home against an outsider and had not believed that Debra's guest was her brother.

When he spoke of the rope about his neck and the tree that was meant to be his place of judgment, and the men who were determined to be his executioners, Ethan felt cold fear that his wife should have been exposed to such tainted men.

"When your neighbor and his son arrived, they turned the tide," Gray Wolf said, his gaze touching upon Debra as he spoke. "Between their guns and Debra's shooting, the men were halted in their mischief, and four of them were left to bleed out upon the ground."

"Debra shot a man?" As if the thought were foreign to him, an unbelievable event, Ethan's voice rang with surprise.

"She killed one and wounded another." Gray Wolf's voice was tinged with pride as he looked up at his sister, his eyes warm as he spoke of her bravery.

Ethan's arm slid to enclose her waist and he tugged her closer to his side, there in the swing, relief flooding him as he considered what the results of the gunplay might have been. The thought of Debra living with a man's death in her memory was harsh, but better that than the loss of his wife and child.

"Surely the men in town were not forgiving of such acts," he said, looking to where Gray Wolf sat, and was rewarded by the solemn shake of the man's head.

"No, they sent out the man who tends to the burials in town, and took care of their dead, but no reprisal was made against Debra or me. Samuel

Shane said that the families of the men who caused the trouble were shamed by their actions."

"And well they should be," Jay said harshly. "To hear of an attack upon a woman goes against the grain of any decent man. I doubt there'll be any more heard about it. At the least, Debra should be hearing apologies from those who rode from here still able to sit upright on their horses."

"Perhaps they'll be sorry enough to come help build a barn," Ethan said scornfully, wondering if he could contain himself should he find out just who the troublemakers were, and in the next breath wishing they would appear before him and give him the opportunity to avenge his wife, to retaliate for her fear and the danger they'd thrust her into.

"We can build our own barn," Debra said. "We'll go to town and order the wood and have it delivered from the sawmill. Mr. Hogan will take care of it for us."

"I think the job will be good for all of us," Jay said, sending Ethan a telling glance. "It'll take all our energy and help us work out the tension we've been under."

"You're probably right," Ethan agreed. "I think a trip to town is in order."

"I've drawn a few ideas you might like to see," Gray Wolf said haltingly. "I didn't mean to interfere, but my sister and I spoke of such a thing and I worked at the table and put some ideas on paper."

"Have you figured out how much wood we'll need?" Ethan asked. "What size did you have in mind?"

"I thought it should be four times what you have already, for Debra's herd of horses is increasing and in another year she'll need at least double the stalls she has now. There is no need to build without looking to the future."

Ethan felt a surge of anticipation as he considered the idea of working at a bigger barn, and he stood, drawing Debra up from the swing with him. "I'll go and harness the horses to pull the wagon and we can make a trip into town right now." He looked down at Debra, pleased by the smile she wore. "Do you need to do anything in the house before we leave?" he asked.

"Yes, but it will only take a few minutes. I'll put on a kettle with a piece of beef in it to make soup for our dinner. By the time we come back, the meat will be tender and I can add the vegetables." She turned from him and went through the kitchen doorway, allowing the screen door to slam shut behind her.

Ethan turned to Jay and Gray Wolf. "We'll need your drawing and the list of materials," he said to Debra's brother, "and you can help me with the horses," he said to Jay. With a nod, Gray Wolf went to the shed to retrieve his plans and behind him Ethan and Jay worked at hitching up the horses to the farm wagon.

THEIR ARRIVAL IN TOWN was a matter of much hustling about once the lumber mill operator recognized the men who had come to deal with him. His young son was sent to the mercantile to deliver the news of the men who were buying wood for a barn and before the three men and Debra had made their full selection, a contingent of townsfolk had gathered in front of the lumberyard.

Fearful of more trouble, Ethan held Debra at his side and waited for the spokesman of the group to approach. With hat in hand, the gentleman stood before them, his look one of apology.

"I hear tell you folks are planning on putting up a barn, Mr. Tyler. We'd like to offer our services to lend a hand with the job."

Hitting him over the head with an ax handle would have produced the same results, Ethan thought, for he was stunned by the offer made on behalf of the men who had gathered before them. "I'd be most happy to take you up on that," he said, aware of Debra's excitement as she shivered in the curve of his arm.

The man look shamefaced as he offered an explanation of sorts. "The folks are feelin' more than a little upset over things that happened out at your place, Tyler. The young fellas who took it on themselves to form that hangin' party were way out of line. We just want you to know that most of the folks hereabouts are of a different mind than those few men."

Ethan took his time, choosing his words as he

answered the declaration. "I'm pleased that you're willing to make such an effort. My wife was badly frightened by the events, and with her condition what it is, I was angered by the thought of those men terrorizing her as they did."

"Well, we're ready with an apology, Tyler. Things have been taken care of and the town wants to make amends."

Ethan looked down at his wife. "Debra? What do you say?"

"If this will mean that we are no longer considered not good enough to trade in this town, that we will be tolerated by our neighbors and my brother will not be a target of abuse, then I will be happy to accept an apology such as this."

Ethan's heart swelled with pride as he heard her words. His wife was a forgiving woman, a wife to be proud of and his shoulders squared as he stood beside her, listening to her words of peace.

THE BARN RAISING went without event, thirty men or more arriving in wagons early on Saturday morning, their tools at the ready, the wood cut to order and awaiting them. Ethan stood on the porch and watched them arrive in the yard, greeting them with a wave as they piled from the wagons and approached him.

Mr. Hogan held out his hand. "I think we'll make short work of this," he said with a grin. "All these fellas know what they're doin' when it comes to swingin' a hammer. Harry Bartlett is a right hand at building, and he's agreed to be in charge."

The man he waved his hand at looked competent, Ethan decided, and he was more than willing to turn over the leadership role to someone who knew better than he just what needed to be done.

The men rallied around, unloading their tools and heading for the piles of wood stacked beneath the trees near the present structure they would replace. Harry Bartlett called them to order and issued directions they were eager to follow, scurrying around like an army of ants as they hauled posts into the square laid out by that gentleman.

"This about what you had in mind?" he asked Ethan, standing in the middle of the area he had marked off as the boundaries of the new barn.

"You'll have to take directions from my wife's brother," Ethan said, with a proud look in Gray Wolf's direction. "He designed the plans."

"I've already spoken to him," Harry said. "I think this is about what he had figured out."

"Then you're all set," Ethan said, feeling buoyed up by the feeling of camaraderie that surrounded him.

The men hauled the posts to their designated locations, dug holes as directed by their leader, and in less time than he would have believed, Ethan was surrounded by the shape of the barn he'd dreamed of.

Long planks formed the walls and the men who

swarmed over the yard seemed to have the design planned out perfectly. By the time wagons loaded with women and children showed up, the ladies ready to serve a meal to their husbands and neighbors, the outline of the building that would house their livestock was evident.

From the house, Debra watched, relegated to the task of overseeing the food preparation, for she had been deemed too far into her pregnancy to be doing any manual labor, the ladies being protective of one of their own. Ethan was amazed that carrying a child automatically made a woman a member of the group, for the ladies rallied around Debra, almost smothering her with their concern.

The food was served in the yard, long tables being formed by sawhorses with planks laid atop their surfaces. The meal carried out of the house was plentiful and the planks almost bowed with the weight of platters and bowls.

The lady who ran the dinners at the church in town had brought stacks of plates to be used and an odd assortment of forks and knives.

The preacher who had married Ethan to his bride spoke the blessing on the meal, and the men lined up to fill their plates with the food provided. Beef and pork vied with platters of fried chicken; bowls of vegetables and assorted salads were offered; and bread had been sliced and buttered before being served. A part of the surface was covered with an assortment of pies and cakes. The younger members of the group seemed to stall before that area, until their mothers pushed them along, advising that they fill their plates with the more nutritious foods before they ate their share of the desserts provided.

Ethan found his wife carrying a platter of fried chicken and took it from her hands, placing it on the makeshift table and then ushering her to the porch swing. With strict orders to remain there ringing in her ears, she sat down and he went about the business of locating food to tempt her flagging appetite.

The women who served the menfolk and awaited their own turn at the food rallied around Ethan, and upon his return to her she had more than a plateful of tasty morsels placed in her lap. A piece of chicken hung from one side and she lifted it before it should leave a grease stain on her apron, biting into the crisp coating with a sigh of anticipation.

"I always think chicken is the best food there is," she said to Ethan. "I was raised in the village of my mother on venison and rabbit, and considered that to be tasty, but when I think of the best meals of my life, chicken is right out in front."

"Anything I share with you is fit for the gods," Ethan said, his voice teasing, but his eyes sending her a message she welcomed. They had found a meeting place since his return, his worries obviously alleviated, providing a level plateau where they could speak and act as husband and wife, sharing their life in a manner she knew was to his liking.

But they had not resolved his actions of the morning after his return, for he still felt a restraint upon himself, knowing that he had insulted her, harmed their relationship and perhaps damaged the fragile fabric of her trust by his behavior. They had slept in the same bed, shared the same pillow and touched with warmth throughout the long night hours, but he had not turned to her with passion since the events of that day.

Now he sat beside her, coaxing her with small bits of meat and the fluffy dumplings one of the ladies had created in the kitchen just minutes ago. Debra ate sparingly, looking with cautious eyes upon the dumplings that were a staple in the recipe boxes of the ladies.

"If I wanted bread, I would slice it and put butter on it," she said, eyeing the bite Ethan offered her.

"Just try it, sweetheart. It's considered a staple of the farmer's diet around here. All the ladies make dumplings with their soup and stew."

She took the bite he offered and let it sit on her tongue, the flavor filling her mouth as she considered the texture. It was different than she'd known other food to be, yet there was a subtle hint of onion in its depths, a flavor of the meat it had shared a cooking pot with and a salty tang she enjoyed.

"I think I like this strange food," she told him,

chewing and swallowing with pleasure. "I'll have to ask Anna Shane how to make such things."

Ethan laughed at her, enjoying the fun of watching her, sharing with her the happiness of this day, when neighbors joined together to help one of their number. Sam Shane and his son George were the center of a circle of menfolk, given high praise for their help here on the farm where Ethan and Debra lived.

Nothing was said of the gunfight they had participated in, for some of the people from town who made up the group were related by blood to the men who had caused the trouble. Trouble that had almost caused a permanent stain on the community, trouble that all involved were now trying to put from minds.

The afternoon went by in a flurry of activity, the sides of the barn being lifted into place, the nails being driven into the roof and the doors being hung both front and back. Mr. Hogan came to the porch where Debra sat watching the men hustling to and fro, his smile wide as he spoke of their progress.

"We'll be back out next Saturday to build the stalls and get the inside ready for your livestock," he said. "You can use the old building to store your feed until the loft is ready for hay this coming summer. You should have a good crop come May, if the green showing out in your pasture is any sign. This'll be a good year for cuttin' hay, I suspect. And you'll have a loft full of it."

"I can't thank you enough for all your help," Debra said, still amazed that the people of the town had rallied round to support the effort. "I didn't expect to have a new barn built so soon. I'd thought we'd probably be spending the whole summer at it, and now it's well on its way to being done."

"Another week or so will do it," Mr. Hogan said, "and then your menfolk can put on a couple coats of paint and fix it up dandy. I talked to the fella at the hardware, and between him and Anderson over at the emporium, they found enough paint to do the job."

"I feel almost as if I'm in the midst of a dream," Debra said, looking at all the men and women who had made this day an answer to her fondest wishes.

"Ain't no dream, ma'am. Just your neighbors takin' hold and doin' the right thing." Mr. Hogan made his firm statement with a vigorous nod of his head, and then returned to the work in progress. And for the next hours, Debra watched and wondered at the things that had come into being, here on the farm where her father had worked to provide a home for her in her childhood.

Watching the wagons roll down the lane caused tears to spring to her eyes, and Ethan pulled her against his side, careful of the unsteadiness of her balance. "Don't cry, sweetheart," he said softly, bending to kiss the curve of her cheek. "We should be happy today, with everything falling into place, and the only event still on the horizon being the painting of the building and putting together the stalls."

"And the birthing of our baby," she said, even as she considered the time to come when their son would make his way into the world.

"Not today, surely," Ethan said firmly. "You're too tired to work so hard at that today, Debra. It's not time yet, is it?"

"No, not yet, but soon. Perhaps in a week or so."

HE PUT HER TO BED at dark, hearing no argument from her lips, for she was weary and needed the comfort of a mattress beneath her. And better yet, his arms around her, supporting her as she sought a comfortable spot in which to lie.

"This may be your final opportunity to lie with me, Ethan, before the baby is born. I have no signs yet of labor, and it will still be safe for the child to have his father so near."

"Are you certain?" he asked, yearning for the soft warmth of her body, aching for the comfort of taking her to himself as her husband. He rolled her to her back and rose over her, his hands forming her breasts, his mouth seeking her lips, as if this were a time to cherish, this communion between them that spoke silently of their need for each other.

He'd left the telling of his heart's desire too long unspoken, he thought, tasting of the delicate flavor she bore, and his heart beat faster as he spoke the words of love he harbored in his very being.

"I love you, Debra. I love everything about you,

your soft skin, your dark hair that tangles around me in the night, the shape of your body that lures me close and offers me more pleasure than I deserve. I want to love your body tonight, sweetheart. I want to hold you and touch all the places that bring you happiness and make you cry out with the joy of loving."

She held him close, her arms strong around him, her mouth opening to lure him within as she arched against him. Between them, the child they had formed from their seed moved, as if assuring them of his presence, and he was careful to keep his weight from the place where the babe was sheltered. His hands moved over her swollen belly, measuring the width and breadth of the child within her, dreaming of the time when he would hold his son in his arms, and aching with the thankfulness he felt at the knowledge of his woman carrying his child.

She responded quickly to his urging, rising to his touch, her breath short as she knew the pleasure he offered, and then she tugged him into place over her, her dark eyes on him as he knelt between her legs and lifted her, opening her to his manhood. Their union was not as it had been at other times, for he was more gentle, his touch tender as he joined their bodies this night. He did not thrust deeply within her, but took her with movements that took into account the child who lay between them.

His body surged above her, his need for her great

and his desire at a peak such as he'd never known. The restraint he employed seemed to only increase their pleasure, for her cries were those of a woman who has been sated by her husband's loving, and his own joy was equal to that of hers.

They laid together, their passion spent. His head rested carefully against her belly, his cheek knowing the movements of his child, his ear hearing the sound of two hearts beating within her body and his heart knowing the joy of loving a woman and the peace of receiving her love in return.

THE GRAVE IN THE ORCHARD where her father lay beneath the ground was a sacred place to Debra, one she had not chosen to share with anyone else before this day. But now, she gathered those she loved about her and led them to the place beneath a peach tree, where a slight mound told of a grave.

She knelt there, bowing her head, feeling Ethan's hand on her shoulder as she closed her eyes and escaped to that place where her father dwelt in her heart. For long moments she thought of the man who had sired her, who had loved her mother and given the two women in his life all that he had to offer.

She lifted her gaze to Ethan and spoke words he had not thought to hear from her until later on, when what was to be was finally accomplished. But she spoke with certainty, and he listened closely as did the other two men who stood near.

"I feel strongly that I will bear a son and he shall be named for my father and for you, Ethan. He will have a name belonging to two men who gave him life, whose blood will run in his veins, and he will be proud to be known as Ethan David Tyler, son of Nightsong."

Ethan only nodded, unable to speak for the tears that threatened to fall from his eyes, unwilling to display to the other men the joy he felt at his wife's words. And then he chanced to look at Gray Wolf, and beyond him, at Jay. They were both calm, but a tick in Jay's jaw gave him away. Gray Wolf's hand rose to brush at his eyes, a motion that told Ethan, without words being spoken, that her brother was pleased by Debra's decision.

He looked again at Debra. Her heart at peace, she rose and nodded at Gray Wolf, who carried the marker he had made for this very moment. With a small shovel, he and Ethan, with Jay's help, prepared a place for the marker to rest, deepening the short trench in which they would place the piece of wood. And when they were finished and the dirt had been tamped down on either side of the slab, when their fingers had pressed tightly against the soil, forming it to the wood and holding it firm, they rose and waited as Debra whispered words from her past, words she had heard her mother speak here at this very place.

What the soft native tongue expressed did not matter to Ethan, though it was apparent that Gray

Wolf understood her words, for he knew that the
bond she shared with her brother was one of blood,
a closely knit tie that was strong and would prevail
for as long as the two of them lived. He looked up at
her, this woman he loved so deeply, recognizing that
the time they spent here brought peace to her soul,
knowing that he was ever the beneficiary of the gift
of her heart.

For the wooden marker was but a part of the sig-
nificance of this time. The knowledge that the man
who lay beneath the ground lived now in the heart
of his daughter. But in the future would live in the
minds of the children who would be taught to honor
his presence and influence on others while he lived
on this earth.

Ethan watched as Gray Wolf took his sister's hand
and lifted it to his lips, touching the fragile flesh in
a gesture that spoke of his great love for her. How
fortunate she was, Ethan thought, his mind at ease,
that two men loved her so well, that she was the
essence of womanhood to her husband and her
brother. And then there was Jay, the man who had
returned to her the husband she might have lost
without the help of such a good friend. Another man
who cherished the strength of Debra Nightsong, and
recognized it as a tribute to her parents, both the
woman who had borne her, and the man who had
loved her so well.

She stood now, before her father's grave, marked

for all time with the gesture of Gray Wolf's love for her, surrounded by the men who would cherish her as wife, sister and friend, for all the years to come.

EPILOGUE

THE WEEKS OF SPRING were rich with the warmth of returning life to the pastures, the sight of young colts and fillies running the length and width of the meadow, their dams watching from the shade beneath the willow trees. The cats grew fat on the milk from the Jersey cow Ethan learned to milk; the chickens hatched their young, with three broody hens gathering their chicks about them and filling the silence with their clucking, even as the air was split with the crowing of the young roosters who found their voices in the early morning hours.

None of the signs of new life were as precious to Ethan and his wife as the shrill sound of a baby, the child of their hearts, who made his appearance early one morning in April. Although the doctor was in attendance, his presence was not needed so long as Anna Shane was there with her, and their child was born. Ethan watched as his wife labored to bring forth the fruit of his loins.

For as such had Debra described the child that she would bear for him. The ancient words were familiar to him, for he'd heard them during his childhood, read from the Bible his mother cherished, but in Debra's voice they had new meaning.

The fruit of his loins. He heard the sound of that phrase as a blessing upon him and the child he held, the son he had been given. The tiny being wiggled in his grasp and he held him firmly, holding him up before the window where the sunlight flooded his vision and made clear each tiny finger and toe, every inch of fragrant skin the child possessed. He was a fine boy, his long legs and arms promising a man who would stand straight and tall in the years to come. Dark hair crowned his head, straight and black as midnight, a heritage from his mother, as were the high cheekbones and prominent nose that would one day be as sharp and finely formed as that of his uncle's.

Outside the window, Gray Wolf waited, and Ethan held up the tiny creature for the admiration he knew was due him, for the two men who had paced the yard for the past hours were filled now with the joy of knowing that Debra was safe and the child was healthy.

"Bring him to me," Gray Wolf said, his voice audible through the window, and Ethan turned to Debra, lest she should not agree to such a thing. But her smile told him otherwise and with quick movement, Anna Shane wrapped a length of flannel around the tiny form and Ethan carried his son to the back door and out onto the porch.

Gray Wolf waited for him there, Jay behind him, and his tanned hands were strong as Debra's brother took the child into his palms and held him high, as if offering him to the brilliant sun that shone upon them there.

"He is a child who will know love, who will be a blending of two races, a man to be honored and re-spected, for his name is strong and his lineage is that of honorable men."

His words rested on the babe, a blessing pro-nounced by his uncle, and Ethan could only watch with the joy of the moment upon him as Gray Wolf lowered the infant to rest in his hands and touched his lips to the tiny, wrinkled forehead. As if he un-derstood the ritual performed by his uncle, the babe looked up with unfocused eyes and settled his sight on the man who held him.

Then, with a strong cry, his sound of a baby's im-patience split the air, as if he were weary of such foolishness and Ethan laughed aloud at the noise of his son. "He sounds hungry," he said, taking him into his own hands and holding him against his shoulder. "His mother will want him with her."

"He will need her milk to help him grow, and the strong arms of his father and his uncle to lead him aright," Gray Wolf said.

"And what about me?" Jay asked, as if his own share in the child was not to be scorned.

"You will have the place of honorary uncle," Gray

Wolf said happily. "For he will need our wisdom in his lifetime. We will share in his upbringing, the three of us."

Ethan stepped to the bedroom window and peered within, where his wife had closed her eyes in slumber and the doctor was packing up his bag, preparing to leave. He looked back at the two men who were deeply engrossed in speaking of their duties to his child, and his heart was light with the joy of their friendship and the knowledge that together they would form the support that would hold the boy in good stead for all of his growing-up years.

He looked out at the barn, so recently painted, shining in the morning sun, and beyond it, the pasture where a small herd of foals ran the length of the fence line. The mares stood by, watching their young ones, much as he looked at his own son, he realized. The role of parent was the same, whether the child be man or beast. And the love of a parent for his child was the same the world over, he decided. A love that grew from the joining of a man and woman, an unending circle that formed a family.

He carried the baby back into the house, into the bedroom where his wife waited for him, and he saw her eyes open as he approached the bed. "Did they approve of him?" she asked, her voice confident with the knowledge that her son was without flaw, that he was a superior baby to be cherished by each member of his family.

"They agree that he is a wondrous child," Ethan told her, bending to place their son in her arms. "They are out there arguing about which of them will teach him to ride a horse and which will choose his first mount."

"His first mount is already chosen," Debra said. "I knew the night he was born that he was a colt fit for my son."

"The golden mare's colt?" Ethan asked, knowing already his wife's reply.

"The very one. I will train him myself and ready him for our son to ride."

"Those two out there, arguing in the yard have a big surprise coming, then," Ethan said, laughing aloud.

"Gray Wolf will know of my thoughts," Debra said. And as she spoke, she gazed through the window, beyond which her brother waited for her to look upon him. She lifted a hand to acknowledge his presence and he nodded, a grave, solemn gesture that pleased her, if the smile she wore was anything to judge by.

"I am happy," she said, turning her attention back to Ethan. "I have worked hard and given you a son, and my heart is full."

His voice broke on the words he spoke, yet he did not falter, but spoke the thoughts that dwelt in his heart. "Mine is fuller yet, for it holds both you and my son within, yet its limits will stretch to contain all of our children yet to come," Ethan said, the words a vow. And then, uncaring of the presence of the man and woman in the room with them, he told her of the feelings that swelled in his bosom.

"You are my woman, the mother of my child and I love you Debra Nightsong. As no man has ever loved a woman before, I vow to cherish you. And in the all the hours of all the years to come, when the darkness surrounds us, I will hear your song as you speak to me in the night.

"My Nightsong. My own love."

REQUEST YOUR
FREE BOOKS!

2 FREE NOVELS
FROM THE ROMANCE/SUSPENSE
COLLECTION PLUS 2 FREE GIFTS!

YES! Please send me 2 FREE novels from the Romance/Suspense Collection and my 2 FREE gifts. After receiving them, if I don't wish to receive any more books, I can return the shipping statement marked "cancel." If I don't cancel, I will receive 4 brand-new novels every month and be billed just $5.49 per book in the U.S., or $5.99 per book in Canada, plus 25¢ shipping and handling per book plus applicable taxes, if any*. That's a savings of at least 20% off the cover price! I understand that accepting the 2 free books and gifts places me under no obligation to buy anything. I can always return a shipment and cancel at any time. Even if I never buy another book from the Reader Service, the two free books and gifts are mine to keep forever.

185 MDN EF5Y   385 MDN EF6C

Name _____ (PLEASE PRINT) _____

Address _____ Apt. # _____

City _____ State/Prov. _____ Zip/Postal Code _____

Signature (if under 18, a parent or guardian must sign)

Mail to **The Reader Service:**
IN U.S.A.: P.O. Box 1867, Buffalo, NY 14240-1867
IN CANADA: P.O. Box 609, Fort Erie, Ontario L2A 5X3

Not valid to current subscribers to the Romance Collection,
the Suspense Collection or the Romance/Suspense Collection.

Want to try two free books from another line?
Call 1-800-873-8635 or visit www.morefreebooks.com.

* Terms and prices subject to change without notice. NY residents add applicable sales tax. Canadian residents will be charged applicable provincial taxes and GST. This offer is limited to one order per household. All orders subject to approval. Credit or debit balances in a customer's account(s) may be offset by any other outstanding balance owed by or to the customer. Please allow 4 to 6 weeks for delivery.

Your Privacy: Harlequin is committed to protecting your privacy. Our Privacy Policy is available online at www.eHarlequin.com or upon request from the Reader Service. From time to time we make our lists of customers available to reputable firms who may have a product or service of interest to you. If you would prefer we not share your name and address, please check here. ☐

BOB07